THE ONE
with the
KISS CAM

Cindy Steel

ALSO BY CINDY STEEL

Pride and Pranks Series

A Christmas Spark

That Fine Line

Stranded Ranch

Double or Nothing

Christmas Escape Series

Faking Christmas

Teresa,
For a friendship that can always pick up right where we left off.
For all those times we spent laughing until we cried. And for
teaching me that Dr. Pepper is always better when it falls.

1

LET ME GIVE YOU A PIECE OF ADVICE.

When you find yourself on a blind date at a professional basketball game with a guy who shows up wearing sweatpants and his favorite jersey—*only* his favorite jersey—run.

Run far away.

I met Jason on MixNMingle. I was new to the app, thanks to my friend, Mira, who signed me up without my permission, lied hysterically on my profile, and held my computer hostage until I agreed to go on one date. 'One night of fun,' she called it. Not to be an old cliche, but I didn't have time for dates. I didn't even want them.

Jason had been my only swipe right. To be honest, I gave myself about one whole minute on the app before getting frustrated and picking the first guy who didn't look like he lived in some basement bunker or the weight room at the gym. He offered me a ticket for the Jazz game that night, which turned out to be my kryptonite. My starry-eyed lapse in basketball judgment was how I found myself hiking to the nosebleeds and sitting next to my date, who was dressed more appropriately for a NASCAR race than a basketball game.

Mullet included.

Proving, once again, that I couldn't seem to pick men any better than my mother.

Jason leaned in close, his bare arm brushing against mine and the smell of beer already thick on his breath. "Can't believe how packed it is tonight."

I leaned away and gave a polite smile. "I know. It's crazy."

My eyes drifted down to the large mass of dark hair oozing out of his tank top. I get it. We're all mammals, we all have hair. My hairstylist always tells me that I have enough brown hair on my head to cover three different scalps. So, I wasn't hair-shaming anyone, but I didn't need to see all of that on a first date. I don't care how much good luck you think your jersey brings to a game. With hair pillowing out of every opening, I wasn't sure where to look, so I turned my attention back to the court as the teams warmed up and tried to appreciate the fact that I was at the game.

The smell of popcorn and the sound of the warm-up basketballs hitting the court should have left me giddy. Though the Delta Center in Salt Lake City, Utah was only a few minutes from where I live, I had never been to a game. Seeing the Jazz in person had always been a dream of mine. Mira and I spent most game nights watching from her apartment, throwing microwave popcorn at the TV and booing the refs. While I did appreciate the arena's excited buzz in the air, sitting next to Joe Dirt and smelling something sour every time he raised his arms definitely put a damper on the whole experience.

But I refused to let that completely sway my attitude.

Eventually, the seats around us filled in as the game began. Though I didn't look directly at him, a man settled into the seat next to me. From what I gathered with casual glances to my right, he was fairly tall. His knees brushed against the seat in front of him. Brown hair. Baseball hat. A nice pair of jeans. He wore a t-shirt covered up by a light jacket. No jersey. No unnecessary body hair in my face. The best part was the light cologne attached to his body that I discreetly turned toward every time I needed a fresh breath of air.

In my defense, Jason's MixNMingle picture was from his stint in the Army. Excuse me for thinking his green camo army shirt, pants, and short haircut was attractive. I still wasn't sure my date really *was* that man in the picture.

I was going to kill Mira.

"You want a drink or something, Nora?" Jason turned toward me, placing his hand lightly on my knee, his face two inches too close to mine. The beer in his cupholder was nearly empty. He motioned toward the guy walking up and down the aisle, selling concessions.

"No. I'm okay, thanks," I said, breathing easier when he removed his hand. I was not big on touch, though some people were and thought little of it. I was probably being too hard on him. He hadn't done anything wrong, per se, but for some reason, something about him rubbed me the wrong way. I wanted to give Jason zero false impressions. The deliberately casual way his skin would brush mine made my red-flag receptor ping. I wasn't *that* hungry. Although, a pretzel with cheese sauce sounded amazing. But not here. I didn't want Jason to pay for a thing. He flagged the guy down and got a pretzel for himself and offered me a bite, which I politely declined after watching his wet mouth attack the bread.

"Not a big eater, huh?" Was it just me, or did he look happy about that?

By the time the buzzer went off, signaling the end of the first quarter, I stood up to stretch my muscles. Jason looked at me curiously. "You need to use the bathroom?"

"No, just stretching."

It did feel nice to stand up until I noticed Jason's eyes drifting down the backside of my jeans. I sat down and inched a bit closer to the good-smelling guy and zeroed my eyes in on the court.

"The armrest is all yours."

The low drawl at my right came so soft I almost didn't register that it was intended for my ears. Jason was now leaning forward and arguing with a group of guys one row in front of us. I shot a look toward the voice.

Dark eyelashes, long and slightly curled, met my gaze. Baseball hat. Gentle brown eyes. And what might be the sexiest five o'clock shadow I had ever beheld. I was able to keep my mouth from dropping open in shock, but only barely.

I remembered he had said something.

"What?" I asked brilliantly.

He nodded toward my seat. "The armrest. I had it the first quarter. The second quarter, it's all yours."

I stared at him, not quite comprehending that this man seemed to be willfully giving up the armrest. I usually made it a habit to tuck my arms around my stomach to appear smaller, as though I didn't want the extra space. But he was just giving it to me?

He must have sensed my confusion and added, "I figured we should have the talk."

My eyes roamed his face for any sort of clue he might be joking, but not knowing anything about him to be sure. "What do you mean?"

"The talk. Otherwise, we just go back and forth, both of us trying to claim dominance over the armrest. I don't want to live like that."

A smile played around his lips, and I couldn't help but join him. Then I remembered I was on a date and glanced back at Jason. He was now gesturing wildly, his furry armpits flailing about, and shouting mild obscenities to his new friends, who looked equally as rowdy. I turned back to my seat neighbor.

"So, I get it the whole second quarter?" I raised my eyebrows in question.

He solemnly held his hand up in some sort of Boy Scout signal. "On my honor."

"And then what? At the buzzer, you just bump my arm off?"

"Exactly."

I laughed. He joined me, a low breathy chuckle that raised the hair on my arms.

"I was under the impression men always took the armrest. No questions."

His eyes flicked over to Jason for a brief second then back to mine. "Not all guys. Some of us like to have the talk."

"I appreciate that." I made a show of plopping my arm on the armrest between us.

"Don't get too comfortable," he said. "Come third quarter, it's all mine again."

"So, wait. That means I get it all through half-time then, right?"

He blinked. Clearly, he had forgotten about the twenty-minute halftime show. After the dunks, the halftime show was mine and Mira's favorite part of the whole game.

His head tilted as he considered his options. "How about we go halfsies?"

I made a face. "I'm not sure. You said specifically your time started again at third quarter. And even though I know absolutely nothing about you, I'm positive you're a man of your word."

His lips lifted in a smile, but before he could speak, Jason nudged my arm, forcing my attention back to my date.

"Those guys think the Jazz won't make the semifinals this year." His voice was about two octaves louder than it needed to be, and his sour breath singed my nose hairs. "Idiots!" He laughed, yelling his last statement toward the people in question only to get into another spirited discussion on the merits of the team.

I leaned back into my seat. My seat neighbor was talking to his friends on the other side of him, so I took a fresh breath of his scent and enjoyed my turn with the armrest. It was so much more comfortable that way. From sly glances out of the corner of my eye, I discovered he was with two other guys, one of whom had a wedding ring on his hand, but that was all I could discover before I started to worry my interest would be noticed.

The whistle blew, and the second quarter began. The Jazz were up by four points. Jason settled back in beside me, offering me his special brand of commentary. Earlier, when we were traipsing up the stairs to our seats making small talk, I made the mistake of telling him I had never been to a professional basketball game. That confession resulted in him thinking I had also never heard of the sport of basketball. The patronizing way he talked grated on my nerves.

Still, I feigned interest while he droned on and tried not to doze off.

During the halftime dance show, Jason stood up.

"I'm grabbing another dog and a beer. You want anything?" he asked, his voice in competition with the music.

At this point, all I wanted was a hot bath and a Tylenol PM, but that wouldn't happen for about two more hours.

"No, thanks. I'm good."

He frowned. "You sure? I haven't bought you anything all night."

And he wouldn't start now.

"I ate dinner at work today." It was slightly astonishing how quickly a white lie could fall from my lips. I blamed it on me shifting into some sort of survival mode.

A sigh escaped me when Jason made his way down the aisle away from me. I leaned back in my chair. He wasn't a bad guy —that I could tell so far, anyway. But he wasn't for me. That much was certain. A part of me was tempted to bail on him and save ourselves an awkward post-date goodbye, but I couldn't bring myself to leave the game, let alone actually *do* that to a person.

A nudge at my right side had my arm falling off the armrest. I looked over to my seat neighbor who stared forward, an innocent expression on his face.

I waited a long moment before I brought my arm up and nudged his off the armrest, reclaiming my spot once again.

My smile was set free when my arm fell off a moment later. A rush of adrenaline burst through me like a lightning bolt. It was sudden and thrilling and secretive in a way I'd never felt before. An inside joke between two strangers. It almost made being here with Jason bearable.

We played like that for a few minutes, both of us feigning interest in the halftime show, each giving the other a thirty-second turn on the armrest. I hoped he had a big sloppy grin on his face like I did on mine, but I didn't look to see. My eyes were trained on the dancers below, but they could have been monkeys climbing trees for all I registered.

"Kiss Me" by Sixpence None the Richer came on in the arena. It was neighbor guy's turn at the armrest, but since he had cut me short by five whole seconds during my last turn, I was counting extra fast in my head to do the same to him. I became distracted when the kiss cam began to play on the large TV, picking out members of the audience to kiss. It was entertaining watching their surprised faces. Most of them seemed excited, but some were embarrassed to be drawn out like that. They were all good sports, though.

It took a moment to register my face when it showed up on the camera. My neighbor must have recognized his face at the same moment I did mine. We both looked at each other, wide-eyed and with embarrassed laughter, while we waved our hands toward the TV, letting the world know we were not a couple.

The camera kept us in its sights for an uncomfortable amount of time before flipping to another man and woman who were much more willing to play along. I was suddenly grateful my date had been out when the camera turned on us. What if it had been Jason on camera next to me? The thought of kissing him was borderline repulsive. I would much rather kiss Armrest Guy over my actual date. But that was…inappropriate thinking. Right? Goodness, it was hot in here.

"That was a close one," Neighbor Guy mumbled as he took his spot back on the armrest.

"Hey. It's my turn."

He flashed me a cheeky grin. "No, you had your turn just now when you were too busy blushing on camera. Not my problem you were distracted."

I scoffed, trying to hide my embarrassment. "I wasn't blushing."

He met me with a wide grin. "You were SO blushing."

Good gracious, his smile was incredible. I had seen side glimpses of it, but looking at the full-blown effect straight on, I almost forgot my name.

"Is that guy your boyfriend?" He motioned toward the empty seat next to me.

I shook my head. "No. That's a dating-app match gone very wrong."

A smile touched his lips. "Ah. I wondered."

He wondered. About me? Cute, neighbor-seat guy had been wondering about me?

Suddenly, his eyes widened. He pointed toward the TV. "It's happening again."

Sure enough, there I was, looking pale and sick to my stomach. My brown hair looked flat, and my soft curls had begun to come undone. Whose idea were these kiss cams? How did they know who was a couple?

The people in our area began to recognize us and started chanting for us to kiss. The growing attention caused my stomach to clench while my heart began pounding through my chest.

"I don't think it's going to leave us alone until we do it," the low voice next to me said.

Those words brought a rush of heat to my face. Perfect.

A small thrill flashed through my body at his suggestion. I didn't date much, but even I knew that kissing someone while on a date with someone else was bad form—no matter how much I didn't want to be on said date.

The camera finally moved on, and I breathed a sigh of relief. I definitely didn't feel any other emotion. The disappointment swirling around in my belly had to be related to something else. I didn't know this guy—although we had pretty much been flirting the entire game.

For a moment, we sat transfixed, both of us keeping a wary eye on the TV. How long was this song? This time, the camera focused on a burly man with his exuberant wife, both happy to make out in front of thousands on camera.

"What are your thoughts on giving the people what they want?"

I looked at him. "What?"

He nodded toward the screen. "If it shows us again, I'm thinking about going for it. With your permission, of course."

He wore a small smile and had a quiet confidence that I couldn't help being attracted to. The song was on its last verse before the chorus. Surely they would leave us alone. His buddies on the other side of him kept laughing and nudging his elbow. The blond guy sitting next to him leaned toward me, patting my seat neighbor on the chest before saying, "I'm telling you, he's a stand-up guy. He always puts the seat down. Does dishes like a champ. Very tender and sweet."

My neighbor was laughing by this point.

I looked at him. "Is that true?"

His mouth quirked upward. "The dishes part, at least. I lived with Mike back in college, and he was a slob."

"And you're not dating anyone?"

He met my eyes. "Nope. Single." He glanced at my lips before he turned to watch the TV. He seemed almost hopeful. Or maybe that was my anxiety overanalyzing the situation. I watched the TV too, waiting. Heart pounding. Awash with indecision. It wasn't like the camera would show us again. We had already disappointed our audience. Twice. A few had even booed us at our last attempt. But why did that idea not relieve me as it should have?

"I don't even know your name."

My neighbor flashed me a grin, and I found myself smiling back. "Makes it kind of exciting, doesn't it?"

"Yes, but I'd prefer to make sure I haven't heard your name on *America's Most Wanted*."

He laughed, moving his long fingers to his hat to flip it on backward. His hair was longer than I thought, touching the top of his ears. He reminded me of a young Ashton Kutcher.

"Is that show still on?" he asked.

"No idea."

"I'm Duke."

I swallowed, my mouth starting to feel dry. "Nora."

He held his hand out to shake mine, and just as he caught me in his grip, the crowd around us began cheering once more. Duke's friends shouted and pointed, laughing and whistling.

We glanced at the TV before looking back at each other—a question in both of our eyes.

He held my hand and leaned in closer, his eyes sparking with humor and sweetness. "I'm going to kiss you. You good, Nora?"

I barely had time to breathe out a yes before his lips were on mine.

2

THE CROWD WENT WILD, AS THEY SAY.

The excitement in the arena was everywhere. I could feel the vibration of stomping feet and excited shouts. The song had begun to wind down.

All the noise became a low buzz in my ears because my senses were completely immersed in what was happening to me. Warm hands lightly gripped that place between my cheeks and my neck, holding me close. Long fingers played with the hair at the base of my neck. His sweet cologne, smelling of pine and warm spices, had me almost shuddering with pleasure. And his kiss.

I wasn't sure what I expected being nearly strangers. Cold? Brief? Impersonal? Duke's kiss was none of those things. He pressed his lips to mine lightly at first, his hands at my neck. He breathed me in before nudging my lips open and increasing the pressure. The soft scrape from the stubble on his skin made my face come alive with sensation. My hands gripped his forearms. My mouth trailed after his when he pulled back to look at me. Soft eyes roamed over my face. He smiled at what he saw and pressed another kiss to my lips before he released his hands from my cheeks and pulled away.

I wasn't sure how long the song had been over. They were now pulling somebody out from the crowd to make a shot from half-court to win a car. The people around us must have been watching with great interest and gave shouts of excitement our way. A few random men clapped Duke on the shoulder, and his friends had a great time teasing him. In a daze, I sat back in my seat and stared forward.

It felt as though the roller coaster ride at the amusement park had ended. An abrupt stop right where it had begun, the doors opening to let the dizzy passengers off.

Excuse me, sir, I'd like to go on that ride again please.

A large and hairy body settled in on my other side, crowding my space and waving a blue foam finger in front of my face. The reality of my situation quickly settled back over me.

"Nobody can say no to a foam finger. Am I right?"

He had bought me a foam finger. Meekly, I smiled and took the gigantic offering, setting it on my lap somewhat awkwardly. "Thank you."

Jason took his empty beer cup and tossed it at his feet, leftover beer splashing out onto the floor and a little on my shoes. He replaced his cupholder with a full glass while balancing a chili dog on his lap.

"What'd I miss?" he asked me.

I stilled.

The entire arena had just watched this soap opera of a moment go down. In all actuality, very few people probably noticed, except for those behind me who saw me kiss a stranger while my date was out of sight.

"Nothing much. Dancers, kiss cam, that kind of thing."

"Oh, man, I missed the kiss cam? I've always wanted to do that." He waggled his eyebrows in my direction before he hiccuped out a burp and took a swig of beer. I took that as a cue that I could look forward again. I wasn't intentionally ignoring Duke, but though my heated cheeks had cooled, my hands were still shaking, the last effect of his kiss. He hadn't looked my way either, but when the ref blew the whistle, Duke's arm nudged mine off the armrest.

A grin exploded onto my face, and my heart began thumping all over again. I placed my hand over my mouth in an attempt to hide my unbidden smile. I couldn't contain it, but I was trying my best to look *less* crazy.

I could tell he was smiling too, though I didn't look at him. He kept fidgeting, like he was having a hard time sitting still. I knew the feeling. It wasn't just the first kiss—the heart-stopping, bone-melting, fire-inducing, entire-arena-watching first kiss. Although, that one definitely got me. But it had been for show. The one everybody had been expecting. They asked. He delivered. But there had been a second kiss. I wasn't sure the camera was even still on us by that time. I hoped it wasn't. He had pulled back, looked down, smiled, and kissed me again. Quick and sweet. Like he couldn't help it. As though we were on much friendlier terms than we actually were.

"What's so funny?" Jason's voice crowded into my space. Instantly, my smile faded, though it didn't go away completely.

"Oh, nothing. I was thinking of something that happened earlier."

"What was it?" Jason had chili drippings on his goatee. He took another bite and waited expectantly for me to fill the silence. I wondered how *he* thought this date was going.

"Oh…nothing. It was from work earlier. It would take too long to explain." I gave him an apologetic smile. "Sorry."

To my right, I felt the distinct shaking of shoulders. I raised my arm next to his and nudged him. I meant to remove my arm but found there was enough space for both of us on the armrest, if we pressed close enough. I left it there—half expecting him to nudge me off. He didn't.

"You're a waitress, right?" Jason said.

"Yeah."

"Can you tell me the special for tonight?" He raised his eyebrows at me again in a way that made my skin crawl. I looked away, giving him no encouragement to continue his thought process. If MixNMingle had a star rating, he just lost a few.

The crowd around us suddenly took an explosive turn, shouting profanities and booing down toward the court.

"Oh, come on, ref!" Jason exploded in an affront at the game, leaning down to discuss the last play with his new friends in front of us.

I folded my arms across my chest and sunk down in my seat, my previous good mood having taken a turn.

"Where do you work?" Duke's low voice spoke to me. Our eyes were both on the game, but his head was tilted toward me.

Jason was still in a heated debate, so I braved a glance at Duke's face. He met my gaze with a friendly smile. I didn't feel threatened by him in the same way Jason made me feel. But I'd gone from 'girl who never went on dates' to 'girl who went out with one guy only to kiss another guy on the same date.' It had been a busy night. My mind was a whirl of over-stimulation. I wasn't sure how comfortable I felt about giving him my personal information. I had done my best to vet Jason before I went out with him—though a fat lot of good that did me.

I mean, I could kiss him, of course, but telling him where I worked seemed crazy.

"Downtown," I said, giving him a little smile. "How about you?"

His eyes grazed over my face before the hint of a smile played across his. "In my garage."

I pressed my lips together and shook my head. Now I had the uncrushable urge to know exactly what he did in his garage and why. But in order to get that information, he would surely expect a bit more from me.

"That's nice," I said, stealing back the armrest.

"It is nice." He grinned, leaning back in his chair and folding his arms, giving up the armrest even though it was technically his turn.

My date was two and a half beers into the third quarter when he made his first move. I had leaned forward to give my body a new position in the uncomfortable chair. There I was, minding my own business, trying to politely ignore the guy on my left and stop thinking about the man on my right, when a heavy hand plopped onto my back and started massaging. My body froze. I never questioned the hand. I knew exactly who it belonged to.

I immediately leaned back in my chair, Jason barely moved his hand out of the way before it got squished between my back and the seat.

"Whoa, jumpy tonight, huh?" He grinned down at me, retracting his hand before holding out his drink. "Want a little? To take the edge off?"

"No," I said. All my nerves were sending jolts of warning to my brain, my fight-or-flight sense suddenly activated. Not because the touch was necessarily inappropriate, but because it was unwanted.

I faced forward again once I was sure Jason's hands were occupied with his beer and my foam finger that he had confiscated during a streak of points from the Jazz.

"If it gets too crowded over there, I'm happy to trade you seats anytime," Duke said in my ear. Goosebumps rose up on every inch of my exposed flesh at his words.

"I'm okay," I insisted, touched by his protective nature. "Thanks, though."

"Sure." He adjusted his position, his long legs butting up against the seat in front of him, before clearing his throat and adding, "It's gonna be a blowout. We're probably gonna bail early in the fourth quarter to beat the traffic. I know you don't know me from Adam, but…these are my friends, Mike and Ryan. They're both married. Mike's got kids. Ryan's got one on the way. So, if you need a ride somewhere, we'd be happy to take you."

"You're not a serial killer, then?" I asked, smiling slightly.

"Not on a Friday. I try to take the weekends off."

Mike and Ryan leaned forward to smile at me. Mike, with his Hawaiian shirt and spiky blond hair seemed so familiar to me, though I couldn't place him. The one called Ryan reminded me of a snowboarder. It wasn't just the easy way he smiled and his lazy movements, but the black beanie on his head and the Vans he wore on his feet that rounded out the effect. They did look like decent guys. Old college buddies out for a guys' night. Mike kept yawning. Nine-thirty probably was late if he had kids. I wished I wouldn't have gotten in Jason's car to come to the game. I hadn't been comfortable enough with the arrangement to allow him to pick me up at my house, so I met him at a well-lit Chick-fil-A parking lot a few miles away from the arena.

While I was thinking, Jason's beefy arm settled around my shoulders, pulling me close to him in a weird side-hug squeeze. Again, my body tensed, stiff as a board.

I hated situations like this. I hated making a scene. Dreaded it, in fact. But I couldn't let this go on.

"Please don't touch me, Jason."

My heart banged wildly in my ears. I could sense Duke listening intently to our conversation. He hadn't moved a muscle since Jason put his arm around me. Even after my rebuke, his arm still hung limply around my shoulders.

Jason was staring at me like I had grown two heads. "I don't mean anything by it. I'm just being friendly. I do the same thing with my grandma."

The tips of his fingers stroked my shoulder.

I jerked forward. "I'm not your grandma. Stop."

He rolled his eyes. "Good hell, does your MixNMingle profile say prudish bit—"

Suddenly, Jason's arm was jerked off my shoulder and flung over my head toward him like a kicked rag doll.

Duke leaned across me to lock eyes with a livid Jason. "She told you not to touch her, so don't touch her, jackass."

Holy crap.

Jason leaned forward, eyeing Duke with obvious annoyance. "You want to take this outside?"

Beyond the obvious ridiculousness of traversing approximately eighteen thousand stairs downward to then take the escalator down even more stairs until we actually got outside, I didn't think Jason was worth a meeting by the flagpole for a fight. I jumped up between the men. This date was officially over.

Turning to Jason, I said, "I don't think this is going to work out. Thanks for the ticket, but I'm going to go now."

"I'm your ride, remember?" Jason said, still looking annoyed and eyeing Duke with obvious disdain.

"We're leaving now," said Duke, standing up and motioning for his friends to do the same. "We can take you home."

"Hold up! Excuse me." The four of us turned to find a man wearing an official Utah Jazz vest making his way down our row, past a floor littered with popcorn containers and drinks. When he caught my eye, he asked, "Were you two on the kiss cam?"

"Yeah."

"What?" Jason demanded. He looked like he wanted to stand up, but the man in the vest stood in his way.

The man held out a paper to me. "You both get a free cookie at the Chocolate Melt cookie store in Murray. Thanks for participating in the kiss cam. It took you long enough, but you were definitely a crowd favorite."

"Uhh, thanks." I took the coupons from him, and he turned to leave.

"I didn't figure you for a two-timer, Nora from the Block," Jason muttered, quoting the horrifying MixNMingle handle Mira picked for me.

"We never one-timed."

Jason scoffed, his eyes finding mine. "You sure you trust these guys?"

I turned to meet Duke's gaze, clutching my purse. His fiery yet warm eyes waited patiently for me to respond. I didn't know him. Or his friends. But I had had more meaningful interaction with Duke's elbow tonight than anything Jason had said to me.

"Yeah. I think I do," I said before following Duke and his friends down the row, squeezing past knees and legs.

And when Duke held his hand out behind him, his fingers beckoning to me like a lifeline, I took it.

3

DUKE WAS TALLER THAN I HAD ORIGINALLY GUESSED. AT 5'7", I
reached the top of his shoulders. The large walkway littered with
concession stands was nearly empty. Beyond the hallway, the
crowd in the arena erupted in shouts and claps. We must have
scored another point. As the four of us walked toward the escala-
tors, my mind relived the past few minutes with surprising alarm.
What had I done? These guys were strangers to me, and I was
contemplating getting into a car with them.

I slipped my hand out of Duke's, immediately feeling more
grounded. He looked at me.

"You alright?"

"I don't know," I replied honestly.

"I still think you should have taken that guy outside," his
blond friend, Mike, said, playfully punching Duke as we shuffled
onto the escalator. "I would have loved to see that."

"His mullet could have probably taken me down," Duke said
easily, shoving his hands in his pockets as if he had no cares in
the world. I stood one step below him on the moving stairs, and
my eyes drifted briefly to his arms and had to disagree.

"Aww, he's too sweet to fight anybody," Ryan said, putting

his hands on Duke's shoulders and squeezing, giving Mike a pointed look before motioning to me with his head.

Duke shook his head, but the hint of color growing on his cheeks made him seem adorable.

"Take it down a notch, Romeo," he said.

I finally figured out how I knew Duke's blond friend, Mike. I had served him and his wife and kids a couple of days earlier at the cafe. It was the bright shirt and spiky blond hair that gave him away. Somewhere inside of me, that tiny interaction–not to mention the memory of his sweet wife and crazy-messy but super-adorable children–helped me to rest…if not easy, then at least a bit lighter in my current predicament.

Ryan stepped in front of me once we got off the escalator and stuck out his hand. He was eye level with me, with light-brown hair and a lazy grin on his face. "I'm Ryan, Duke's oldest friend. I know everything about him, including how many times he wet the bed growing up, so if you have any questions, feel free to ask."

Duke punched him in the arm while my smile broke free. My nerves were beginning to quiet, but I was still unsure of how to proceed. They all seemed so nice, but so did Jason. Should I go with them? Call an Uber? Mira? My mom was working at the cafe tonight. My car was about five blocks away, but walking alone down the dark streets didn't appeal to me either. We were now rapidly nearing the outside doors. As if reading my mind, Duke stopped suddenly, and we all followed suit.

"Let me talk to Nora for a sec." He reached into his wallet and pulled out a ten-dollar bill and held it out toward Ryan and Mike. "Here, kids, go buy some hot dogs, but stay where I can see you."

It took some prodding on Duke's part before the guys meandered off to the concession stand, amid teasing and exaggerated eyebrow raises in my direction.

I tucked a piece of my hair behind my ear, braving a glance at Duke. "I was under the impression that you didn't have kids."

Duke's face lit up in mirth. "I only get them one day a month. And that's usually enough."

Wrapping my arms around myself, we stood in silence for a moment. I was trying to process that I had kissed this man only a short while ago. I didn't even know his last name. Up until now, the craziest thing I had ever done in my life was not return a library book on time.

"Nora, I'd love to ask you out to go grab that cookie, but if this is all too fast or too weird for you, I'd be happy to wait with you while you call for a ride. I don't want you to feel uncomfortable."

He shoved his hands in his pockets as he looked at me. His brown eyes held a gentle confidence with a touch of vulnerability in their depths. A woman could fall in and get lost in eyes like that. The kind eyes, baseball hat, the light scruff on his face, and a quiet confidence were all working very nicely for him. I couldn't tear my gaze away, and I couldn't stop wondering why he was looking at me. Like that. I shouldn't do this. In three days, I was moving away for an undetermined amount of time. I couldn't get involved in anything right now. It had been an interesting night, but I needed to end it.

"Sorry. I'd love to, but I've got to retake a test tomorrow morning. I need to study."

"Oh, you bombed it before or something?"

Bombed was definitely not accurate. "More like got a B, and it was going to bother me enough that I wanted to redo it."

He stared at me incredulously. "Hold up. You're retaking a test because you got a B?"

"Guilty."

"Well, maybe it is best we part ways. For me, getting a C was cause for celebration at my house growing up."

I looked up at him then and smiled when I saw he was teasing, "Alright then, Nora. Is your car somewhere around here, or did your date pick you up?"

"I met him at a Chick-fil-A parking lot a few blocks away."

He nodded and seemed to be waiting for me to make a decision.

I opened my mouth to say something, but I couldn't remember what it was. An unfamiliar feeling of reckless abandon replaced the usual calm and order flowing through my body. I *wanted* to go with him. I wasn't scared for my safety. There was no warning alarm in the back of my mind when I thought about leaving with him. But could I?

At my hesitation, there was something else that grew in his eyes as he looked at me. Hope, maybe? As if he felt my hesitation, a half smile broke out across his face. "Just a cookie?"

Was that…a flutter…in my stomach?

"Okay," I said boldly before promptly losing some of my nerve. "But just a cookie. Then I have to study."

He grinned and gave me a salute, his face lighting up with boyish charm. Back in the arena, I thought he might be in his mid-twenties, but there was a calm vibe about him that alluded to a maturity that now gave me late-twenties vibes.

He motioned toward his friends walking back toward us, each carrying hot dogs. "They rode with me, so if you want to hop in with us, I'll drop them off, and then we can grab our cookies. Then I'll drive you back to your car. Sound okay?"

I nodded, sucking in a breath. "Yeah, sounds great. Thanks."

Mike and Ryan graciously squished into the back seat of Duke's white Toyota Tacoma amid lots of jokes and complaining. It had seen a few years, had a few minor dents, and the inside…looked lived in. Duke seemed a little embarrassed as he scooted fast food wrappers and bags aside to make space for me to sit.

"Dang kids," he mumbled.

"If you'd just taken your fancy car, you wouldn't have to worry. We're not allowed to eat in that one," came Ryan's reply.

Duke ignored them, pulling out of the parking lot, and made his way toward State Street before heading east. He glanced over at me. "You doing alright?"

"I don't see any shovels or duct tape. So far, so good."

He grinned. "I told you, not on Fridays."

"So did you all grow up together, then?" I turned sideways to speak to the guys in the backseat.

Ryan, the brown-haired friend, leaned forward in his seat. "Me and Duke grew up together, and in middle school, we allowed Mike to join the inner circle of awesome."

"You guys were in the chess club," Mike said, looking out the window.

"And the basketball team. Women like a well-rounded man."

"You were that too."

Ryan punched Mike in the arm.

Mike and Ryan razzed each other until we arrived at Ryan's house on the outskirts of Salt Lake. With a wave, Ryan slipped into his house, a split-level home in a subdivision of new starter houses. Mike lived a few minutes away, in a similar neighborhood.

"See you at work on Monday, boss." He said the words sarcastically while Duke shook his head.

He backed his truck out of the driveway, the sudden silence engulfing us, and I immediately missed the back and forth of Mike and Ryan in the backseat. They took all the pressure off of me to think of conversation. Jason had talked mostly about himself the five minutes we'd been alone on the car ride to the arena. Duke reached up and adjusted his hat. I watched as he placed his hands back on the wheel again, his forearms flexing in all the right ways.

Must think of something to say.

"I feel like we're doing this backward," I said.

He glanced over at me, eyebrows raised. "So you save your kiss for the end of the date? No imagination."

"No. I don't usually kiss on the first date." Or date, period.

"There was one interesting word in that sentence." Duke held up one finger, checking his rearview mirror as he eased his way back onto a main road.

"What?"

"Usually."

I laughed. "Does seven minutes in heaven in the eighth grade count?"

He threw me an incredulous look. "Do people really play that game?"

"It was a dare at one of my friend's parties. Her first boy-girl party, and she must have searched the internet for terrible ideas." It had been Mira's party. One of the few parties in middle school I remembered going to.

"And did you kiss for the whole seven minutes?"

"Rob definitely would have, but I made us play a get-to-know-you game for six minutes and forty-five seconds first."

"Poor guy. So how was that kiss? Better or worse than ours?"

Ours.

What an utterly sexy word. And completely inappropriate, given that I didn't know this man. But regardless, flutters made their way in a flurry around my stomach.

I pretended to think. "Rob had braces, so that made it exciting."

He grinned, pulling onto the freeway, heading south. "I feel like I know a lot about you and also very little at the same time."

"What do you know about me?"

"I know you work somewhere downtown, you've got a killer smile when you let it loose, and that you'll flirt with another guy while you're on a date."

"What?" I protested loudly while his deep chuckle warmed the empty space between us. "You started it!"

He gave me a sidelong glance. "You kept snuggling closer and touching my arm, giving me very mixed signals. I was beginning to feel sorry for poor Jason."

A smile lit my face even while I protested loudly. "You were not."

"No. I wasn't."

"So you can admit that it was ALL you."

He turned to look at me, eyebrows raised, looking like he was holding back a grin. "Really? *All* me?"

I could feel my face heat up as I remembered exactly how forward I had become at the game. But I couldn't admit that. "It was mostly you."

"Mostly. You add the most telling words to your sentences."

I could only shake my head. "You were the one talking to me while I was on a date."

"I was trying to be a gentleman and share the armrest."

"You're a saint. You did smell a lot better than my Jason, I'll give you that."

"*Your* Jason?"

"My *date*, Jason."

He chuckled, his fingers flexing on the steering wheel.

"I'm not usually like that," I said, breaking into the five seconds of silence. I was suddenly desirous for him to know that tonight had been a very unusual moment in my extremely boring, work-all-the-time, go-to-school, non-dating, just-missing-the-cats, cat-lady life. "I'm always very loyal to my dates right up to the doorstep."

"I'm not usually like that either."

"Usually?" I gave him a side-eye.

Another smile. "Usually."

He took the next exit. "I've always wanted to be on the kiss cam, though, and look at that…got my wish," he said.

"You're telling me that being on the kiss cam is something you've actively thought about before tonight?"

He huffed out a laugh. "No. But it got put on my list in bold capital letters real fast."

I looked over at him, suddenly feeling shy. "What's on your real bucket list?"

"It's all been checked off. I can officially die a happy man."

"Your ambitions in life are inspiring," I said.

He glanced in the rearview mirror before switching lanes. Was getting turned on by watching your date be a conscientious driver a sign of maturity? Asking for a friend.

"What's on your list?" he asked. "Maybe I just need some ideas."

"I wish I could tell you, but I save all my deepest thoughts for the second date."

"Is that an invitation?"

The retort itching to leave my lips halted before it could escape. I shouldn't have been flirting with him like this. I usually didn't flirt with *anyone* like this. I was moving to North Dakota in three days. It seemed dishonest to lead him on—unless, of course, he was just being friendly.

He pulled into the cookie shop parking lot, and in a super-suave way, I blurted out, "I'm moving in three days."

His mouth had been open, as if to say something before my confession, but he closed it, glancing at me with furrowed brows. "Huh?"

"I just…thought I should tell you that I'm moving to another state in a few days. Just in case."

"Just in case what?" He put the car in park.

My heart stopped until I saw his lips twitch.

"Just in case you fall madly in love with me during this cookie date," I sputtered, trying to keep my wits about me.

"What if I'm already halfway there?" His alluring grin my way was over the top and, strangely enough, put me at ease.

I breathed out a soft laugh and unbuckled my seatbelt. "Ha ha."

"Where are you moving? And why?" he asked as we walked toward the entrance. The Chocolate Melt had several flavors, but the poster outside boasting about the chocolate chip cookie that was voted the best in the city two years back already had my whole heart. I didn't need to see any other flavor.

"My grandma lives by herself and needs some help for the next while. So, I'm moving to Fargo."

"North Dakota?"

"Yeah."

He made a noise of disbelief. "I've heard of the Dakota states, but I didn't think anybody actually lived there."

I laughed, brushing the hair off my shoulder. With my work in the cafe, I usually had it up in a bun or ponytail. After being down all night, the constant feel of it at my neck was starting to annoy me. "A few people do. The entire state of North Dakota is as flat as a pancake, but Fargo is actually a pretty cool city."

Duke opened the door for me, the smell of butter and sugar and chocolate making my mouth water. I had seen this cookie store and many more like it all around the city, but I had never gone inside.

A few minutes later, we sat at a small table in the corner, both of us eating a warm chocolate chip cookie, and I determined I would have said yes to Jason's date a thousand times over if it led me to this moment.

"So, I thought you were in school. What are you going to do about moving to Fargo?" Duke asked.

"I'm almost done with finals for this semester, then I'm switching to online classes. I'm retaking my last test tomorrow. My grandma offered to pay for my degree in exchange for helping her out."

"And what are you going to school for?"

"Graphic design."

His head turned toward me in surprise. "Really?"

My brows raised in question at his interest. "Yeah."

"Me, Ryan, and Mike started a marketing company."

This time, my head turned to him in surprise. "You did?"

"Yeah."

"In your garage?"

"Yeah. It's probably not going to work out. I don't have the greatest track record for new business ideas. How long are you going to be at your grandma's?"

I wasn't sure how much to say. Telling someone about a terminal illness seemed like a mood killer on a date.

"I'm not sure. She's got dementia and is starting to slip more and more and doesn't really have anybody else to help her." I was going to stop there, but for some reason, the mood hadn't been killed, and he waited patiently for me to finish my explanation. "I'll be there as long as I need to be. Could be six months or five years."

"Could your parents go instead?"

I shook my head. "My mom still has my little sister at home, but this is my dad's mom. My parents divorced when I was a baby, so…" I trailed off.

He nodded thoughtfully. "Are you and your grandma close?"

"Sometimes." Memories of her visiting at brief intervals throughout my life had always been pleasant. A nice diversion.

"So this is probably the only date I'll get with you. Is that what you're saying?"

"I guess so," I said, trying to keep things light even as the tiniest hint of disappointment laced my body at his words.

There was a pause in the conversation, and when I finally looked up, he had his arms folded and a glint in his eyes. "The way I see it, Jason would have probably taken you to dinner after the game, so that would have been, what…another seven hours?"

I smiled, feeling my stomach tingle but shaking my head. "I would have turned down Dinner Jason."

"What about Bucket List Duke?"

"What?"

"All your talk about bucket lists got me thinking," he said. "What's on your list? Besides making out with a stranger on the kiss cam."

"Don't pull me into your dreams, buddy." I broke off another piece of cookie and popped it in my mouth.

One side of his lips curved into a grin even as he shook his head, probably graciously resisting the urge to respond to the opening I left wide open for him. Which was impressive.

I didn't have a list. Of course I had places I'd love to go, but on what planet would that happen? Currently, North Dakota was as exciting as it was going to get, and I was secretly ecstatic about the change of scenery. But one look at Duke and I knew that the answer of Fargo would not satisfy.

"If I were to have a list, most things would be like…getting my picture taken in a red phone booth and seeing the Eiffel Tower. You know, really original stuff like that."

His eyebrows raised. "You said *most* things?" There was a challenge in his statement, bubbling just below the surface.

And not for the first time all night, I wondered again how I had gotten here. After MUCH protesting to Mira, I had penciled the Jazz game—I mean, Jason—into my schedule for a generous four hours. Neat and tidy. I had pushed back studying for my make-up test to accommodate and to get Mira off my back. Fun was a luxury I rarely could afford.

He tilted his head back and considered me. "I'm thinking… what if we use tonight to check a few things off the bucket list?"

When he saw I was about to protest, he held up his hand. "You're moving in…how many days?"

"Three," I said, feeling my body begin to stiffen.

"One night to write home about? To send you off in style."

I held up my half-eaten cookie. "We got our cookie. That was fun."

He went on as though he hadn't even heard me. "From what I gathered, you got roped into your date with Jason, right?"

"Yeah."

"You seem like the type who has to schedule in your fun. What if tonight we did that? No worrying about being out late. No worrying about tests, or bills, or whatever else. Tonight, we'll be one hundred percent spontaneous and live in the moment."

I stared at him long enough to make sure he was serious. He was. A part of me wanted to tell him that spontaneity was what landed my mom with a baby in her belly three separate times. Those *fun* nights had given her children three deadbeat dads who had quickly found that their idea of a good time didn't include diaper duty or child support. The *fun*, spontaneous actions of others are what drove me to a life made up of barriers and lines and boundaries.

No. Fun had never been something that I particularly sought out.

"Why do you want to do this with me? This can't go anywhere."

"That's the beauty of it. A night as friends. Nothing more. One wild night." He must have seen my eyes turn terrified and quickly added, "Platonically wild night. Friend stuff. Crossing off some bucket-list items. Life can't just be studying for a test you don't need to retake."

I gave him a look that tugged his lips upward. "I didn't mean that as bad," he began.

"Yes, you did."

"Don't you want to make a few memories? Throw the schedule out and live up the night. Give yourself something to remember while you're freezing in Fargo."

I didn't do things like this. My wild nights consisted of movies on the couch with Mira or my sisters. So why was I contemplating saying yes to his crazy scheme? It wasn't his smile or the way his body filled out his jeans. It wasn't. A handsome face, while admired, did less to impress me than you might possibly imagine. There was a challenge in his eyes when he spoke, and the urge to prove him wrong hit me strong.

"You don't even know what's on my bucket list. What if it's singing Disney showtunes at the top of my lungs down Main Street?"

"Just tell me what part to sing." There was a grin on his face now, and he regarded me for a long moment. "So are we doing this? Want to check a few things off your list tonight?"

I stared at him before answering. "I have rules."

He folded his arms, amusement lining his expression. "I can't wait."

Ticking the first one off with my finger, I got comfortable. "Number one: No flirting. Number two—"

He leaned forward, catching my gaze with his. "We can't fall in love with each other."

Though I appreciated his nod to the romantic-comedy genre, I kicked his leg.

"That was it, wasn't it?" He laughed.

"I'm not that cheesy." I raised my chin. "Number two is no getting attached. No strings."

"Same thing," Duke declared. "But I agree. You're leaving. I don't want to get attached either. That's why this is so brilliant. No pressure. No strings. We both know how tonight ends."

Rules were kind of my thing, and my body immediately relaxed once they were in place. I checked the time and mentally cringed. Eleven-thirty.

PM.

"What do you say?" he asked. "You in?"

The idea began to be appealing. Even in the late hour. A night free of worry sounded so luxurious and foreign that I couldn't help myself. Maybe it was the sweet excitement in Duke's eyes or some sort of adrenaline side effect from escaping my date with Jason. Either way, I had been effectively swayed.

"I'm in."

His eyebrows rose slightly. "Really? Great."

"I have one more stipulation. I have time for two things and two things only. One from your list and one from mine. Nothing crazy. And I have to be home by two at the latest—non-negotiable." At the light that leapt in his eyes, I quickly added. "Two in the morning. AM."

He folded his arms, looking suspicious. "What time's your test?"

"None of your business."

He laughed. "Let me guess. Noon? 5 pm?"

"Seven in the morning, buddy. I have to be home by two so I can get up in time to study." To be honest, seven was when the test became *available* to take, but Duke didn't need to know that. Though...he probably did, but he let it slide.

"Okay," he said, considering me. "One more thing. You said yes. So you can't be worrying about what you're not getting done while you're with me. You have to be all in. Deal?" He held his hand out to me to shake and had the look on his face like he had won something.

Eyes narrowed playfully, I tamped down all the giddiness rising rebelliously throughout my body, met his hand with mine, and shook on it.

4

"So where am I headed?" Duke asked as we settled back into his truck.

"Let's do yours first," I said. My list could change based on whatever he pulled out for us to do tonight. I'd either match his crazy or be significantly less crazy.

"I've always wanted to buy a ticket to Europe and hop on a plane, spur of the moment," he said. "No plans. Just up and go and buy the ticket at the counter and take off."

"What about hotels?"

"I'd find something when I got there."

"What if there's nothing?"

"There'd be something."

"What about exchanging all your money into Euros?"

"I can do that there."

"What about work?"

He shrugged, so casual at the thought. "It will be there when I get back."

I laughed, somewhat bitterly. "Your work must be different than mine."

He leaned forward, tugging his hat around until it was backward, and started the engine.

"What if you don't speak the language?"

"Google translate."

"My blood pressure just spiked listening to you right now."

He tapped on the steering wheel, lost in a memory that put a dreamy look across his face. "One time, back in college, me and Mike had two days off of school and work. Middle of the week. Really random that we both were free. We decided to up and go to New York City. We bought tickets that afternoon, boarded a red eye that night, and spent the next day doing a twelve-hour tour of the city before catching a flight home the next morning. And it was the best vacation I've ever been on. No agenda. No money. We stayed in the scariest hotel in downtown New York. We ate hot dogs off the street, carried a backpack with all of our stuff, ran across the Brooklyn Bridge, yelled at drivers on the road just because we could."

I smiled at that. The idea of a free few days with no responsibilities was mind-boggling on its own, but to hop on a plane with no planning beforehand. To have money not even be an issue...

I cleared my throat. "Well, I don't think we can make it to Europe and have me home by 2 am, so you'd better pick something more attainable."

"Ladies first."

I was all set to tell him I wanted to get a fake tattoo or steal the idea of being in two places at once from *A Walk to Remember*. I was ready to borrow ideas from a movie. That was how far removed I was from a bucket list having any sort of impact on my life. But there was a part of my soul beginning to waken. However, with my current bank account situation, it would have to be a cheap type of spontaneous.

"I've always wanted to crash a wedding."

He looked confused. "Why?"

"They have the best cake. And food. And it would be free."

34

"I always thought wedding cake tasted like sugared Crisco."

"You must have been to all the wrong weddings."

"So we show up and eat the cake? That's the goal?"

"That's my goal."

Duke checked the time. "I'll bet most wedding parties are wrapping up by now. Well, actually...I've got a cousin who does catering. Want me to call her to see if she's working anywhere tonight?"

"Yes, please." The tiniest thrill of excitement shot through me as he phoned her, and I immediately tried to push the feeling away.

"Alright, thanks, Jess. See you in a bit." Duke ended his call and tossed his phone on the dash of his truck. "Okay, my cousin, Jess, is working at a party in the downtown event center here in town, and she said they have the place rented all night, and it's starting to get crazy. Sound good?"

I sat on my hands. "Sounds perfect."

He pulled his truck out onto Main Street. "So, from what I know about you, this bucket list item surprises me. You don't seem like the party type."

"Don't let my love of wedding reception food fool you. I'm not."

"So...what's our end game?"

"What do you mean?"

"Is it the thought of getting away with something that's appealing about this? Or are we playing a part?"

I thought about his question. I had no real interest in playing a part. What was it about sneaking into a reception and basically eating food we weren't invited to eat that appealed to me so much? A safe way to sow some wild oats I never got to sow in my childhood, perhaps?

"I'm not sure," I said, looking out the window as we drove downtown, watching the lights and the motion of nightlife blurring past my window.

"Here's the thing," he began. "I'm down for this, but I think we need to make it a little more interesting."

I gave him a wary look. "What?"

"I think we need to go full-out *Wedding Crashers*—we eat the food, dance on the dance floor, tell guests stories about the bride and groom, hug the mother of the bride...that kind of thing. Our goal here is to make memories and do the unexpected. Sneaking into a reception and grabbing a slice of cake isn't something I'll remember in five years."

"I already gave you the kiss cam. You've got plenty of material you'll remember in five years."

He laughed. "I think I gave *you* the kiss cam."

"It was definitely a joint effort."

"Fair enough. So what do you say, Nora? You up for going *Wedding Crashers* on this reception?"

There it was again...that yearning to be reckless. To do something off-kilter. Throw my tidy world off its axis. There had never been a guy that had so much sway over me. Was it like a gateway drug? One approving smile from Duke and now I'd do whatever he asked? Or was it the idea that I'd probably never see him again that made our night seem full of possibilities? Full of the unknown.

Ah, dang it.

I was going to say yes.

THE MOTHER of the groom was named Sandy, and it turned out she was a delight. Of course, if the whispers throughout the venue were true, she was six glasses of wine into the evening by the time we showed up and had been living up the night, dancing with every available—and sometimes not available—male in the building, if not to have a good time, then to most definitely stick it to her ex-husband who was at the wedding with a tall, young, and very attractive red-head.

Duke and I were sipping our drinks on the side of the dance floor after casually stuffing our faces with two slices of cake each, which Duke had deemed delicious, when Sandy shimmied up to us. She wore a sparkly cream-colored dress that glistened in the disco lights above. Her dark-blonde hair had been pulled up in what looked like an elegant updo, but after two hours of dancing, it looked more like a deflated balloon.

"I don't know you two," she proclaimed loudly as she draped her arms around our shoulders. "Tell me your names. How do you know my sweet Timmy?"

We had already concluded Tim was the name of the groom, based on a picture the size of a small school bus with a sign above reading Tim and Jori, Forever in Love—which was ironic because we had just witnessed the happy couple shouting and swearing at each other in the hallway after a very spirited and messy cutting of the cake.

"I'm actually second cousins with Jori," Duke said smoothly. "We used to play together as kids."

"How nice!" Sandy yelled pleasantly at both of us. "You're from South Africa, then?"

Duke blinked. I bit back a smile, suddenly catching the vision of immersing ourselves in our roles as wedding crashers. "Oh, he loved South Africa," I supplied, my hand on his arm. "He always tells the best stories about growing up there." I nodded toward Sandy. "Tell her one, Duke!"

There was a brief pause before Duke sunk easily into his new role. "Oh, you mean that time you came to visit? And you ate the elephant dung? You tell it, honey. It's funnier coming from you."

A smile brimming at the edge of my lips threatened to expose us both, but I held it in. "That never happened, remember? I *almost* took a bite. You thought it was some sort of medical cream and smeared it all over your bug bites."

Sandy laughed a little too loud. "Jori always told us it was quite a volatile place." Sandy wobbled a bit on her feet, her alcohol-addled head moving back and forth between us. Then her eyes turned to me. "Can I steal him away for a dance?"

Duke's eyes widened at that, making me smile brightly at Sandy in return. "Of course you can! He *loves* to dance."

The look Duke shot me as I blew him a kiss and Sandy pulled him toward the dancers made the entire night worth it. A memory I would happily remember for the next decade of my life. Alcohol and vengeful glances at her ex-husband gave Sandy octopus arms. Duke did his best to hold her at a respectable distance, occasionally moving her hand back up to somewhere on the north end of his body, as needed. When he threw me a helpless glance, I could only turn away, hiding my laughter behind my Dr. Pepper.

The smell of alcohol and sweat filled the room of partygoers. More drinks consumed led to more dancers out on the dance floor. I eyed the impressive tower of partially full wine glasses in the corner of the room in concern, one drunk stumble away from disaster.

"I've been bad!" Sandy slurred, her voice in my ear causing me to jump. I turned as she pushed an amused Duke toward me. "I shouldn't have taken this man away from his sweet wife. You two, full of love in your eyes." At this point, she let go of Duke to squish my cheeks. "Go dance." She stared at us in complete adoration in that hollow, glassy-eyed way of hers.

Duke's forehead was glistening in sweat after his passionate dance with Sandy to a wedding classic, "Don't Cha" by the Pussycat Dolls and Busta Rhymes. He held out his hand to me, his eyes glinting dangerously. "Hey, wife. Wanna dance?"

The wife comment sent actual waves of sensation up and down my spine. Or maybe it was the way the universe was spinning so randomly for us tonight, but I could not keep the smile from my face as I placed my hand in his and allowed him to lead me to the dance floor.

It was the second time that night I had held Duke's hand. My mind wanted to go down the rabbit hole of acknowledging how crazy it was that I had only met him five hours earlier, but I forced it to stay in the present. The feel of his hand holding mine, the pounding in my chest as he pulled me close while dancing to "Another One Bites the Dust." The songs from this wedding had a vibe all their own. The way the lights from the disco ball lit across his face was enough to consume me at the moment.

Showing up at a function where we only "knew" each other created a cozy sense of togetherness that I hadn't been prepared for. It was hard to remember we had barely met by the way his eyes repeatedly found mine across the room, to the way he mouthed, *Help me*," just before Sandy dipped him. Or when a balding, middle-aged man with sweaty hands approached me for a dance while Duke was in the restroom and Duke cut in to whisk me away twenty seconds later. Or the way he lightly stepped on my toe with his foot when Sandy stumbled up to us once more, asking another question about South Africa.

It was disconcerting. That was all. I was moving away. There would be no strings. It gave me leave to relax the tiniest bit. In his arms, knowing it was all pretend, I could imagine what it would be like to actually be with a guy like Duke. I could live in a romantic fantasy world like the best of them, and for tonight, I was Cinderella at the ball. The clock would eventually strike midnight, and there was a feeling of both relief and disappointment at the thought.

The fast song ended, and he held me close until the next one started. A slow song. I didn't allow myself to process how it might be the most fitting song of the night—Tom Waits' classic, "I Hope That I Don't Fall in Love With You."

Duke adjusted his arms slung low around my waist, pulling

me closer. "Hopefully this song will keep you in line. I saw you checking out my dance moves. You better keep your hands where I can see them."

My head was turned into his shoulder, hiding the bliss on my face. "I think this song is the universe keeping *you* on track."

He pulled back to look at me. "Too late. You're my wife now. Didn't you hear Sandy?"

"You wish."

"I'm starting to."

I stiffened, swatting his shoulder. "Hey! We have rules."

"It's your fault. I only said it because your cheeks turn pink when I tease you. No man on this earth would be able to resist trying to make that happen over and over. Strings or no strings."

I made the mistake of looking into his eyes. They were filled with sweetness and teasing, and combined with the raspy voice crooning above us, suddenly a flaming arrow of tingles erupted down my veins.

"Okay, time to go." I pulled out of his arms and began walking toward the exit, snatching our coats off the backs of our chairs as I did so.

He hurried to catch up. "Why? The song was just getting to the good part."

"You start breaking the rules, then we have to leave."

He jumped ahead to fling open the door for me. The December evening was the perfect cool blast to the face we both needed.

We were silent, walking toward Duke's car before he turned around, walking backward to face me. "You know what this means now, don't you?"

I eyed him. "What?"

He grinned. "It's my turn."

5

THE AIR OF THE TRUCK WAS THE SAME TEMPERATURE AS OUTSIDE. Duke idled in the parking lot, each of us blowing warm air on our hands while the heater took its sweet time warming up.

I settled down in my seat, bringing my feet up on the dashboard and taking a long, fortifying sip of the Dr. Pepper I'd taken with me from the reception. I was hoping for a shot of energy to get me through the next hour. Glancing over at Duke, I motioned toward my feet. "Is this okay?"

He nodded. "I guarantee you're only improving the look of this truck."

My body stilled as I glared good-naturedly at him. "Pretty bold statement for someone who is already on very thin ice."

He drummed his fingers on the steering wheel. "That wasn't flirting. Believe me, I would never. It's a statement of fact." He glanced at the can in my hands. "How's your Dr. Pepper?"

I looked down. "It's fine."

"Just fine? I thought there was a cult following with that stuff."

He self-righteously took a sip of his Coke.

"You're one to talk," I said. "There isn't much a DP can't fix, but it's better when it falls."

He leaned close, brows furrowed. "What now?"

"There's a gas station by my apartment, and when I'm going to treat myself, I get a large Dr. Pepper with light ice in a cup. It's better when it falls out of a fountain."

His lips broke out into a wide smile. "Good to know. Here I am just drinking a Coke from a can like an idiot."

I shrugged. "The same rules might not apply to Coke. I'm sure it's still gross either way."

"Hey…watch your mouth."

I felt a smile tugging at my lips. "Okay, the clock's ticking. What's your pick?"

"Alright…you did *Wedding Crashers*. I'm sensing a movie-reenactment theme here tonight."

I folded my arms. "No. I wanted cake. You turned it into *Wedding Crashers*." He shot me a lazy grin that caused me to blurt out a warning. "I have to be home in one hour. ONE. Take whatever crazy is going through your head and bring it down twenty-seven notches."

To my dismay, his smile only grew wider. "I've always wanted to reenact the lift scene from *Dirty Dancing*."

My shoulders relaxed. "At the end of the movie? Like they did in *Crazy Stupid Love*?"

It would be a little weird having him lift me up, but if his muscles did what they looked like they could do, it was reasonable to assume we could knock that bucket list item out in about ten minutes.

"Nope. The one in the water."

It took me a moment before I connected to what he said. I peered closer at him. "That has never once been on your bucket list until two seconds ago."

He bit his lip, but his grin would not be contained. "If we're going with a movie theme…"

42

"We're officially not!"

He laughed. "I wish I had thought to bring my actual list to show you, but I guess you'll have to trust me."

"I don't have extra cloth—" I stopped and eyed him warily. "I am NOT going skinny dipping with you, so don't even think about that."

He held his hands up in mock offense. "Look, lady, I just met you tonight. Even though we've kissed and you got a bit handsy once, you're making me very uncomfortable."

"That was Sandy!"

"It was dark. How could I know for sure?"

I leaned forward to swat at his leg.

"See! There you go again. The first time was a lot gentler."

I covered my face to hide my laughter. Sandy giving Duke a three-swat pat on his rear end after her dance should give her ample reason to be embarrassed tomorrow morning. Though, I didn't think she'd remember any of it.

"Okay, I have a gym bag in the back with two shirts and two pairs of shorts. One pair is dirty and the other is not. You can take your pick."

"It's December. I'm not jumping into a lake with you. It must be a swimming pool or no deal."

He looked offended. "Swimming pool? That's not how they did it in the movie. It was definitely a lake."

I gaped at him. "I don't do frozen lakes."

"It wouldn't be frozen. It's early. There might be a few ice chunks, but that's it."

"It's the middle of the night."

"I didn't say this bucket list would be easy. I only said it would be worth it."

"You didn't say any of that. You forget, we only just met. I'm not driving to some mountain lake in the middle of the night with you. I need a place with witnesses."

"Geez, you're feisty." He checked his watch as though he

43

was unsure about something before saying, "Fine. My parents have a pool. We'll go there."

"Of course they do."

"Lucky for you."

"Is it outside? Won't that be freezing?"

He hesitated, before speaking carefully. "It's outside, but they have it covered. It will be cold either way."

With those promising words, I allowed him to lead me up the mountain on the east side of the city. Minutes later, the old, white, beat-up Toyota Tacoma passed through the gate of the Wild Rose subdivision in the hills along the east bench, overlooking Salt Lake City. I watched as Duke rolled down his window and punched in the passcode. He studiously ignored my gaping as we passed home after multi-million-dollar home.

We pulled into a driveway with a towering three-level home with eaves and alcoves and balconies...you name it, gracing the front. The front boasted a beautiful mix of creamy rock and stucco, lit in the dark by warm, glowing lights in the eaves. I didn't even know what it was called, but Duke drove us through an arched, rounded, covered bridge connecting the house with some other garage or building and parked in an area behind the house. He killed the engine and I looked out on a courtyard complete with a basketball court and a swimming pool with a cover over the top.

I looked at Duke who only scratched at his neck almost sheepishly.

"You ready?" he asked.

"Yeah, just waiting for the butler to come catch my door."

"Butlers don't do truck doors, Kiss Cam. But I can grab it for you."

My fingers clutched the door handle. "I've got it."

The crisp winter air nipped at my face as I stepped outside onto a cobblestone driveway. I turned to face Duke as he rounded the truck.

"Is there really a butler?" I assumed he was joking, but now, taking in the twinkle lights over the pool area with the amazing slide made fancy by decorative rocks, I couldn't be sure.

"No," Duke said.

"There is a maid, though, right?"

He ignored me, his hand light at my elbow, propelling me toward the building I had first mistaken for another garage. He punched the code on the pad outside the door before leading me inside.

A boat house.

It was a boat house.

And a car house. I would just say garage, but that was what we passed on the other side of the arched driveway.

A fancy white boat, rimmed in crisp blue, was the first thing to catch my attention. Two jet skis and a rogue snowmobile were lined up perfectly next to the boat. Then three fancy cars stacked in tight next to each other filled out the other side of the building. I had no idea what make or model the cars were, but they were sleek and sporty and looked like something you'd see on a magazine cover. To the left of the main door to the garage were two bathrooms, each with a man and woman sign over them.

He propelled me toward the woman's door. He was hurrying us, which seemed out of character for the man who hadn't been in a hurry all night. I wanted to linger and appropriately gawk at all the details. For some reason, seeing Duke's childhood home —though the word *home* now seemed laughably modest— relaxed me. I didn't have anything to worry about. This date was indeed a one-night-only kind of date. Even if I hadn't been moving, Duke and I were from two different worlds that rarely collided. My weird attraction to him would stay just that...attraction. I knew this wasn't 1800s England, but it only took living in a run-down apartment in the city to understand that the class system hadn't totally dissolved.

"Are we going to wake up your parents?" I asked, my hand

on the door, ready to enter with Duke's clean pair of gym clothes tossed over my shoulder.

Another sheepish look crossed his face. "They're in Europe right now."

I froze. "What?" I smacked him with his shorts. "I said we needed a place with witnesses!"

"You want people to watch us attempting the lift?" he asked. "You said you needed a pool. This is the only place I knew I'd be able to get in at one in the morning." He must have seen a look on my face that didn't convince him I was okay, so he added, "If it makes you feel any better, my parents have cameras all over this place. They're probably being alerted to someone on their property right now."

I blew out a sigh. I did my best to go about my daily life, making the kind of decisions where I wouldn't wind up the victim on a true crime podcast. This whole night had blown my cautious nature to bits, but so far, my decision to live in the moment with Duke had been rewarding. Fun, even. Duke no longer felt like a stranger. We had inside jokes, for Pete's sake.

"Alright, let's do this."

He gave me a salute. "I'll meet you out here in two minutes."

The bathroom smelled like the perfect mixture of lilacs and chlorine. I hadn't thought of the logistics of my wearing his clothes like a swimming suit. After deciding it would be too weird to completely strip down in his clothes, I kept my bra and underwear on underneath. I'd probably freeze the rest of the night, but according to my calculations, our night would be over soon. I checked my complexion in the mirror. To my surprise, my skin didn't seem the pale color it had been at the start of my date. I wasn't used to seeing a splash of color on my cheeks, but for a long moment, I couldn't look away. I wasn't sure who I was tonight. My hands shook as I pulled my hair up in a familiar high ponytail, looking the most like myself I'd been all night long.

I didn't allow my mind to overthink the grand marble counters, or the fancy above-counter sinks in the bathroom, or the toilets that flushed themselves. And this was *just* the boathouse. I'd kill to see the inside of Duke's actual home. I pushed open the door and found Duke waiting for me, wearing his "used" set of gym clothes that looked almost identical to what I was wearing—black shorts and a gray top.

My eyes trailed down his shoulder to his arms before I remembered myself and yanked them back up. In all reality, I should have felt frumpy. The clothes were too big and awkward, and I didn't even like the gym whose name my shirt boasted proudly, but the way his eyes drifted down my body, taking in the shorts that went past my knees and the oversized shirt with sleeves that hung past my forearms…I felt anything but frumpy.

"You ready?"

"If I say no, can we be done here?"

Placing his hands lightly on my shoulders, he led me out the door and into the night, which suddenly seemed significantly colder than when we had arrived, which was probably due to the fact that I was wearing shorts and was now barefoot.

"Wait here." Duke's warm hands left me as he jogged over to the pool and pressed a button. The cover began retracting, opening up to a glittering pool filled with water. I danced on the balls of my feet for warmth.

Duke walked back to me, his arms folded across his stomach in an attempt to ward off the chill. Though, with his arms folded, it only made his muscles seem to burst out—

Never mind.

Rubbing my arms briskly, I began searching for which side of the pool was the shallow end when Duke stopped me with his hand on my arm.

"We have to run and jump."

"What?"

The brisk air turned the concrete into shards of ice at my feet as we moved barefoot past patches of snow.

"That's how I've always imagined they did it in *Dirty Dancing*."

"No, you haven't!" I said to his laughing face. "It was a lake. They HAD to walk in."

"Nah. I'm sure they had a dock. They totally jumped."

It wasn't true. And by the gleam in Duke's eyes, he seemed determined to create zero shortcuts in our bucket list scheme. I didn't want to jump, but I was also standing in Duke's clothes in the middle of the night, ready to re-enact a movie scene. I was already fully committed to this bit, and I wasn't about to back down now.

"Fine."

His eyebrows raised. "Fine? Really?"

A reckless smile slowly appeared on my face. It felt as familiar to me as the ultra-plush guest bath towels I'd just wiped my hands on. Before I could overthink, I took off running down the concrete pathway leading to the pool, cheered on by Duke's whoops and hollers behind me. Today, I was going to be fun. I was here. I was ninety-five percent certain I wasn't going to get murdered tonight, which still left a five percent chance Duke would turn on me, but that was probably just life. I kept going, picking up speed, fully embracing the unpredictability of fun. Fun. I could do it. I could *taste* it. I could *be* it. The lights around the pool shimmered against the water, beckoning me closer, even as I braced myself for the cold. I, Nora Griffin, was going to be FU—

My foot caught on a patch of black ice as I neared the pool, my momentum forward-spiraling into skittish turns and flailing arms and a loud crack, and then ended with me sprawled out spread eagle on Duke's parents' extravagant pool deck.

6

"I AM SO SORRY," DUKE SAID AGAIN.

I turned to him, sitting next to me in the uncomfortable hospital chair. We were still dressed in his shorts and t-shirt, though I had my coat over me. Dozens of people filled the cracks of the waiting area at the emergency room, ranging from limps and scratches to hacking up the black lung. We sat in the corner of the room as far away from everyone else as we could.

"I know. And you really should be. It was completely your fault there was a patch of ice on the ground."

"I made you run."

"I could have stopped if I wanted to."

He was about to say something else when he looked at me. "So...you wanted to jump in? That's interesting because I remember a lot of swearing and mild threats on the drive to my parents' house."

We were interrupted by a pretty nurse with graying hair and a plump figure, who looked like she could use a fresh dose of caffeine.

"I'm so sorry about the wait," she said with a slight Southern accent. "We had a big multi-car crash with patients coming in an

49

ambulance about ten minutes before you arrived. It might be a while still. Can I get you something?" She looked at me sympathetically.

"Will everyone be okay?" Duke asked.

She sighed. "It sounds like everyone will survive, so that's good news, but some are in pretty rough shape." She motioned to my foot. "Do you need another ice pack?"

"I'm fine. It's probably a sprain. I only came because of him." I motioned my head toward Duke.

"It made a popping sound when she went down," he said.

She smiled at Duke. "You did the right thing." Then to me, she added, "It sounds like he's a keeper." She began walking toward her desk. "Let me know if you need anything."

Duke waited until she sat down at her desk before he elbowed me. "Did you hear that? I'm a keeper."

I settled back into my chair and closed my eyes with a sigh. "I kind of hope it's broken so I can justify the cost of this ER visit."

We were silent for a long while, both of us lost in our own thoughts. Me because my last statement to him sounded flippant, but it wasn't. Duke felt so terrible about my leg, and when I began limping upon standing up, he was so insistent we come here. I didn't want to make the money a big deal, but I cringed at how long it might take me to pay this off. But I was here, living in the moment, and at the moment, my brain was too fuddled to try and make sense of anything, because it was two-thirty in the morning, and his arm was currently smooshed against mine on the armrest.

I pushed his arm off with mine. "My turn."

He nudged my good foot. "We haven't had the talk yet."

"Since I'm injured, I call it for the rest of the time we're here."

I could hear the smile in his voice. "You think because I feel bad about you getting hurt that I'll just give you the armrest?"

I peeked one eye open at him. "I kind of do, actually."

He folded his arms in his lap and slouched down in his seat, head on the back of his chair. "Alright, Kiss Cam Nora. We may be here all night. Tell me about yourself." Before I could protest, he turned his face my way. "And before you tell me we can't have strings, just think of me like one of your romantic-comedy movies. A mysterious and handsome stranger asking the hot babe a few questions about herself in a waiting room. It's just small talk."

"I'm a cafe expert on small talk, and that's not how you do it," I said, mimicking his position on my chair, proud of myself for feigning a relaxed pose after being called a hot babe.

"Oh, really? Let's hear it, then."

"Are you not allowed to speak to the common folk where you live?" He gave me an annoyed look that only served to excite me. "It goes like this: 'I can't believe how cold it is already. It's only the first of December. I'm scared to see what else is in store for us this month.'"

There was a pause before Duke spoke. "Yup. It does get cold in the winter."

I tapped on his foot. "You have to pretend to be shocked that it's so cold."

"It happens every year."

"I know, but we don't say it like that. We are always surprised that it gets cold so early in Utah. Always."

"I'm bored. Can you please just tell me why you have a tattoo on your foot?"

I froze, but before I could shut him down, he continued. "I want to know why the foot? Did that hurt? And what does it mean?"

Granted, if I wanted to not have people ask me about the tattoo, I should have gotten it on a more private part of my body, but that didn't mean anyone was entitled to the real reason.

"How did you see that?"

At the pool, before you went down."

Fair enough. Feeling a slight headache, probably from the late night, I massaged the tension in my eyebrows. "I got a tattoo because I wanted one. And the foot seemed like a great place."

"Nope. Try again."

I looked at him. "What?"

"You're not the kind of person who wakes up and decides to get a tattoo. It doesn't fit your MO."

"My MO?"

"Your modus operandi. Your way of operating." When I didn't say anything, he said in a softer tone, "You don't have to tell me if it's personal. I just noticed it and got curious."

"You're forgetting something, though. You don't really know me." I made a show of checking my phone for the time. "It's been exactly six hours since we first met."

"Is it our six-hour anniversary already? I didn't get you anything."

The smile on my face came without warning.

He continued, "The way I see it, we've packed almost three and a half dates into those hours, so, technically, this is date three and a half...we're getting pretty serious now."

For one tiny millisecond, I had a pang of sadness that I was leaving for North Dakota. And before you go all elderly lady wisdom on me, I know I can't stop love if it happens, which is why I had made it a habit to avoid relationships in general. At least until I had a career and could take care of myself. But Duke was on a whole different level of life than I was. No strings attached was now the most important rule of our night.

"I can change my question, if you want." Duke's soft voice filtered into my ears.

I was making it a bigger deal by hesitating. The actual reason wasn't a hidden, dark secret, but it would open doors between us I wasn't sure should be opened. I would be giving him a piece of myself, and I couldn't help but wonder if it would be better for my heart to keep it all reined inside. Then again, this night had brought out a strange version of myself, so maybe it would be good to clue him in a bit more on the real Nora. Everything had gone to whack the moment he sat next to me at the game. I had a sudden urge to dip my toe in the water.

"It's not random. It's Latin. It means, *To the stars through difficulties*. I got it when I turned sixteen and got my first real, tax-paying job to help my mom cover the rent."

Okay, that was less like a toe and more like plunging my entire body into the water.

He seemed confused by this. "What do you mean your first tax-paying job?"

"My aunt's boyfriend at the time owned a cafe by the freeway. He used to let me wash dishes there when I was thirteen."

"All under the table?"

I nodded. "I didn't understand any of the legal stuff at the time, but I had overheard my mom crying to my aunt about not being able to afford the rent that month. So I told my mom I wanted to help, and my Aunt Cathy got me a job at her boyfriend's cafe."

"So you've been working since you were thirteen?"

"Mostly. It depended on my mom's boyfriends or husbands. Some of them had money and moved in with us for a while, and then I didn't have to work. But they never lasted."

"What about your mom? Does she work?"

I nodded. "After I turned sixteen, I'd go to work right after school until nine or ten at night, and then I'd be home while she went to work the night shift. By this time, we were both working at a cafe downtown by where we lived. She'd get home in the morning just as I was leaving to take me and my sisters to school."

"And do you still pay half of your mom's rent?"

He asked the question so softly an unexpected ache in my

chest formed. "My mom is…complicated." I ended my statement with a shrug of my shoulders.

"What's she going to do when you go to North Dakota?"

"I'm hoping she'll figure it out."

"Are your sisters able to help?"

"Harper has practices and games after school. My other sister is a nanny in New York…" my voice drifted off.

He seemed lost in thought, not saying anything. His gaze locked on the chair in front of us. I chewed on my fingernail until I could no more.

"Do you ever feel resentment?" he asked.

"No."

He eyed me.

I huffed out a noise that seemed a mixture of annoyance and defiance. "I mean… Maybe. A little. When I was younger, I sometimes wished I could have had time to play sports instead of working after school. But it is what it is. I've spent my whole life watching my mom struggle and dig herself into holes she can't ever seem to get out of. She needs help. She has an addiction to jerk-face losers."

"Jerk-face losers. Is that the technical term?"

The smile appearing on my face was interrupted by the nurse from the front desk. We both sat up, ready to stand, before she stopped us and bent over next to me, whispering in that way elderly people often do, broadcasting loud and almost shrill throughout our entire section—specifically right in Duke's ears.

"Sorry, sweetie, it's not time to go back yet. I was just processing your paperwork, and you didn't fill out the date of your last period."

If the shaking shoulders next to me were any indication, it would seem that Duke heard that—as well as the three sections of chairs near us.

I leaned forward. "I didn't think it was necessary information for a sprained ankle." Also, because I never tracked it and had no clue the date of my last period.

Her drawn-on eyebrow crinkled, bringing the paperwork up to her eyes to see better. "A sprained ankle? I thought you were here for the"—she leaned even closer, her sour breath a puff of air shooting into my nose—"anal abscess."

My eyes widened. My mouth opened and closed before opening again. From the corner of my eye, Duke definitely brought a hand up to his mouth.

I gave a tight smile and motioned toward my foot. "No, just a sprained ankle. Are you sure you have the right person?"

She squinted down at her paperwork. "Debbie?"

"Nope. Nora."

The woman's cheeks colored as her hands flew to cover her face. "Oh, my lanta, if that wasn't a HIPAA violation, I don't know what is. I'm so sorry."

At this point, a laugh escaped me. "You're fine. I hope you find Debbie."

"I tried calling out, but nobody heard me. I was sure she was you." The distraught nurse backed away, mumbling to herself as she frantically searched the now packed ER. With great regret, I turned my attention back toward Duke.

I put my hand in front of his face. "Not one word."

He groaned, clutching his chest. "Come on. I can't keep this in all night."

"You can, and you will."

He laughed again, this time his fingers pinching the top of his nose. "I guess we should be grateful it's only an ankle issue."

I swatted his arm, making the mistake of meeting his eyes—crinkly and brown and twinkling in a way that had my toes curling. I couldn't help but smile back, the heat on my face lessening.

"Anyway, go on." Duke motioned me forward with a flourish of his hand.

Where to even start up again after that? "I love my mom, but I've worked my entire life to *not* be like her."

"In what way?"

In that moment, Duke was my best friend I had just met. The words flowed out of my mouth and into the air between us, where I felt sure he would catch them and hold them safe. I'd never experienced anything like this night, and a part of me wondered if I stopped talking, would the magic between us be over? So I kept talking, the words leaving my lips and healing a part of me as they did.

"Well, I already didn't get pregnant at sixteen and married at seventeen, so that's one hurdle crossed off the list."

He held out his hand for me to give him a high five. "Same."

I laughed and gave him a high five.

After a moment, Duke asked, "Your mom works, right?"

I nodded.

"Why can't she pay her own rent?"

If this were any other day, I probably wouldn't have answered. But tonight...

"She's been divorced a lot and has a credit card problem," I said simply.

Duke nodded. "You moving away will be good for her, then. Give her a chance to fall."

"Fall?"

"Yeah."

I leaned back in my seat, examining my nails. "I'm enabling her, right? Isn't that what they call it?"

Duke shrugged.

"I get that. But things aren't always so black and white." Suddenly, I was desperate that he know more about her than her shortcomings. "My mom can't pick men, and she can't manage her money. Those are two pretty big things." I waited a beat before continuing. "But she has a singing voice that makes people stop and stare. She can do impressions of people in ways that have everyone snort laughing. She always told me and my sisters that we were beautiful and funny. Sometimes she'd let us stay up past our bedtimes, and we'd watch movies with microwaved popcorn and a handful of candy she'd bought for each of us from the dispenser at the cafe. She always gave the homeless people on our streets whatever change she could—or whatever change I had." Duke snorted at that while I huffed out a laugh and brushed away a tear leaking from my eye. A beat of silence fell between us before the two of us were lost to the moment with shaking shoulders and hushed wheezes.

Eventually, I added my last thought. "The point is, it's not all black and white with my mom—there's a lot of gray."

"Probably true for all of us," Duke said, letting out a big breath. He paused, then added, "So that's why you don't date much? You're scared of being like her?"

"Yup. In my dream world I'll have a career before I get into a serious relationship. I also keep pretty busy. I work at the cafe and go to school full time. The jury's still out on whether or not I'm like my mom. I definitely haven't been blown away by the quality of the two guys I've dated in the past."

"You sure picked a stinker tonight," he said.

"Aww, don't be too hard on yourself."

He nudged my arm. "Your pick was terrible, but thankfully, there was an amazing kiss-cam interception."

My eyes fell to his teasing lips. It took much less effort than it should have to conjure up the memory of his kiss.

We sat quietly for a moment. There was more I could have added about my mom, but it would have been too much for our night together.

My entire life, I watched men who used my mother like a bar of soap. Then a year ago, I met Derek. He was different. He wasn't just good looking; he was ambitious. My mother never dated ambition. This was different, and I clearly wasn't my mother. Turns out, I couldn't have been more wrong. Within a month, I'd found that I had attracted the same quality of guy my mom always had—a liar and a cheat. Quite the blow to my ego, realizing that I was a carbon copy of the woman I'd spent my entire life trying not to be. A heavy blow indeed.

"Tell me about you now," I said, attempting to lighten the mood, a playful smile at my lips. "Let me guess," I began, shifting toward him in my seat. "Your parents bought you a car for your sixteenth?"

The guilty half smile came almost unbidden on his face.

"What was it?" I pressed. "A Ferrari? Lambo?"

A wrinkle furrowed across his brows. "As if I would stoop that low."

"Aston Martin?"

"They couldn't get it custom-made in time for my party."

My smile dropped, and I peered closer. "Seriously?"

He shot me a look. "They did buy me a car, but then I bought my truck when I was seventeen. And I did have a job in high school, smarty pants."

"The truck you're driving tonight?"

"The very same."

I tried not to be impressed that he still used the old truck he drove in high school when all signs suggested he could probably afford newer and better—or at the very least, his parents could.

"I keep the Lamborghini parked in the garage on guys' night so I don't make Mike and Ryan feel bad."

I leaned back in my seat. "So considerate of you."

"I try."

"What was your job in high school?"

He adjusted in his seat before doing an almost convincing job of faking a cough.

I leaned forward, wolf on the scent. "Come on...what was it?"

"When I was in high school, my dad was a lawyer. I worked at his office as a runner."

"They hire people to jog for them?"

A smile crept across his lips. "They hire people to run documents that need signed all over town, grab coffees, wash their cars…things like that."

I tried to imagine a young Duke grabbing coffee for people. I could see it, strangely enough, though it definitely shouldn't have fit his MO. "You said in high school. What does your dad do now?"

"He starts up companies and sells them."

"And now you're going into business with your friends?"

He stretched his legs out in front of himself. "Ryan and Mike talked me into starting a marketing company with them, so I guess I'm going to try that for a bit."

"For a bit? Why? You don't think you'll work well together?"

He shrugged. "We used to blow up mailboxes as teenagers, and now they think we can run our own business."

I jolted. "You blew up mailboxes?"

"It was a dark time in my otherwise spotless existence."

"Did you get in trouble?"

"I replaced all the mailboxes and was sentenced to a summer living at my grandparents' farm—to get away from all the bad influences." His voice was dry, almost sarcastic, though he said it with a smile.

My eyebrows raised. "Did it work?"

Another shrug. He was giving me bits and pieces, which made me instantly annoyed I had given him so much.

"Hey! I gave you stuff on my mother." I pushed his shoulder lightly. "And you think I might have an abscess, so you'd better start talking."

His laughter was quick, and our easy camaraderie started up again.

"The summer on my grandparents' farm became my whole

personality, and I ended up choosing to stay with them every summer until I finished high school."

"Every summer?"

"Yup."

"Did you start wearing cowboy boots and a hat?"

He leaned back. "You'd like that, wouldn't you?"

I didn't answer, suddenly struck by the alluring image of Duke in a cowboy hat.

Thankfully, he kept going. "My parents are also a little gray. They're good people. They mean well. They do lots of good in the community. But what if I told you that I was only sent to my grandparents' house because my parents already had a trip to Europe planned for the summer? They paid for all the mailboxes and then told all their friends they were sending me away to the farm to straighten up."

My brow furrowed. "They didn't make you pay for the mailboxes?"

"I had never had a job at that point. Honestly, I think it was easier to just pay for it than to take the time to teach me to work. Probably a big part of why I spent so much time goofing off."

"More like damaging personal property, but go on." I motioned him to continue with a wave and was rewarded with a sheepish smile.

"Anyway. Let's just say that I owe my grandparents a lot." The softness in his tone and the pride in his voice caused my heart to burn for some reason. All the while, my mind reeled with this information, though I was still not even close to knowing the full picture.

"So…back to your company. Why do you not think it will work? Is it the money to start up?" Instantly I blanched, remembering myself. The waiting room was full, noisy even for the middle of the night, but we were tucked away into our own corner, leaving a cozy kinship kind of feeling. That had to be the cause of my loose tongue.

Duke didn't seem worried by my tactless question. "No. My parents are planning to loan us the money to move into a building downtown, but I'm not sure. We hired a designer, and we have one client so far. I'm just having a hard time getting into the idea of it all."

"Why?" The freedom and money to do whatever he wanted felt like a lavish dream to me. That he would be so flippant with the idea made my insides physically ache.

"I just... I've tried a few business ideas before, and they've always fizzled out. We lost quite a bit of money on the last idea I had. I'm having a hard time finding something I'm passionate about long term."

"We?"

He shifted. "My parents."

"Do they hold it against you?"

He scoffed, laughing a little bitterly. "Not really. They're so focused on me becoming successful that they don't care about the money."

"Is there a family business they want you to take over one day?" I asked, folding my arms and turning in my seat toward him.

He tapped my foot. "You watch too many movies."

"Am I close, though?"

His teeth were pearly white and perfectly aligned in his mouth. I'd know, because I was learning that Duke was the jovial sort who'd happily flash me a smile even when nothing we were talking about was particularly funny.

"They don't care much about what I do as long as I'm as successful as them or close to it."

"Did your parents fund all your other ideas?" I couldn't get off the money thing. The idea of this was so foreign to me.

He seemed a bit embarrassed. "Not completely. But yeah, they've helped a lot." He ran his hands through his hair and gave me a wan smile. "Sorry, this all probably seems so dumb to you. I just need to get out of my head and do it."

What would it be like to have been raised like Duke? His life wasn't as perfect as I'd imagined in my head, though he had at least lived in a somewhat functional family setting. They could go to school without having to worry about how much food was in the cupboards over the weekend. Their rent was a mortgage, and it was always paid. He could play sports and be in the chess club instead of working to make ends meet. To have parents that were in a position to help when needed. Parents who *wanted* to help. A flame of jealousy shot through me before I squashed it. I couldn't blame Duke for his upbringing any more than I could be blamed for mine.

"Anyway...not sure why I went off like that. Probably your intimidating demand for more information."

"Hey. You gave me unsolicited advice. Do you want mine? It's only fair."

He laughed, motioning with his hands for me to continue. "I'm all ears."

"Don't take your parents' loan."

He stilled. "Why? I'd just have to go through a bank if not them. This way we don't have to deal with interest."

"I can't help but think that with your parents backing you, the feel of the whole company is different. It's hard to take ownership in something if it never feels like it's completely yours. They'll always have a say. And I think you feel differently when you know you didn't work that hard for it. I don't know you or your life beyond what you've told me and impressions I've gathered, but being completely invested in your life can only happen when it's your own skin in the game. Maybe that means keeping your business out in your garage for a while longer before moving into an office space."

He leaned forward in his chair, his elbows resting on the tops of his knees, rubbing his fingers together, his eyes trained intently on the floor.

"Thank you for coming to my TED talk," I said.

"I'm guessing your TED talk comes from some real-life experiences."

"You'd be surprised at how motivated for success you can be when you don't have anything to fall back on. I don't have anybody around to catch me if I fall, but sometimes I wish I did."

"That's because you're the one who does all the catching."

A pensive air filtered between us as we both grew lost in our thoughts, our heads resting against the wall behind us. We were still sharing the armrest, but neither of us moved to pull away. The rush of the night had begun to catch up with my body. Yawning, I checked the clock. Three-thirty in the morning. Duke followed my gaze.

"I'm sure they'll get you back soon."

"You know that for a fact, Doctor?"

"Sure. Soon is relative. I'm really sorry again, by the way."

I bumped his arm off the armrest. "I can still bend it. There's no way it's broken. We're wasting our time." Not to mention whatever this ER bill was going to cost me.

"It's not a waste." His voice, low and smooth, skittered down my spine. Somewhere in the foggy recess of my mind, I wondered if that statement meant more than how it sounded. And...why did I wish it did? Would he feel disappointed like me when the doctor actually called me back and popped this little bubble we'd created?

"You're probably just faking it 'cause it got you out of doing the lift."

I grinned, my eyes closed, relishing in how comfortable I felt around him. For the first time in a long while, I felt my body relax. My head bobbed toward his shoulder before I jerked it back. "I was saving you and your weak muscles from attempting the lift. You should be thanking me."

He snorted, putting his well-sculpted arm around my shoulders, giving my head a place to land. "This is pure Utah gym-rat muscle, with a little Idaho farm boy thrown in. And maybe a pinch of couch potato."

"*Idaho* farm boy?"

He smiled. "My grandparents live in Idaho, just across the border. I still go a few times a year to help them fix their fences and brand their cattle."

"Are you trying to lure me in with your sexy farm-boy talk?"

He curled into me slightly. "Is it working? Are farm boys what do it for you?"

"I don't think it hurts anything."

He laughed while I yawned again. I should have told him to remove his arm, but I didn't. Instead, my head dipped even closer.

"Why does your armpit smell good?" I was getting delirious now.

"Uhhh. Men's Speedstick. I'm too tired to think of something to counter your weirdness."

"That's fine. My foot hurts."

"I'll kiss it better."

"Gross."

"Fine. I'll kiss you better."

I ignored the thrill that shot through me at his words. "No strings."

"Oh. Right. I'll just sit here, then."

We stayed like that for the longest time, my head on his shoulder, both of us spouting nonsensical words as we drifted in and out of an exhausted but completely contented haze.

7

ONE AND A HALF HOURS LATER, WE LEFT THE HOSPITAL AT 5 AM on a high, snorting at dumb jokes and laughing at things like seeing a squirrel in a tree. Not to mention that we spent three hours in a hospital in the middle of the night for the doctor to take four seconds looking at my foot before telling me it was a sprain, which caused us to break out into more fits of laughter. The wheezy, breathless kind that I could only assume was what flying felt like. We weaved toward his truck in what probably looked like a drunken haze.

"You still owe me the lift," he said, wrapping his arm around my waist as he led me toward his truck. I was still limping slightly, but his extra concern was probably overkill, although I found it hard to care at the moment.

"Next time, for sure," I lied.

"Hey. You can't say that unless there *will* be a next time."

"Guess I'll always owe you one."

"Such a tease."

He opened the door and helped me inside. The little shut-eye we'd gotten in the waiting room before the nurse called us back had breathed new life into us. We had officially caught our second wind. That and the fact that I was back in my own clothes again after seeing the doctor.

Duke started the truck and turned to me. "Breakfast?" When I didn't answer, he added, "I know you probably lied about when you could take your test."

I laughed. "I knew nothing about you. I needed to have an out."

"How long does your test really go?"

"Until five," I said, a reluctant smile peeking through.

"Okay, little liar, you want to grab some breakfast?"

Our end was near. There was some anxiety on my part, which meant we hadn't been as diligent with our no-strings rule. There was a part of me that felt very much attached to Duke.

"You sure you're not sick of me yet?" My voice sounded a bit too vulnerable. I almost hoped he would tell me yes and we could rip this night off like a Bandaid. As it was, lingering would definitely cost me.

He rolled his head to the side to look at me, holding my gaze longer than necessary.

"I'm not sick of you."

There was a look of sadness that crossed his face before it was gone. Which couldn't be right. I wouldn't let it be right. We had made a deal at the beginning of this…whatever this twelve-hour passage of time was.

"Hey. No strings. No weirdness," I said, repeating a version of our mantra for the night.

He held his fist out to mine to which I gave him back the knuckles.

"The fist bump. Do people still do this?" I asked.

"We do."

When he realized I still hadn't answered his question, he leaned across the bench seat, whispering sexy things like, "Bacon. Eggs." At my smile, he came even closer, sending a puff of warm heat down my neck. "Pancakes."

And so, after a night of crazy, interesting, thought-provoking, maddening excitement and fun...he bought me breakfast. Which resulted in both of us yawning over the table, eating pancakes and waffles drenched in syrup, trying not to get delirious again but getting so anyway. Laughing at things not funny and telling stories that didn't make sense. A perfect way to close out the night. The end of our time rushing in on us. We traded social media handles, but not phone numbers because we were only casual acquaintances who spent a fun evening together. Texting and phone calls could lead to attachment. And no matter how much it hurt to say it, I wasn't getting attached.

My heart pounded for some unknown reason as he pulled up to the Chick-fil-A where my car was parked. I tried to chalk up our time as exactly what Duke had said it would be...something off the wall and spontaneous. It had truly been a night for the books, which meant that ending this was good. If I stayed...I couldn't deny this pull to him, and I couldn't—I wouldn't—get wrapped up in it. I had plans, and I was leaving.

It just wasn't the right time in my life for a Duke.

I resolved to remember that line so I could relay it to Mira. As a lover of the books with bare-chested Englishmen on the covers, I couldn't help but think she'd appreciate the joke.

We sat in the idling truck for a few long moments, trying to make it seem normal that neither of us was moving. Finally, he broke the silence.

"So...same time tomorrow?" he asked, shooting me a small smile.

"No strings."

"You're no fun."

He was smiling when he said it. Teasing.

"I was fun today," I insisted, suddenly anxious that he know something about me. "But today felt like a fake version of myself."

"It's not fake. It's just the version you might not show the world as much."

"If you think I regularly jump ship on dates and take off with strangers, last night has sorely misrepresented everything I usually stand for."

"It was a night of random fun. Anybody is capable of that."

"You don't really know me, though."

He raised his eyebrows, hurt lining his eyes. "You're going to try telling me I don't know you after the night we've had? I've dated women for two months and don't feel like I've gotten to know them as well as you after twelve hours."

"Well, either way…" I spread my hands out wide. "If I were to stick around longer than tonight, you'd probably be disappointed."

He shook his head slowly. "I don't think that's possible."

I huffed out a noise of disbelief, aware of a growing heat at the back of my eyelids.

"How the night unfolded might not have been your idea, but it was still you. Maybe not the side of you that you show to the world, but it's you. Whether you believe it or not, you're fun, Nora. Smart. Driven. Hot. And fun." His eyes flitted to my lips before raising back up again, his low voice causing sparks to burst down my spine. "You're the whole package, and I hate North Dakota."

A smile crept across my face even as my stomach flipped. That was my cue. My time to exit before the string connecting the two of us grew even tighter. A person could lay a lot on the line when there was no tomorrow. And there *wasn't* a tomorrow. Our time had come to an end, and it felt much more bitter than I had bargained for.

I kissed the fingers on my hand and leaned in, touching his cheek gently, laughing as he moved them to his lips, kissing each finger on my hand and giving me the feeling of flying. He pulled me over to him, a quick hug to end our night, before I gained the presence of mind in my sleep-addled brain to slide out of the car. I leaned in before closing the door.

"See ya."

If he was disappointed in my goodbye, he was careful not to show it. I closed the door and rounded the front of his truck, headed toward my car, when I paused, my fingers sliding over the white hood of his Tacoma. My old Honda Civic that had seen way too many miles sat before me. Ready to take me home. Take me back to my life.

It was then that I understood what exactly Duke had given me. This night. This beautiful, chaotic, charming, gratifying, and thrilling night that would be hard to forget. Something I hadn't realized I needed. I didn't let myself feel the nerves. I just acted, my feet taking me toward his door. He was already out of his truck when I nearly launched myself into his arms. There was no hesitation on his part, and I found myself cocooned in an embrace so tight I almost lost all my senses. His arms cradled and held and kept trying to bring me impossibly closer. I relished the feel of him holding me, my head lingering on his chest for a few long moments.

Warm eyes looked down at me as I dragged myself out of his embrace, backing up slowly while holding his gaze.

"Thanks for the date, Duke."

"See you around, Nora." His eyes were firm. His gaze locked on mine, and I truly believed he meant it.

And then I turned and walked away, a smile on my face and a touch of sadness in my heart, knowing that was not a possibility for us.

8

I SMOOTHED DOWN MY SHORT-SLEEVED, BLACK T-SHIRT BEFORE tucking it into black yoga pants that were fitted just right they could almost pass for something dressier. The mirror leaning against the floor in front of me was not helping any with my ego. My brown hair, tied loosely at my neck from working the diner all day, looked flat and lifeless and smelled faintly of bacon. After a quick debate with myself, I took it out of the scrunchie and fixed my hair. A high ponytail gave me a certain bounce that I definitely didn't feel. I could have really used some blush or something to brighten my pale face, but I ignored the thought as I pulled on my black slip-ons.

"You look like you're going to a funeral," Mira said, leaning against my door frame. My best friend and soon-to-be ex-room-mate stood, wearing her blue scrubs, about to head out the door to go be a nurse and save lives and stuff.

"Aren't I?" I smiled over at Mira to let her think I was joking.

I was not joking. Black was the appropriate color for where I was headed.

"If you're going to a funeral," Mira began, striding forward to grab the blush off my vanity desk in the corner, and proceeded to put some on my cheeks. "Then I'm going to try my best to help you look like a guest and not the main event." My eyes drifted to her curly black hair resting prettily on top of her shoulders. Though I knew she'd have her hair up in a ponytail before long.

I snickered. "Thanks. The people working late tonight will probably thank you." The light floral smell radiating off my beautiful friend worked as a smelling salt.

"How long do you work tonight? Here, mascara too."

Moving toward the mirror on my desk, I applied a few swipes on my eyelashes, silently appreciating how much better I felt with these tiny adjustments to my tired face. "I'm signed on until nine. Probably nine-thirty by the time I get home. How's Loverboy?"

"He's good. He's taking me out to dinner tomorrow night."

"Anything new on the wedding plans?"

"I decided I hate planning weddings, and we might just elope."

Laughing, I said, "Good luck getting your mom on board with that."

"I'm twenty-five. I'd only have to ask forgiveness, not permission."

"Not sure she'd ever forgive you." I stood up from the table and turned to face my friend.

"I wish you didn't have to do this," she said, her eyes sunken with dread on my behalf. "It just sucks. How long until you pay it off?"

I shrugged, not really wanting to think about the sinking debt that caused all of this. "If I throw everything I make at this job toward the bill, maybe two years?"

Mira sucked in a breath. "I can help a little."

"Don't even think about it. It's my problem. There are lots of worse things in the world."

CINDY STEEL

"Yeah, but most people pay it off while working in a career, hypothetically."

"Or a second job," I said brightly, ready to move on from this conversation.

"Have you heard anything from your mom?"

I laughed. "No. She doesn't come around unless she's in between husbands or boyfriends. So..."—I checked my watch—"according to my calculations, that will be another six months or so."

"I hate that for you."

"I think there's a marketing firm somewhere in the building. Maybe I can rub shoulders with some of the graphic designers who work there and dazzle them with my wits."

"A meet-cute in an elevator." Mira's voice turned excited. Our love for romantic comedies usually infiltrated our conversations more often than not. "What if you accidentally touch his hand while you're both pressing the same floor number?"

"Aww," I said, plucking my keys and phone from my desk and turning toward her. "And then he'd look me in the eye and whisper, 'Is that the hand you used while you were scrubbing the toilets?'"

She smacked me on my butt while I scooted away, laughing. "Get out of here! Go save a life or something."

Our two-bedroom apartment had seen better days—about fifty years ago. The light-colored linoleum floors had a permanent dirt stain that gave the surface a cloudy effect, no matter how hard Mira and I scrubbed. The kitchen appliances were made in the eighties and worked about like you'd expect. Located close to downtown, it was close to the cafe and not too far from the office building where my aunt's cleaning service was located. In the tight, galley kitchen, I threw together a peanut-butter-and-jam sandwich to scarf down on my way.

"Did maintenance come and fix the fridge?" I called, noticing how the jam felt cold to my touch.

"No. They've still never shown up. Brock fiddled with it when he was here last night. Is it working better?" her voice called out from the bathroom. I could hear the water running, like she was washing her face.

"The jam is cold! So are all our pretty condiments!" I yelled, grasping at every bottle in the door of the fridge. "If you decide not to marry him, I'll take him."

"Yeah right."

Sandwich in hand, I ignored the mail on the counter and made my way to the exit. "See ya tomorrow."

Her reply was muffled as I closed the door, taking the outside apartment stairs two at a time to the parking lot while I focused on one more thing that made my stomach fall.

My first day at a new job.

MY FLAT SHOES didn't click on the pavement like I always imagined they would. It was more of a sliding sound as I trudged my way down the city streets in my practical shoes—shoes with drops of soup on them, I noticed, upon closer inspection. I wasn't wearing the high heels all the women in the romantic comedies wore as they gracefully clip-clopped with other career-obsessed natives into their fancy office buildings. By this time in the afternoon, most people were done with their workday, the shine worn off of their faces, hair limp, and grabbing takeout on their way home.

I checked my watch. I would be fifteen minutes early at this pace, so I slowed down next to a coffee cart that was parked on the sidewalk. The temptation to grab a cup for the burst of energy I needed was strong after a day of working in the cafe. Instead, I kept my pennies where they were and stared at the impressive building before me. From what I understood, my aunt's cleaning service was contracted to clean a few floors of the massive building. Aunt

Cathy's business was a new company and occupied a small office space on the fourteenth floor of the huge skyscraper. Well, maybe not a skyscraper. Not sure Salt Lake City actually had any of those, but the tall gray building with dark windows seemed impressive. My phone buzzed with a text.

Mira: Don't let anyone tell you that morticians aren't sexy!

Me: It's the black loafers, isn't it? Does the trick every time.

Mira: Send me pics if you find anything interesting.

Me: Like what?

Mira: I don't know, but speaking as a nurse, people can be disgusting. Just keep the phone handy.

Me: Does Brock know how weird you are?

Mira: He does, and he loves it.

Me: Putting my phone away now.

Mira: Good luck. Can't wait to hear all about it.

I HAD BEEN SLOWLY INCHING my way down the sidewalk, texting Mira, when an older gentleman, probably in his mid-fifties, held open the door for me. I took that as my cue to stop procrastinating and stepped inside, giving him a grateful smile as we made our way toward the elevators.

A group of men and women looking very much like executives of some sort milled around outside the door, talking loudly but looking as though they weren't planning on going inside, so the older gentleman placed his hand in front of the open elevator and motioned me to enter first.

"Thank you, again." I smiled kindly.

"You're welcome." The man stepped beside me, his hand hovering over the buttons. "What floor?"

"Fourteen." I took in a deep breath and expelled it quietly.

"Oh, do you work at RDM?"

"No." I smiled as the door began to close. "Cathy's Cleaning Service. They share the same floor."

He raised his bushy eyebrows, taking me in with a closer look. Probably noting my casual attire in a building full of suits and silks. "Oh. Well, that's nice."

My reply was cut short when, at the last second, an arm attached to a business suit stopped the door from closing.

A man in his thirties, with reddish brown hair, smiled politely at us, his eyes impassively scanning over our faces. "Sorry. Is there room for, like, twenty-seven more?"

My older friend laughed. "As long as you guys in the fancy clothes aren't lawyers."

The entire group of executives, mostly men but a few women in pantsuits and dresses, began filling the cracks inside the elevator. The older gentleman and I stepped back together in the corner to allow more room.

The younger man laughed. "No lawyers in this bunch." He motioned toward the other men spilling inside. "I'll bet most of these suits are rented." He nodded toward someone by the door. "Pretty sure Mike's is an old prom suit."

The blond-haired man in question laughed and craned his head to make eye contact with the other man. "Plaid polyester never goes out of style. Don't let anyone tell you different."

There was some chuckling and a brief pause as we all faced forward, waiting for the door to close.

The man named Mike, with the blond spiky hair, who was indeed wearing a bright-green plaid polyester suit, caused a wave of familiarity to come over me. I was tucked away in the corner, crowded behind shoulders, but I knew him. I just couldn't place how or when I had ever spoken to him. My eyes skittered around the side profile of the tall, brown-haired man he was speaking with standing next to him.

When the man turned his face, my heart immediately began racing.

Flashes of a basketball game and a kiss cam had me biting my lip to keep from smiling. Elbows and armrests and hands lightly touching my face. The wedding crash, his house, and our night at the hospital. Breakfast. Teasing, flirting, and talking the entire night. Exchanging social media information instead of phone numbers. Saying goodbye. The moment when I called the hospital months later to inquire about the bill I'd never received and was told it had already been paid in full.

On occasion, during the dark and cold winter in North Dakota, I'd pull up his account and look at the three pictures total he had on there and relive the moments of the Jazz game. But that had slowly stopped. Soon after, he got himself a girlfriend, and somehow, pictures of him with his arm around a beautiful brunette kept making their way into my feed. I ended up unfollowing him and forced myself to stop looking him up.

A woman with blonde hair stood next to Duke, leaning in to tell him something, her hand resting on his back just below his shoulder.

Out of the almost nine thousand days making up my entire life, I had shared one night with him. One. A few hours. A date. I had no reason to feel weirdly possessive. I didn't understand the surge of jealousy that burned for the briefest of moments. I wasn't sure whether he worked somewhere in the building or if he was just here for a meeting. He probably still had a girlfriend. Or maybe a wife by now? No sense reliving something that was only a fluke. The back of his head was enough for me. He probably wouldn't remember me, anyway.

I thought back to the kiss cam...okay, he probably remembered me. Crossing off a bucket list item of that magnitude with a stranger seemed like something a person would remember. Maybe he wouldn't recognize me. My hair was in a ponytail and...okay, not much had changed for me, but for some reason I couldn't explain, I didn't want him to see me. A Duke sighting was something a girl needed to prepare for. Work up to. When it was dropped on me like this, my pulse shot through the roof. My frame of mind was a complicated mixture of dying for some interaction between us and staying hidden in the corner.

Tomorrow, I'd be ready—which, of course, meant that I would never see him again because I would now be *looking* for it to happen.

Okay. New plan.

I'd wait for him and his posse to get off the elevator first before I attempted my fourteenth-floor drop-off. The last thing I wanted to do was shimmy past all these people.

Ding.

The elevator came to a sudden halt. My eyes shot up to the number above the door, indicating we were stopped on the four-teenth floor. The door opened. Nobody moved a muscle.

Apparently, he didn't work on my floor.

I had imagined this going much differently. Fine with me, I would just wait them out and come back down by myself. I swal-lowed, trying to shrink myself in the corner while everybody glanced around, looking for the person who had obviously planned to get off on floor fourteen. Now it was too awkward to change my mind. I had waited four seconds too long.

The door had begun to close when the older gentleman nudged my shoulder. "Isn't this your stop?"

An arm somewhere in the front shot out, stopping the door from closing while heads turned to look my way.

Yes, this was much worse.

"Thanks," I mumbled and began moving out from my corner, squeezing past broad shoulders and suit coats.

I felt Mike's eyes on me as I passed, but I couldn't bring myself to look up, not when the floor at my feet was so interest-ing. When I stepped around him, Duke was holding the elevator door open, and when I inched toward the threshold, he moved his arm out of my way. My head had been turned slightly, but good manners dictated I give him a smile or a thank you. And I couldn't *not* give him that.

I braved a look at him as I passed. "Thanks."

To my utter delight, recognition flared into his widened eyes almost immediately. His mouth dropped open slightly as his gaze swept over me. The energy in my veins moved like a shot of caffeine zinging straight down my body, curling my toes and hitching my breath. An unbidden smile crept across my face as I stepped out. The fact that he recognized me made me breathe in this moment a little easier.

"Hey!" Duke's rushed, soft voice carried to my ears. I turned and met his smile with mine, both growing wider by the second. He had a look on his face, almost calculating, as if he had a thousand things to say to me but couldn't pick which to begin with.

And like all good romantic comedies, we were interrupted before we could speak. The doors shut, blocking his handsome face from my view.

All the adrenaline coursing through my body dissipated the second the elevator door closed. My shoulders dropped while my breath expelled in a dramatic whooshing sound. I hid behind my hands, not ready to face the world quite yet. I wanted to hide away in a room somewhere and relive every delicious second of the twenty spent in his company.

9

"Nora?"

I spun around, dropping my hands and forcing myself to remember the reason I was here. My Aunt Cathy stood just past the elevators, waiting for me, her eyebrows furrowing in question as she walked toward me.

"Hey." I tucked a wayward piece of hair behind my ear and remembered myself. "Hi, Aunt Cathy."

Cathy reached toward me and gave me a hug, a mixture of chlorine and citrus enveloping me as she did. Her curly blonde hair was down, and she wore dark-rimmed glasses and loose-fitting gray slacks with a stylish tucked-in t-shirt and a relaxed blazer. Her style was effortless and simple in a way that made me jealous. She was so much the opposite of my mom that it was always a trip seeing a nearly exact replica be so different.

"Thanks for hiring me last minute."

"Sure, sure. Let me show you to the office. I need you to sign a few things before I turn you loose." She turned and led us down a small hallway and into a doorway marked CCS - Cathy's Cleaning Service. The room held a small office with Cathy's nameplate on the front, and she gestured to me to sit down.

"Your call came at the right time. We just had someone quit, and I've been a bit shorthanded."

"Good. Glad it worked out."

"Your call did come as a surprise, though." Cathy peered at me through her stylish lenses. "Last I remember talking to you, I thought you were close to finishing your degree? Shouldn't you be out of school by now?"

I swallowed, feeling the drop in my stomach. "Yeah. I'd hoped. I had a few setbacks. I'm working at the cafe most days and hoping to start school again in the fall." I failed to mention that I'd be finishing once I was accepted into a program again since I had flunked out previously.

"And this job on top of all that?" Her face looked incredulous, and I wanted nothing more than to move us past all of this.

"Yeah. I'm good. I like work."

"I thought you were living with your grandma the past few years. I can't imagine you being an impulsive spender. Your mom's not hitting you up for money again, is she?"

I glanced at her, startled, before looking away. She sounded so aghast. Cathy had never been one to beat around the bush if she sensed something was off. I should have figured this meeting would be more than just hooking me up with my cleaning cart.

"No. She and Kip are on a big RV trip at the moment—last I heard. I had some things come up that set me back a bit." I smiled brightly at her. "But I'm so grateful for this job. I'd love to get started."

Cathy paused a few long moments before she cleared her throat and started in with her new hire information. A half hour later, after signing a stack of papers, she led me down a small hallway and into a room full of cleaning carts packed full with treatments for windows, floors, vacuums, toilet paper, and dusters.

"This is your cart. Your assignment every day will be the entire office at RDM, down the hall, and The Computer

Company office space one floor above us. Vacuum and dust all the offices as needed, take out the garbage, clean the bathrooms." She eyed me critically. "There is a card on your cart that tells you detailed information about how and what things should be done each day. Read through that. Every Friday, we vacuum the entire space, but during the weekday, we only do touch-ups as needed. If you have any further questions, come find me. I'm in my office until we close at nine. Don't touch the desks or any personal items."

"What if people are still working in their offices while I'm there?" It was five, so most would probably be going home, but according to my extensive knowledge of movies, there was always somebody staying late.

"If I were you, I'd do upstairs first and RDM last. Half the office is usually working late. If you've done all you can do on the floor and some are still in their office, I'd just knock on their door and see if they'd like their garbage emptied and then call it a night."

I nodded.

"Alright, well, I'm headed back to my office. Let me know if you need anything." She gave me a small smile as she left the room.

The door closed behind her with a thud, leaving me alone in the lifeless room. For a moment, I stood in the quiet and looked around, taking in my new reality. It was one thing to apply for a job, but it was quite another to pull on the yellow gloves and start scrubbing the toilets. I had worked in a cafe for half of my life. I was accustomed to sweat. This didn't have to be any different. Nothing about this job was going to be different, so why were my hands shaking? My stomach about to be sick? Instead of racing upstairs to begin my assignment, I found myself holding onto the cart while I took several deep breaths, trying to calm my nerves. But the air did nothing. My feet stayed planted.

I had just seen the man who'd invaded my thoughts more times than I could count for the past three years. I no longer knew anything about him. He could be married or still be with the brunette I saw in those pictures. He could work somewhere in this office building, and maybe I'd see him in the elevator regularly. Maybe I'd be scrubbing his toilets before too long. Maybe he'd look at me with pity, seeing how I'd actually gone backward in life since our one night together.

What a cruel trick the past three years had played on me.

By habit, my hand reached for my phone, pulling up the student loan bill on my app. Though I'd already paid as much of it back as I could, the amount left was a crushing blow. The kind of blow that made it hard to see straight.

When I first saw Duke, I had been transported to a happier moment, an alternate blip in my reality that I thought about a disconcerting amount. I couldn't have predicted how much I would have needed those happy memories over the next few years. But that was all it was. Happy memories. Now, I wasn't sure I could face seeing him again. Knowing it was possible meant that I'd be double-checking for a dark-haired charmer around every corner. I wouldn't hide if I saw him, but I certainly wouldn't seek him out. At least, I was almost ninety seven percent sure I wouldn't hide if I saw him. A ringing phone down the hallway startled me out of my thoughts and turned my emotions numb. I grabbed my cart and began rolling it toward the door. No. I wasn't embarrassed by the work.

I was embarrassed by my life.

10

THE SOUND OF A ROCKET LAUNCHING INTO SPACE WOULD HAVE been quieter than the vacuum Cathy's Cleaning Service issued to me. It was Friday, a week after my Duke sighting and I was vacuuming the long hallway at RDM. I hadn't seen him again. I felt relieved and, at the same time, disappointed, and I hated myself for it. I had worked the afternoon shift at the cafe every day this week, and my evenings were spent cleaning. Exhaustion was beginning to take its toll.

I loved the modern, artistic feel of the office. The main room of the company was occupied by a spattering of cubicles in the center, private offices flanking the sides, and a long hallway with doors that branched off to the bathrooms, the break room, supply room, and a very large board room, made visible by the wall of windows from the hallway.

Turning the corner, I was startled when I saw the board room full of people in suits sitting around a large oval table. I immediately turned the vacuum off, not wanting to disturb them. A few curious eyes glanced over at me before darting away. Their posture around the table didn't give off the vibe that they would be wrapping up soon, so I gathered up the cord and began winding it around the back of the vacuum. The rest of the hallway looked fine. I would officially be calling it a night.

Looking up again through the glass, my gaze caught on a man who looked very interested at the sight of me. I froze in place, a deer in the headlights. This was twice now that our meeting had caught me unaware. He sat at the end of the table, slouched a bit in his seat, wearing a delicious fitted navy suit. He shook his head slowly at me, biting his lip in what looked like an attempt to rein in his smile. My reaction matched his before I could think better of it. He was mouthing something to me, gesturing lightly with his hands. My eyes shot downward because I wasn't curious at all, and I had work to do, and I didn't need him interfering with that.

It took me three tries to finish winding the cord around the vacuum and load it back onto my cart, my trembling fingers and erratic heartbeat making the job nearly impossible. Finally, I stood up, and because it was literally like attempting to not look at a celebrity when you were told they were in the same room, I caught his eyes again before I could disappear down the hallway.

"Wait," he mouthed. Very clearly.

"What?" I mouthed back, cupping my ear.

His eyes flashed with a knowing look as he motioned his hands in a stop pose. "Wait," he mouthed again.

I hesitated. Ohhh, it was tempting. So tempting. Maybe if we had met again on the elevator, we'd have our chance at small talk. I'd tell him how nice it was to see him again. He'd say something like, *'Wow, you're cleaning toilets now?'* And I'd say, *'Yeah, isn't life crazy?'* We'd both remember fondly our night all those years ago and breathe a sigh of relief that things turned out like they did. Then we'd high five each other a goodbye. Or was it a fist bump? Either way, over and out. Clean and simple.

I'd wait for an elevator to chat.

I shot him a smile and tapped my wrist. "Gotta go," I

mouthed. He looked like he was on the verge of a protest before I bolted, my cleaning cart rattling behind me.

I rushed my cart back to the cleaning room, waving at Cathy sitting at her desk through her open door, praying she didn't want to chat today. Cathy had a laugh that could be heard two floors down and an office with lights that beamed brighter than the sun. I'd be a sitting duck. She made no move to get up, and I zoomed past her without incident and into the cleaning room, which was really just a big walk-in closet that smelled like bleach, and closed the door. A sigh escaped me at the relief it was to feel hidden. I had mentally battled a very sexy dragon, and exhaustion settled in my limbs. I leaned against the white wall, pulling the latex gloves off my hands, grateful I'd survived another day without having to speak to—

"Nora!"

I jumped, my gloves dropping to the floor because suddenly he was there.

He was there.

In the doorway. His eyes raked me up and down, a smile lighting his face at the same time pretending affront at my crimes. Five days of dodging shadows and hiding in closets had brought me to this moment. Time to get this over with.

Without asking my permission, my eyes swept over the man I'd been unable to forget. I wanted to scoff at my reaction to him. It really wasn't fair what I was seeing. He checked all the boxes that a man should check. The five o'clock shadow on his face that was still the stuff of dreams. Check. The blue suit that fit him better than any glove I could imagine. Check. The smile that still powered the sun and felt so familiar to me I had to keep myself from touching it. Him. Check. Check.

An undeniable feeling of warm friendship settled over me. I strongly suspected we could talk for the next two hours, and we wouldn't skip a beat in our conversation. Even now, he was not looking at me like a stranger. So, there I stood, breathless and in awe at how fast three years between us could disappear.

"Hey, Duke."

He stared incredulously at me for a long moment. "Hey, Duke?"

I bit my lip, but the tiny laugh escaped. "Yeah. Hey, Duke."

A silent battle waged between us then. He had the look of a man who either wanted to wring my neck or tackle me to the ground. One option definitely sounded more appealing than the other, but I would never admit which one.

"Hi." Doing great on my small talk so far.

"Hi." His reluctant smile felt like a win.

I cleared my throat, digging deep to find my focus. "So, you work at RDM? Or were you just there for a meeting?"

A long pause. His eyes studied mine. "I work there."

"How come you didn't get off on the fourteenth floor the other day in the elevator?"

"We had a meeting with a company upstairs."

Great.

Out of all the office buildings in this city, I wound up cleaning his.

"Guess the marketing dream worked out for you, then."

He shoved his hands into his pockets. "Guess so. How long have you been back in Utah?"

"A couple months."

"Why are we no longer friends online?"

I lifted my chin. "Not sure."

"Liar. I've been blocked. Not just unfriended."

How does one tell another person that, platonically, I couldn't stand any more pictures of him and his girlfriend in my feed?

Platonically.

He went on in my awkward absence. "After I saw you the

other day in the elevator, I tried to find you, but it was like you never existed."

"Maybe I deleted my accounts." It wasn't lying, just spouting off a hypothetical idea.

"Mike and Ryan could find you, though. Easily." My eyes widened. He was looking very much like a cat who had caught a mouse and wanted to toy with it a bit before having a little snack.

"Geez. Stalker much?"

"Not on Fridays."

Then we were lost, both of us trying and failing to hold back our smiles.

He folded his arms, leaning on the doorframe. "Alright, Kiss Cam Nora, I'll let you off the hook from answering that question if you answer another one. What are you doing here?" He motioned to my cart.

My body froze. I wasn't sure which question was worse. Or how to give him just enough that he'd no longer be curious.

"Cathy is my aunt."

"Cathy's Cleaning Service," he said softly. "All this time, I was working right across the hallway from your aunt?"

"I just moved back and…she needed some extra help, so I'm working here for a few months." *Or years.*

It was good, honest work. It was just…I had plans. Bigger plans than a moment like this might lead some people to believe. I hated that he was here in a suit and catching me at such a low point.

Before he could ask me anything else, I added, "What do you do at RDM?"

He held my gaze for a long moment before speaking. If this was going as well for him as I thought it was, I shouldn't have to worry about running into him any more.

"I manage a few departments. Are you doing any work in graphic design?"

I opened my mouth, ready to evade an answer, when something puzzled me.

"Wait, did you run out of that meeting while it was still going?"

"Yep."

My mouth dropped open. "Why?"

"Because I wanted to see you."

"You can just do that?"

"I did."

"Would your girlfriend have any issues about you chasing down random women while you're supposed to be working?"

He cocked his head, one side of his lips curving into a grin. "Nice pivot."

I scoffed. "That wasn't a pivot. I…just…" I ended my extremely intelligent sentence with an annoyed look at him.

He huffed out a laugh. "I don't think she'd mind me catching up with an old friend. And you're not random."

The heart inside of my chest skipped a beat at the way he said random. My brain scrambled for something else to focus on besides the dark gaze intent on me.

"So…um…how long have you been dating?"

A sliver of disappointment crossed over his face at my question, but it disappeared quickly. "Rachel and I have been together for almost three years."

So it was the same brunette.

"That's great," I said brightly, hoping my eyes matched the tone of my voice.

"What are you doing right now?" he asked.

"Huh?" His low, sexy voice had scrambled my brain.

"Why don't you come back to the office, and we can catch up. My meeting is probably done by now."

It all sounded so inviting. The words were breezy. Casual. Old friends catching up. But his eyes did not say casual. His body language was not casual. The underlying string between us tightened with tension—the very smoldering, sexy kind of tension that had my nerves pinging overtime.

He had a girlfriend. The way my body was reacting to him, I knew I definitely shouldn't be alone with him.

"I'd better not," I said. "I've got to get home."

He paused a moment before he went on in conversation like I hadn't said a word.

"You were in school, right? Did you get your degree?"

Talk about salt in the wound.

"No." My fingers absently toyed with a bottle of cleaner. "I had a few setbacks in Fargo. I'm hoping to enroll again soon."

He looked like he wanted to ask more but hesitated. Clearing my throat, I said, "But it's all good. It's been fun seeing you again." Except, he didn't look like a man who believed a word I'd said.

"Do you need anything? Any help? As a *friend*," he added, emphasizing the word.

"I'm okay. I'm on track again. I've got everything I ne—" I moved my hand for effect, swinging awkwardly backward and landing a direct hit on a stack of toilet paper rolls sitting on my cart. We both watched them fly before landing and immediately rolling all around the room.

I looked around for a hole to crawl into. If I had wanted to try and make Duke forget what I was doing in his office building, the toilet paper really helped to bring us back full circle.

With jittery hands, I began picking up the rolls. Duke pushed himself off the door and bent to help me.

"You don't have to do that."

He ignored me, stacking the rolls back onto my cart. "How did things go with your grandma?"

"Fine."

"Fine?"

As usual, the ache whenever I thought of my grandma was

still there. "She passed away six months ago, if that's what you're wanting to know."

His eyes grew soft. "I'm sorry."

"Thanks."

He didn't bat an eye. "Is this your only job?"

"I work at a cafe during the day." *Please go away. Go away. Go away.* All of these details in my life he remembered only reminded me how full of hope I'd been three years earlier.

"During the day?"

"My schedule rotates. Sometimes I work the morning shift and sometimes the afternoon."

"Are you still interested in graphic design?"

I needed to start holding my own in this conversation. He had come upon me so suddenly it had disconcerted me. I mentally took a quick breath.

"Yes. Are we finished with the interrogation? I haven't even had a chance to ask whether your suit is Italian or French made."

A reluctant smile tugged at his lips. "Smart aleck." He turned toward the door, his hand on the knob. "Well, if you don't want to catch up with an old friend, I'd better get back to my meeting."

"Just out of curiosity, how often do you have late meetings?"

He opened the door and stepped out. I didn't need to see his face to hear the grin in his voice. "Pretty often."

I made a mental note to change RDM's cleaning time to midnight. Should be fine. "Good to see you, Duke."

"You too, Nora."

And then he left, almost as quickly as he arrived, leaving me feeling all kinds of emotions but the biggest being…unsettled.

Very unsettled.

11

"I HAVE AN OFFER FOR YOU, KISS CAM."

I yelped, jumping back from the window I'd been cleaning, swearing as I rammed into the corner of the cleaning cart. My body flailed to the side while my corded earphones caught on a bottle of cleaner and proceeded to rip themselves from the phone and my ear, sending my phone clattering to the ground. All of a sudden, the kiss scene in the romance book I'd been listening to began blaring with startling volume between us.

"...THIS time, the shy meeting of our lips had passed, deepening to something heated."

HORRIFIED, I scrambled upward, my limbs in such a state of shock they refused to move fast enough.

"HIS MOUTH MOVED AGAINST MINE—DARTING, clinging, tasting. He pressed me closer..."

. . .

I DOVE FOR MY PHONE, my fingers fumbling with the mechanics, frantically pounding at the screen.

"HE PUSHED me back against the wall with my body. His lips took full advantage of my gasp, while his hands held my neck and caressed my face, moving my head to whatever angle would satisfy..."

HOW DO YOU TURN THIS THING OFF?!!

The buttons were frozen—my phone unresponsive to my desperate efforts—so in a last-ditch attempt to make it all stop, I grabbed my earphone cord and shoved it into the connector.

The room fell into blessed silence. I was sweating and panting like I'd run a marathon when I stole a glance at Duke. His eyes could not contain any more delight. His cup was full.

"Why'd you turn it off? It sounds like it's just getting good."

"Shut up," I said miserably, my heart racing. "Where did you come from?"

A grinning and moderately repentant Duke answered, "Sorry. Didn't realize you had earbuds in. Or that you were so busy getting some very useful tips."

"I was not getting tips. And I thought everyone was gone."

"Not all of us."

I set the bottle of window cleaner and my squeegee down on the window ledge. He looked so good it almost hurt my eyes to look at him. What was it about him in a suit that sent my heart pounding?

"What are you doing here this late?" I demanded, taking a breath to calm myself.

He didn't look at me as he took a seat on a desk nearby. "Business things."

My hands found my hips. "Business things at eight p.m.?"

"Marketing never sleeps."

I peered down at him. "Is that the phrase?"

His arms folded. "Either way, I have an offer for you."

My body stiffened. "What?"

"As it turns out, my company is doing an internship program for our graphic design department."

My ears perked up, but I kept my face passive. "Okay."

"They're going to pick three candidates for the program, hire them for the summer, train them but also be running a contest during the last month."

"What's the contest?"

"Each intern would have to design an entire marketing package for a company of our choosing. Everything from a logo, branding, social media, and website for a company. The person who wins the competition at the end of the summer gets hired on as a full-time intern with the idea that once they complete their training, they'd move up to a graphic design position."

I stood still as his words trickled over me. Inside, I was jumping up and down, but I forced myself to keep it together. This sounded suspiciously too good to be true. Before I could counter, he added another spoonful of sugar to the pie.

"One more thing. The winner of the internship will be eligible to have their schooling paid for, if it's a graphic design program approved by the company. They'd have to study nights and weekends while they work full time with us, but the company will pay for it."

School would be paid for, which meant I could quit the cafe and focus everything toward paying off my student loan bill. Just thinking the words made me want to sob with relief. If I won, I'd be able to quit the janitor job much sooner than I'd anticipated. I was vaguely aware of Duke picking up the squeegee and the squirt bottle and spraying a window I hadn't gotten to yet.

"What's the catch?" I asked, moving closer. "Why do you all of a sudden have the perfect solution for me?"

He grabbed a towel laying on the cleaning cart and wiped the squeegee before dragging it down the window. "No catch. I'm just relaying information, in case you're interested."

"I'm not interested if this is some sort of handout." *Yes, I am*, my traitorous mind screamed at me.

"Not a handout. Our company is growing, but we can't afford to hire on as many employees as we need—at least not yet. So we thought we'd open it up for a little competition." His voice had a hint of distraction as he grew more comfortable with the squeegee. "I've got to get me one of these."

I refused to be diverted by the cute furrow on his face as he worked at keeping his lines clean and smudge free. "Why didn't you tell me about the internship the other day?"

"I was too busy catching my breath after chasing you down."

I would also not be distracted by his sweet little grin, though he still wasn't looking at me.

"Nora. This is a good thing. It's not a trick. Haven't you ever heard that it's all about who you know?" he asked.

"Yes, but…Duke, is this your company? Are you the boss? Something about this feels weird."

"Do you know how much a squeegee runs at the store? This works amazing."

He ignored my questions, but still my mind raced. I took the trash out of his office every night, but he had nothing personal in his room. The sign at his desk just said Duke Webber, no title.

"My company needs some extra help. That's all. You have to earn your place here either way. I'm only passing on information to a friend. If it works out and it's something you're interested in, then great."

Those words. Casual. Breezy. Almost flippant. The casualness of it was made even more so by watching a handsome man dressed in gray suit pants with his white shirt rolled at the sleeves cleaning windows. My windows. He was right. I needed to calm down. Life was more about who you knew. I was janitorial proof of that. I didn't owe Duke anything. If he wanted to help me out in a time when even I could admit (silently) that I really needed a boost, then who was I to say no?

"Where do I sign up?"

He smiled. "I'll sign you up. I'll just need your phone number."

"I'll sign up myself." I smiled at him sweetly.

He bit back his grin. "Email?"

Once I determined that email would be the less-intrusive threat, he typed my email into his phone. When he was finished, he slid his device into his back pocket and picked up the squeegee once more.

"Is this your company?" I asked again, suspicion etched in my voice.

He sounded distracted as he worked on making his dry lines straight. "I'll send you the info tomorrow."

"You can stop cleaning now." I held my hand out for the squeegee.

"It's kind of fun. What's next?" He ignored me, spraying the last window.

"Nothing. I'm finished for the night."

"Bummer. Maybe I'll stop by tomorrow to try my hand at vacuuming."

"Duke."

"Nora."

"Go home."

"After you."

I still had all the trash to empty, but I didn't want him to know that. "I've got to clean my...brushes." I didn't have any brushes that needed cleaning, besides maybe my toilet brushes, but I wasn't about to get up close and personal with those. Cathy kept me in high supply with new toilet brushes. But the excuse sounded good. Before he could offer to help me, I snapped my fingers, holding out my hand for the squeegee and spray bottle. "I'll see you later."

He set down the cleaning supplies on the cart like they were weapons, giving me a salute before backing toward the doorway. "I'll let you get back to your…book. Have a great night."

I threw a dry sponge at him, enjoying the sound of his chuckle in spite of myself.

THE NEXT DAY, I wasn't scheduled to work at the cafe and had some rare time off. I rolled out of bed at nine and made myself a luxurious breakfast of waffles from a boxed mix with fresh strawberries and half a can of whipped cream. The strawberries had been too soft for the cafe to use but not bad enough to be thrown away, so I had saved them from the trash can. Mira was sleeping after getting home from her night shift at the hospital, so I kept my noises down to a minimum.

Until my phone rang, and my shoulders sagged, the peaceful morning about to be obliterated.

"Hey, Mom."

"Hey, Nora Bora." Her voice was muffled, swallowed by the background noise.

"Where are you?" I stood from my breakfast of half-eaten waffles and slipped out the front door so I didn't wake Mira. The calm May morning greeting me was a direct contrast to my phone call.

"We're at a karaoke bar in Florida. We spent all morning on the beach, but now we're eating lunch." My mom laughed and shouted at something. "Sorry, Kip just got up to sing. Go, babe!" she shouted into the phone.

I pulled the phone away from my ear.

After a few long moments of laughter and snippets of my mom's conversation with other patrons at the bar, she remembered she had called me.

"Nora? You still there."

"Mom, I'm going to hang up. Sounds like you're having fun."

"No! I need a favor real quick, sweetie. You know that storage unit I put all our stuff in before Kip and I got married? Anyway, I forgot to get that bill sent my way, so you probably have a stack of them on your counter. They just called me, and they put a lien on it. If we don't pay in time, they're going to auction off all our stuff. Can you believe that? But my credit card keeps declining. I think it must have gotten hacked. Anyway, would you mind paying that? I'll have Kip send you some money."

If I had a dime for every time my mother's credit card had been *hacked*, I wouldn't be in this mess. I had indeed seen the bills that my mother had so kindly forwarded here when she took off on an RV road trip adventure a month ago with her new husband, Kip.

"Mom, I'm sorry, but I can't help you out. I'm saving for college again."

"But we'll pay you back, sweetie. Some of your things are in there too. And Harper's and Candice's things. They're going to sell it all if it's not paid by the fifteenth."

To be honest, I couldn't think of anything tangible from my childhood that I was dying to save, but her mention of my sisters' things gave me pause—and a sinking stomach. My three years in Fargo had imploded on me, but the one good thing that came out of it was the natural space carved between my mom and me. I had stopped paying part of her rent, though not long after I'd left, she began dating Kip. I guess that was a small blessing in disguise that Harper could finish out her senior year playing basketball and not working at the cafe to cover my mom. Kip had been there.

They had actually dated longer than any of the other men she'd married, but he hadn't won me over yet, by any means. I thought about the meager eight hundred dollars I had saved from the cafe over the past couple months for tuition and wanted to cry at the thought of parting with any of it.

No.

I needed boundaries, or I would always be in the exact same place–forever my mom's cushion.

"Mom, I really don't have the money to pay it. You and Kip will have to figure it out. I'm sorry."

She spoke faster, her voice a little desperate. "We'll pay you back, sweetie. We're just waiting for Kip to get his paycheck at the end of the week."

There was a slight sway on my part before I held strong. I needed to let her fall.

"Sorry, Mom. I've got to go."

And then I hung up on her.

I numbly let myself back into the apartment and finished my cold waffle. As I ate, I flipped through the stack of mail piling up on the counter. Three bills had come from the storage unit and a handful of others. I had put good faith in the idea that perhaps my mom was paying them online. But apparently not. I opened one of the bills, aghast at the amount. Three months of unpaid bills had led to a collection threat and notice of a lien if not paid in time.

Though definitely tipsy, my mom had also sounded happy on the phone. Not a care in the world. Whenever my mom thought herself to be in love, she became the best version of herself. No matter how many times she'd been burned before, she was all in with any relationship. Which was all part of the tragedy. There was light in her eyes, excitement on her face... Though she loved us girls, we rarely got that part of her all on her own. It was always attached to a man, her self-worth literally held in the balance of a selfish, scheming, and conniving man out for a good time. And my mom fell for it. Every. Single. Time.

Harsh?

Maybe.

True?

Yes.

I pushed aside the bills and the guilt, not sure what to do with myself. I eyed my computer. Duke said he'd send the email today. Beyond two emails from a clothing company I bought from one time three years ago, there was nothing. I even checked my spam folder. It was probably too early. He could have forgotten. I hadn't allowed myself to be that excited about the idea in front of him. Maybe he decided to cut his losses before he started.

I spent the next part of the morning cleaning the apartment as quietly as I could, disinfecting the countertops and dusting the furniture while mentally berating myself for even considering the job. It wouldn't happen. And even if it did, who was I to think I'd ever win the permanent position? My mind wanted to reject the whole idea because it felt like some sort of handout. I wasn't sure, of course, but it was all so sudden. Convenient. Not to mention, Duke was...hard to figure out. I wasn't sure what his motives were.

I checked my email again. My heart dropped because, this time, there it was. One unread message shown in bold from RDM Marketing.

Not Duke, specifically. From Mel at RDM.

I opened the email. Might as well have all the info to make an informed decision. I squinted closer. It wasn't an application as Duke had led me to believe. This was an acceptance email.

Dear Nora,

Congratulations on being chosen to take part in the internship program at RDM. We, as a company, are looking for highly motivated and creative individuals who are interested in helping to grow the company. This is a paid internship position. You will be tasked with entry-level assignments to grow your knowledge base and hone your skills while working under a highly reputable graphic designer. Three candidates will be accepted into this three-month program. As part of the last month of the program, each candidate will be required to design and create an entire branding package for a business of your choosing, including a website, logo, social media campaign, etc.

The winner of this competition will receive a full-time position with RDM as an official intern. After the employee gains the necessary education and experience, they will be promoted to a full-time graphic design position. The winner of the internship will be eligible to choose a graphic design program approved by and paid for by RDM Marketing to complete their schooling.

If you would like to accept the terms of this program, please click here to sign…

I SKIMMED through the rest of the email, my cursor hovering over the link to complete the signup. Okay, so Duke's company sent me an email offering me everything I could possibly ask for, beyond just skipping the whole competition thing and hiring me full time. Even the idea of having the rest of my education paid for brought on such a feeling of relief it was almost hard to breathe.

The struggle to make and save money was an uphill battle I'd never quite conquered. Whenever I got something substantial tucked away, an unexpected bill would appear, or my mom would wreck our car, or one of my sisters would need money for dance camp or a basketball tournament. I could never get ahead. Not fully. And then North Dakota happened and blew everything else out of the water.

I clicked on the link, finding more detailed information. With a sigh of relief, I discovered that the internship would pay about as much as I earned from the cafe. Which meant that I could quit my job as waitress and use the extra hours working for Cathy to throw towards my bill. It would leave me in the same position, money-wise, but at least I'd be working in a job with potential. If I did end up winning the competition, my education would be paid for. I couldn't say no even if I wanted to.

Looked like I would have to find a way to co-exist with Duke Webber at the office. There was no way I would be giving up this opportunity.

12

ONE WEEK LATER, I FOUND MYSELF WALKING ON THE CITY sidewalk leading up to my building, this time the heels on my new shoes clicking pleasantly on the pavement. The fashionable pants and stylish top I wore felt like a step up in the world. For the first time ever, I was not wearing clothes or aprons covered in stains. Instead of my hair being tangled into a messy ponytail, it bounced against my shoulders, leaving me feeling soft and feminine. I wondered briefly if Duke would notice, until I pushed those thoughts away. I didn't care if Duke liked my hair. And the second I did care, I vowed I'd quit.

Well.

Maybe not quit…

This time, the streets were bustling all around me. A motorcycle's loud engine roared as it passed by, zipping way too fast down the crowded streets. Large city buses and a handful of taxis sped past. A certain buzz was in the air. A crisp morning full of possibility. There was underground parking for all companies in the office building, but today I parked in a lot above ground, two blocks away. Just this one time, I wanted to bask in the feeling of my romantic-comedy moment. I stopped to grab a coffee from the street vendor, smiled cheerfully at other men and women making their way to their offices, and put some change in an open guitar case while a man played an old Bon Jovi song for his mobile audience.

I opened the doorway and breathed in the smell of paper and coffee and some sort of pastry sold in a shop on the first floor. The first floor was nothing new to me. Nothing had changed but my own circumstances, and it was hard to keep the grin from my face. I stopped in front of the elevators, but as I reached for the button, another finger got there first.

Duke.

He was wearing his fitted gray slacks and white button-down shirt with a yellow tie and his sleeves rolled up halfway. Handsome and effortless and sinfully sweet all rolled up into one delicious package—an extremely off-limits package. He had been in meetings a few of the nights I'd been working my janitor shift, and he'd only waved, which I very much appreciated.

"Hello." I spoke casually, breezing into the empty elevator when the door opened. My voice sounded level and smooth, for which I gave myself a mental pat on the back. For all the effort it took to hide my own jitters, he seemed as calm as a summer's morning.

He followed languidly behind me, turning to stand shoulder to shoulder next to me. I moved a couple inches to my right so as not to accidentally bump him.

"Kiss Cam Nora."

The elevator door closed.

"Hey, you can't call me that here."

He furrowed his brow. "Where? Here? The elevator?"

I gave him a look. "In the office. If I'm going to be taken seriously, you need to forget you know me. Just call me Nora."

"Why can't I know you here?"

"I don't want anybody to think I had a leg up."

"You didn't. Are we going up?" He pointed toward the

button pad, and I noticed neither of us had pushed any button yet.

"As soon as you promise me you won't interfere with anything I'm doing up there. I have to earn my spot, Duke. No special treatment."

He seemed distracted. "The second somebody pushes the button on the outside, it's going to open. And we'll be waiting here again forever."

"Promise me."

"I won't do anything to help you in here."

"There."

"What?"

"You said, 'in here.' Like the elevator. Don't think I didn't hear that."

"I don't know what you want from me."

"Promise me you won't help me in—"

The door opened and we were swarmed by a group of people dressed in business clothes headed upstairs to their various offices. Duke seemed a little too smug as he allowed himself to be pressed into the opposite corner of the elevator wall than mine. We then endured the awkward kind of silence that happens when nobody wants to finish their conversations while trapped in an elevator. A handful of people got off on the ninth floor, then the thirteenth, and finally the fourteenth.

Duke smiled at me as he moved to step off the elevator, following a man who must work for us. "Hey, Troy. Your wife have that baby yet?"

I didn't hear the man's reply as they walked toward RDM's office door. The elevator started to shut before I bolted forward.

Up ahead, Duke glanced over his shoulder and gave me a smile before opening RDM's doors. I vowed to find him later and run over a few rules.

A woman named Holly with a friendly smile, long blonde hair, and dimples greeted me at the reception desk.

"Hey there. How can I help you?"

"Hi. I'm Nora, I'm here for the internship."

Her eyes widened, and she took me in once more. "Of course. Great. I'll show you to your desk, and I'll get the guys in IT to set you all up. Welcome to RDM."

"Thanks," I said, sucking in a deep breath as I followed her down a hallway that broke out into a large room with cubicles strewn about in the center. A healthy mix of men and women milled about, and the conversations seemed full of happy chatter as the room buzzed with the sounds of phones ringing, coffee mugs clanging, and the copy machine humming. And for the first time in my life, I stood in the middle of it all, not with a vacuum or a mop, but with a laptop. The urge to both cry and dance across the room to the loudest version of Pharrell Williams' song "Happy" hit me hard, though I resisted. Even if I was fired tomorrow, I had lived through two romantic-comedy moments this morning, and I couldn't help the smile that crossed my face.

Also, off the record, I must take note of how clean the office looked this morning. Not a speck of dust in sight.

The next couple of hours were a blur of new faces and setting up my cubicle, all while trying not to feel like a stranger. Others around me were bustling about with assignments, while I set up my desk, signed more paperwork, and waited for my manager to get out of her meeting and show me the ropes. While the IT department set up my computer, I met the other two interns occupying the cubicles next to mine.

Shawn and Anita were both younger than me by a few years. Shawn seemed nice enough. Standing tall and lanky, he had flaming-red hair and freckles covering his cheeks. If *endearing computer geek* had a picture in the dictionary, Shawn's face would pop up. The same could be said for Anita and Cruella De Vil. Her long, jet-black hair and the over-the-top cartoonish way she laughed sent chills straight down my spine. With a laugh a little too fake, eyes a little too calculating, and the way she'd stare at me with a blank expression after I finished speaking was enough for me to gather that we'd probably never be great friends.

I saw Duke a handful of times, running in and out of the office, chatting with Ryan or Mike, taking phone calls or meeting with a designer and a client in the conference room. Not that I was trailing him, specifically, but the office wasn't that big. I had nothing to do yet. My eyes just naturally wandered…where they wandered.

The designer over me was a vivacious woman with ultra-curly black hair and creamy black skin. She wore a neon-green dress and a headband on her head, and I couldn't help but be jealous of her fashion sense. She was striking, owning the room when she walked in. I looked down at the tame-by-comparison outfit I had been so excited to wear, but she had me laughing before my insecurities could run too far. I wasn't sure if it was because she was my manager or if she was this genuinely nice, but I was grateful for her sitting by me in the break room at lunch. I figured I would eat at my desk, as I'd seen others do, but when I went to grab my food out of the fridge, Tenisha motioned for me to sit beside her at one of the four round tables placed around the break room.

"So, how many clients are you working with currently?" I asked, taking a bite of my peanut butter sandwich, wishing I would have brought a more grown-up lunch for my first day. It had been a long time since I'd had a real first day of work. And I'd never had a job where lunch wasn't already included in my pay.

Tenisha looked at me like I had asked her to take me to the moon. "Honey, I'm on lunch break. I do not talk about work on my lunch break."

I blinked. "Oh, sorry."

"I'm teasing. Goodness, you interns are going to be fun."

And then she laughed, the sound echoing all throughout the room.

Anita and Shawn joined us soon after at the table with their lunches and their managers nowhere in sight.

"So when do we meet with the owners?" Anita asked Tenisha.

Duke's face blared in my mind. He had never told me outright, but if my suspicion level had a number, it had shot past ten and was inching toward fifteen.

Breaking her own rule, Tenisha supplied, "They've been in and out of meetings all morning. They'll be here for the staff meeting at two. You'll meet them all then."

"I heard they're all young." Anita raised her eyebrows, not even attempting to seem discreet. "Office eye candy."

Tenisha had been about ready to take a bite when she paused mid-air. "Who did you hear that from?"

Anita laughed off the question. "Oh, I don't remember."

"Well, two are married with families, and one is in a long-term relationship," Tenisha said, peering over at her frankly.

"Duke, right? Is he the tall, dark, and handsome guy I've seen in and out?"

Hearing his name fall out of her lips triggered a spiteful reaction inside of me. I channeled the emotion into attacking my sandwich.

"First of all, they're all handsome, but nobody's that dark," Tenisha said, making me and Shawn laugh. "And second, I'd suggest not talking like that ever again in this office."

"I didn't mean anything by it," she clipped, laughing obnox-iously. "I was just teasing."

And that was lunch.

After an hour spent attempting to look busy going over more office policy, we were pulled into a staff meeting. I counted about fifteen employees, including the three interns, all sitting around the big conference table. I sat next to Tenisha at the table, taking my notepad out and placing it in front of me, feeling antsy over my less-than-productive first day. At the café, there were always things to be doing. If I wasn't taking orders, I was delivering food, or clearing plates, or rolling silverware into napkins. This first day had been nothing like I had thought. Of course, I was an intern, and I had no idea what to do yet, but my fingers itched to be set free on an assignment.

An RDM sign hanging above the doorway in the boardroom caught my notice. R.D.M. Ryan, Duke, Mike, perhaps? I felt so stupid that I hadn't seen the signs. Of course it was his company. Their company. A surge of unreasonable jealousy shot through me at the thought of his dreams working out exactly as he'd planned. The stars just aligned for some people. He was only a few years older than me, yet here he was, part owner of a company with their own floor in an office building—all in under three years. In talking about his company that night, he'd told me it probably wouldn't work out. Deep down, I'd agreed with him. That thought came much more naturally to my thinking than something actually working out.

And that was sad. Right?

I felt him the moment he entered the room. He suspiciously kept his eyes averted from mine as he greeted the entire staff. Like a boss.

Outwardly, I sat rigid in my chair as he made his way closer to me, shaking hands and checking in on his staff.

"Nora, right?" Duke smiled, holding out his hand for me to shake.

I looked up and met his gaze. "Yeah."

"So glad you're here."

I made sure my eyes spoke volumes to this man, even as I shook his hand.

"Thank you, *sir*. Glad to be here."

He grinned. "Oh, just call me Duke. Nobody goes too wild with titles here."

"I'll call you a lot of things," I muttered.

"What was that?" Duke asked, leaning closer to me with a big fake furrowed brow.

"Sounds good."

Soon, Ryan and Mike filtered in, each greeting the staff and adding noise and humor to the entire meeting. Mike wore his soft-blue suit with a bright-green tie. Ryan dressed in a black suit with a classic gray tie.

All three owners sat around the conference table, pulling out an open seat wherever they could find it. I had figured they'd sit at the head of the table, but I immediately liked the sense of camaraderie that came from having them sit with the group. While Duke welcomed everybody into the meeting, Mike and Ryan caught my eye and both raised their eyebrows in sync. I could do nothing but bite back a smile and shake my head slightly.

"We'd like to welcome our three new interns," Duke said, pointing toward the three of us sitting next to each other. "In fact, why don't you each take a minute to introduce yourselves. Tell us your background, a few of your favorite things, and a bucket list item you plan to complete this year." He made a show of checking his notebook. "Hmm, Nora? Why don't you go first?"

He met my gaze with a hint of a challenge. I swallowed the nerves collecting in my throat and decided that I would match whatever he threw down.

"Sure. I'm Nora Griffin. I grew up here in the city. I love Chinese food and romantic comedies."

I stopped talking, hoping he'd forget, but Duke never let me off that easily.

"And how about something on your bucket list?"

Mike leaned forward on his elbows, suspiciously covering his face. Ryan looked up toward the ceiling, a half-smile toying across his lips, but neither looked at me, for which I felt grateful.

Duke kept it together, but there was mirth in his eyes. Straight up mirth.

"I'm not sure yet."

"Or you can tell us about an epic bucket list item you've already completed."

Props to him for keeping his composure, because his two friends were fighting smiles. I bit my lip and put my game face on.

"I can't think of one. I'm pretty boring, I'm afraid."

He held my gaze for a smidge longer than necessary, before he said, "No worries. I'll circle back." Speaking louder and to the entire room, he added, "At RDM we believe in setting goals in all areas of our lives. What's the point of a bucket list if you don't start checking a few things off? If you work hard for our company, we'll work hard to allow you the freedom and schedule to have a life outside of this office. For some of us, that means making goals and scheduling in time for some fun."

He moved on to Anita, who immediately droned on about taking her parents' yacht to Lake Powell sometime this summer. She couldn't believe she'd never boated Lake Powell, and oh my gosh, it's just so beautiful. My mind was transported to my evening with Duke three years earlier. Our talk on bucket lists had obviously affected him. Now he was running a company dedicated to helping employees not be like me. He had taken our talk and did something about it. I had taken that same conversation and somehow turned into *less* of a risk taker—if that was even possible.

"Does anybody have a bucket list update?" Duke asked the entire group.

The office manager, an older woman named Susan with graying hair, probably in her fifties, raised her hand, her cheeks turning pink as she spoke. "My husband and I booked that trip to Europe for this fall."

Ryan and Mike started clapping, and the rest of us joined in.

A wide grin spread across Duke's face. "Nice, Susan! For how long?"

"Two weeks." Susan beamed in a shy way.

"Question. Will your luggage fit me?" Mike quipped, gaining a few laughs in the room.

"I've been training to hike to the top of Mount Timp later this summer. Some friends and I scheduled a weekend in July to get it done," Tenisha piped up.

"I've done that hike before. You're gonna love it. I mean, you'll actually hate it, but you'll love it by the end," Ryan said. Everyone chuckled.

A few more bucket list items were announced while the rest of the table reaffirmed their commitment to take action.

"Alright, Nora, back to you. What do you got?"

I felt the eyes of the room on me again. I had known Duke wouldn't let me off the hook, so I'd spent the last few minutes internally freaking out while my mind stuttered and stalled, rejecting ideas before they came to full fruition. Too expensive. Too epic. Too far away. Too dangerous. Any mention of the kiss cam was out. Of course, a trip to Europe sounded lovely, but since the entirety of my bank account was down to three very low digits, I'd have to think of something else. If Lake Powell was ever on my bucket list, it was officially off now.

I cleared my throat and stilled my shaking foot. Everybody was staring at me, waiting. "Umm..." I began, "I've always wanted to...ride a..."—the flash of the man on the street came flooding into my brain—"motorcycle."

I wanted to kick myself the second that came flying out of my mouth. Someone booked a trip to Europe. And I basically said that I wanted to hitch a ride around the block with someone on a motorcycle.

Anita snorted lightly before covering it up with a cough.

Shoot me now.

"Anybody drive here on a motorcycle?" Mike said. "We might be able to make that happen today."

Thankfully, nobody raised their hand. I desperately wanted to explain that if I had had more than three minutes to think about my bucket list, I might have come up with something better that didn't cost any money. But instead, I said nothing. I was in this now. I didn't even think I liked motorcycles. Did I?

Duke's cheery eyes settled on me. "I like it. For you interns, we follow up on bucket list items every month at our staff meeting."

"What's yours, Duke?" Anita asked, her greedy eyes roaming all over his face.

He specifically didn't look my way, but I could feel my face heating as he spoke.

"I've always wanted to re-enact a scene from a certain movie."

My stomach clenched. I lowered my gaze when his began to wander toward me. I would not engage, though my lips fought against my will not to smile.

"With your girlfriend?" Anita purred, leaning closer like she was in on some great secret.

He shook his head and grinned. "That's classified. I'll report back if I get it done."

The meeting finally began. For the first two months, we'd be working closest with our designers, learning the ropes while alleviating some of their workload. The last month of our internship would be the design competition.

"After two months, Mike, Ryan, and I will give each of you three different business options for the marketing package we feel would best represent our work as a company. You'll pick the company you'd be most interested in. From there, you'll have four weeks to curate your marketing package for whichever business you choose."

"Nora, you'll be working with Tenisha and me," Duke stated.

"Anita, you'll be with Susan and Mike. And Shawn, you'll be with Ryan and April."

The meeting continued with everyone giving reports on projects and companies they were working with, while I sat watching Duke lead the discussion, impressed by his ability to command the room with such friendliness and ease. And I realized something. What we knew of each other before I came into this space wouldn't matter. We shared a moment a long time ago. He was my boss and he had a girlfriend. In a lot of ways, that simplified my entire objective and nullified my concerns. I could now spend my time focusing on doing my best to win my position here at the end of the summer. We had become something like friends a long time ago, but that was officially over. Back to the real world.

My eyes drifted to his forearms, of all things, as he spoke. Honestly, I was getting tired of looking at his face. He had laugh lines around his eyes that crinkled when he smiled, and his dark hair was casually mussed in the most attractive way. It was too perfect. Though, the forearms weren't much better. Only when he sat down and Ryan stood up to speak did Duke look at me. I felt it before I saw it, my gaze meeting his in a flash of heat that had me shifting in my chair. My arms, which were folded very normally against my stomach, suddenly felt ten feet long and absurdly awkward. When a smile began curving his lips, I shot my gaze down to the floor. Unfortunately, there were no dark eyes piercing through mine. Though, I will say, it was spotless.

13

DUKE'S GIRLFRIEND WAS EVEN MORE BEAUTIFUL IN PERSON THAN she appeared on social media. And that was saying something. I knew I shouldn't compare, but it was difficult not to. Her chestnut hair was shiny and rich compared to mine—so dull and lifeless. I hadn't the time nor the money for expensive conditioners or salon visits. Everything about her, from her toned body all the way to her professionally manicured nails, outshined me in every way.

It was a small office. She came in at least two to three times a week. My desk was near the center—close to Duke—so my observations of her weren't really abnormal given my proximity to Duke's desk. It was my location. She was quieter than I imagined her to be, which surprised me for some reason. She'd arrive at RDM and immediately sequester herself in Duke's office. At face value, she could pass for whatever she decided to be. She could be nice and sweet. She could be pouty at something Duke said to her. She could be a guy's girl, high-fiving Mike and Ryan and laughing loudly at something they said, or chatting casually with Anita. She could be smiling while delivering a clichéd, meaningless compliment. She could also be clingy and annoyingly touchy. Some days, she'd attach herself to Duke, and he would have to literally remove his arm from her grip to get away. It was happening more and more in the couple of weeks I'd observed the awkward dance between them.

Or so it seemed to me. I'm sure that my judgment wasn't the least bit cloudy.

And then there was yesterday. Duke stood in a group by the copy machine in front of my desk with Rachel, talking with the other owners about something. Again, the proximity, I couldn't help my eyes flitting over to the group while they chatted. Rachel had been grabbing his hand or linking her arm through his throughout the entire five minutes they were in front of me. Duke found a gracious way to step out every time. His eyes met mine suddenly, and I startled at my desk, my computer immediately demanding my attention. But when I glanced back up again, his gaze was still on me.

VOICEMAIL: Nora, honey. I promise Kip will send you money, but now we have to wait until his next paycheck. I didn't realize he had some...outstanding bills that were more pressing. Anyway, we're good for it. I could just use a little help. I would use my credit card, but it's maxed at the moment, and Kip doesn't want me to get another one. Anyway, the storage unit called me again and...I just...I don't know what to do. Those blankets grandma made for you all are in there. Your baby things. I...could you pay it for me? Please? We'll send you a check as soon as we can. Please let me know.

ACCORDING TO MY MOTHER, the lien on the storage unit would take hold on Monday, if not paid beforehand. I wasn't going to do it. I had to put my foot down with some boundaries. If it wasn't this, it would be something else. There was always something else. She was the one who quit her job to go gallivanting around with Kip in an RV. She was just as capable as I was to pay her bills. Although, capable wasn't quite the word I would use to describe me or my bank account. Reliable was probably more accurate. But not this time.

Her voicemail came on Thursday evening. The plea in her voice played in my head on repeat all through Friday and Saturday. My maternal grandma's handmade blankets she'd sewn for me and each of my sisters before she passed away kept me company while I worked on a new logo for a client of Tenisha's. I scrubbed toilets to the thought that Kip's outstanding bills probably had more to do with the new Jeep I spotted in their social media pictures than anything meaningful. On a Sunday afternoon, I drove to my mom's storage unit. The office was closed, but I didn't need to speak with anyone at the office. As an attempt to assuage my guilt, I had planned to grab a few things that really meant something to my sisters and me. If I had room in my car, maybe a handful of things for my mom.

Except, the storage unit now had an extra lock on it from the storage company, blocking my entrance and halting my entire plan.

On the quiet drive back to my apartment, guilt kept me occupied in the form of old picture albums, the pretty plates my mom had inherited, our couch, and my mom's old record player and albums that we girls would spend hours making up dances to in the living room. Did we need the tangible proof? Or would our memories of those times be enough to sustain us? I was still pondering that question as I walked up the flight of stairs to my apartment, let myself in, grabbed the storage bill from the counter, an apple from the fridge, and flung myself onto my bed.

The answer to the question still hadn't found me as I reached for the laptop, set up an online account for my mom's storage unit, and paid her bill in full.

THE NEXT DAY, I checked the clock on the oven and shoved in my last bite of cereal, milk dripping down the side of my mouth before I wiped it away. I had only been working at RDM for a couple of weeks, and the thought of being late gave me pangs of anxiety.

Mira had just gotten home from her night shift at the hospital. Her car was in the shop, so she'd taken mine. I'd spent the last ten minutes frantically stress-texting her, asking where she was. She had gotten held up by an emergency patient. At this point, I wasn't going to be late beyond one or two minutes, but I'd be tense the entire drive to work.

"Sorry I'm late," Mira said, plopping her purse on the counter. "But do you want the bad news or the really bad news first?" She set two envelopes on the counter next to me as I rushed to rinse my bowl in the sink.

I reached for my glass by the sink and took a big drink. "No news."

"Your student loan bill arrived."

I swallowed and wiped my hands on a towel before accepting the document.

"I told them to stop asking me for money. It's rude," I said with a lightness I didn't really feel as I ripped open the document. I had made several large payments, but it never seemed to go down.

"What's the other bad news?" I asked, searching for my Chapstick on the table. Might as well hit me with everything or else I'd be more anxious not knowing.

"The rent is going up."

That stopped me. "What?" I would have preferred not to know that one. Picking up the letter she held in her hand, I scanned the document. "Two hundred dollars more a month? How can they do that to people?"

"Everything's going up. The apartments Brock and I were looking at the other day were crazy high. I'm so sorry."

I bit my lip and put on a good face. "Maybe you and Brock could move in here," I said. "I'd be a fun third wheel. You'd seriously never know I was here."

She grinned wickedly. "You'd definitely know we were here, so maybe you want to re-think that invitation."

"Okay. Nope. Nope. Nope. Offer revoked." I smacked her arm as I strode out the front door, purse and keys in hand. "See ya."

I'd be okay. I'd made it through worse. I either needed to find a new roommate before the end of summer or a new apartment. I was sure it would be hard finding something cheaper than what my rent was now, even with the two-hundred-dollar hike. If Salt Lake City was a car lot, I was definitely living in the used section. After paying for my mom's storage unit, I had four hundred dollars left in my savings account. I vowed to protect it like gold. I mentally calculated where that extra rent would come from. Instead of the entirety of my cleaning job going directly to my student loan, I could pay the minimum balance and use some of that money for rent. I could make it work. Maybe I could get a couple roommates. Share a bedroom with someone. The lack of privacy made me physically ache. But I could do it if necessary. It would take me years to save up for tuition again, but lots of people go to college in their thirties. It would be fine. This was a hard season. I'd get through it. I always got through it.

I had almost convinced myself of that fact as I drove to work. My heart had settled into just enough denial that I turned up the volume on the radio. A pop song was playing, and I needed a distraction. I'd be fine. I'd get through this. I would still be able to pay off my student loans in—

Suddenly a booming pop exploded in my ears, and my car jerked toward the sidewalk at my right. Instinctively, I tried to turn back toward the road, but the wheel felt tight, almost impossible to budge the other way. I stomped on the brakes. A man walking down the street jumped out of the way moments before my car came barreling onto the sidewalk and then to a heaping stop. It took a few seconds for my brain to catch up to what had just happened.

The next half hour was a merging of emotions. Thankful I hadn't been driving down the freeway when my tire popped. Thankful for the man on the street who didn't get run over but, instead, helped me call a tow truck to take my car to a tire shop. A thudding in my gut, trying to calculate the cost of a tow truck. The tall thin man at the tire shop with the greasy white uniform telling me he could not sell me just one tire. It would be too unsafe. My three remaining tires were all threadbare.

"You'll be back in a week, maybe two, with the same problem. That is if you're as lucky as you were this time. You could have been seriously hurt. It's too dangerous to be on the road."

Utter devastation clenched my heart, and all my attempts at being positive seemed to vanish. Just like that, I handed over the last of my meager savings for four new tires on my rusty, old, beat-up Honda Civic.

"So nice of you to show up to work," Anita barbed, her eyes peeking over the partition separating our desks as I dropped into my seat, three hours late. I didn't say anything. I couldn't. Apparently, my emotions were equipped to deal with a lot of unexpected things today, but my co-worker's snide, clueless comments were going to push me over the edge. I spent what little energy I had left going through the motions of turning on my computer and putting my purse in one of the pull-out drawers of my cubicle.

She huffed at my silence, her eyes drifting down to my rumpled outfit, probably reeking of rubber from sitting in the tire shop. "Calm down. I'm just kidding. Holly told us about your car."

The receptionist's motive had been pure. Of course she had to tell those who worked near me why I would be late, but I still detested people knowing my business. I forced myself to take a deep breath. So far, it had been a horrible day—after a horrible weekend—but I was determined to push the emotions aside until a later date. Hopefully never, with a side of…wait until I'm alone.

"I think I parked by you the other day. How old is your car, out of curiosity?" Anita asked, her sickly sweet voice grating my insides raw.

"Not sure," I said. "And it was the tires. Not the car." Thankfully, the car had been working great.

"My dad won't let me drive a car with over 75,000 miles on it. He always said he never wants to worry about me on the road."

My toes clenched inside my white Keds, and I forced myself to take a breath to re-focus and calm myself down. In my moment of attempted Zen, I noticed a large cup of what looked like some form of pop with a lid and straw next to my computer. I hadn't had anything but a bottle of water at my desk the past couple of days. I peered over the lid to see a dark liquid with bubbles, which immediately made my mouth water. I wouldn't be drinking a stranger's soda, but I could only imagine how much a caffeinated sugar-laden drink would help lessen the day's sharp edges.

"Whose drink is this?" I asked the area around me.

"I don't drink soda," Anita declared. "Too much sugar."

From behind me, Shawn's voice finally spoke out. "Yours maybe?"

I looked around the office, but nobody looked like they'd sat down at my desk for a second and left their beverage. Sighing, I picked it up, moving it to the edge and out of my way, when a small wadded-up paper underneath the cup gave me pause. I set the drink back down and unfolded the note.

> Kiss Cam,
>> Heard about the tires. I was once told there wasn't much a DP couldn't fix.
>>> PS. I made sure it fell.

I SAT THERE for a long moment, not moving, chewing on the insides of my cheeks, the words on the paper blurring at the edges. When the tears had been pushed back and I'd finally collected myself, I slid the drink closer to me and proceeded to have the longest and most satisfying drink ever drunk in the entire world. The combination of caffeine and Duke's kindness pumped enough life back into my veins to get me through the rest of the day.

14

After my disastrous morning in the tire shop and only bills to greet me when I got home, I had no desire to hurry through my cleaning tonight. I finished the upstairs office much later than usual, which gave me exactly what I wanted when I arrived back at RDM—everyone gone. I began working through the rooms, spot cleaning when needed and emptying the garbage cans. I found the repetitive tasks soothing in a pathetic kind of way. I was about to enter the women's restroom when I heard a door open somewhere down the hallway. Panicking, I dove through the doorway to hide.

Of course, diving somewhere was difficult when lugging a huge, squeaking cleaning cart behind me, but I thought I made it through the doorway without being seen. In the bathroom, I moved efficiently, cleaning toilets, sinks, and mirrors before mopping the floor. When I finished, I peered out into the hallway, taking my earbuds out to listen before pulling the cart into the men's bathroom.

I'd gotten into a rhythm with the cleaning that suited me. I didn't hate the work. Okay, to be fair, I did hate cleaning the men's bathroom. Not that it was ever too disgusting, thank goodness, it just felt wrong to be inside. Like I was doing something I shouldn't be. I made sure to check underneath the stalls twice before allowing myself to relax.

The mindless work allowed my cluttered brain to run rampant with every anxious thought I had pushed aside throughout the day. Bills and rent and tires circled in and out of my thoughts. And of course, the one question it all really boiled down to—how I could be saving up my entire life but never really get ahead. I scrubbed and plunged, anxiety and anger taking hold of my fingers as I wielded a brush and cleaned in and out and around the men's urinals.

Since our meeting a week ago, the talk of bucket lists had been prominent on each intern's mind. I hadn't expected a company to take interest in something like that. Duke's influence, no doubt. Maybe in Duke's world, bucket lists were a dime a dozen. Spend a pile of money to go somewhere exotic in order to feel fulfilled in this life. A big life meant doing big things. Big trips. Can't write home about something if there's nothing to write home about.

In my world, the idea of a bucket list only created guilt. Guilt that I was somehow doing this life wrong. No matter how hard I tried, how hard I worked, it might never be enough. And that thought made me physically ache. Maybe I'd always have guilt for not being more fun or for always covering for my mom.

I flushed the urinal, watching in depressed satisfaction as the soap swirled around the bowl before being sucked down the pipe. I had guilt because I *was* embarrassed to be working as a janitor in the same office I was interning at. The same office I worked at with Duke, even though it shouldn't matter because he had a girlfriend—but somehow it did. I had guilt for wanting to put a career ahead of my personal life. I even had guilt for accepting this stupid internship and for the fact that I not only wanted it, I *needed* it. I hated the idea that Duke had seen me so low.

And there, in the quiet of the men's bathroom, all the emotions I'd pressed down came to me full force. A tension headache behind my eyes had me clutching my head and sitting down on the only seat within sight. There is a certain cathartic release that happens when a person cries. I had held myself so stiff and rigid, my body taut with anxiety, I had almost been begging for this moment of release.

It was also unfortunate that Duke, of all people, decided to walk into the men's restroom at that precise moment to see me crying while sitting on the men's urinal.

"Nora? Hey! What's wrong?" he asked, alarm lacing his voice.

I jumped up, horrified, choking back snot through my nose while he strode over to me, his eyes examining every part of me as though he expected to see me bleeding out on the floor.

"Nora." He stopped in front of me. "What's wrong? Are you hurt?"

"No." I wiped at my face. "I'm fine. Why are you still here?"

"I had a meeting. Why are *you* still here?" he countered, his eyes scanning my face as though he didn't believe me.

"I work here, remember?" The smile I attempted was most likely a cross between a circus clown and serial killer. For all I knew, the mascara had gone the way of the tears. I wiped under my eyes, doing my best attempt to clean them up. "I'm fine now. Sorry."

"What do you have left to do?" Duke took in the bathroom, his gaze scanning over the mirrors still speckled with water stains and the dirty sinks.

Panic laced my insides. "Nothing. Go home."

"Tell me." He grabbed a toilet brush from my cart and held it up like it was a hostage situation. It was a new brush, thank goodness, still wrapped in plastic and attached to the bottom compartment. Duke stood with his disheveled brown hair, suit pants, tie, and rolled-up sleeves and was brandishing a toilet brush as a weapon. And dang it all if it didn't make me smile.

"I'm done," I said brightly, inching my way closer to him.

"No, you're not." He moved the brush a bit higher out of my reach.

"I am. I was just sitting down to have a quick cry before leaving. I did that. So now I'm going home."

I began straightening up the things on my cart, untying my apron and waiting until he dropped his guard a fraction of an inch before I attacked. I flung myself toward him, surprise on my side as I grabbed his arm holding the brush and used all my weight to pull it down. By that point, Duke was on to me, trying to shake me off like a wet dog. My fingers clung to him, a rush of adrenaline on my side. There was no way on this green earth he would be scrubbing toilets for me.

But then he did something unexpected. He dropped the brush on the floor and wrapped both arms around me and pulled me into his chest. I froze. The subtle scent of pine from his cologne infiltrated my nose and left me comatose. It was all so appropriately inappropriate, and my right-and-wrong sensors were pinging. He had a girlfriend, and we were hugging. But we were also friends…or something. I stood there, a statue in his arms. It must have been like hugging a tree trunk. Undeterred, he pulled me closer and held me tighter until something deep within me let out a great gaping sigh of relief. He was the wrong person to be hugging, but there was nobody else around, and so, ever so slowly, my head melted against his chest. My arms went around his waist. And for a moment, a brief millisecond in the history of time, I let Duke Webber, my boss, hug me in the men's bathroom.

"Why were you crying?" he whispered a long moment later, his voice low and in my ear.

I swallowed, remembering myself. "Because I'm cleaning the men's bathroom. Happens every night about this time."

I felt his small chuckle before he released me and stepped back. I adjusted my shirt and bent over to pick up the clean toilet brush he'd held hostage from my cart. In that time, Duke had managed to grab the cleaner and the toilet brush I'd actually been using and strode into one of the stalls.

"Duke. Please don't." I could only handle so much humiliation in one night, and the idea of him cleaning toilets for me was too much. I didn't want his pity. I didn't want him to be so nice.

"You're in luck. My mom always assigned me to clean the bathrooms growing up because I would much rather clean toilets than any other chore." His voice sounded muffled inside the stall, but I could hear the squeak and spray of the cleaner.

"You better hope you're not lying, because when you get married, I'm going to tell your wife what you said, and you'll be done for."

"Great. I love it."

"Liar."

"Tell me why you were crying."

"Is this some weird form of blackmail?" I asked.

Duke flushed the toilet and moved into the next stall. I couldn't watch it any longer, so I began cleaning the countertop and sinks.

"Nope. Just asking a friend if she's okay."

A friend. The words should have brought me comfort. And maybe they did to some small degree, but a huge wave of humiliation washed over me again.

"I don't really want to talk about it. I'm okay. I got a little sad. The end."

Duke was quiet for a bit after this, the sound of toilets being scrubbed a constant reminder of the mortification of it all. "Just tell me this, is it anything at RDM making you sad? Is someone not treating you right?"

"No. Nothing like that." My mind briefly shot to Anita's face, but I dismissed the idea. I could handle mean girls. And after the summer, one of us would be going home, so I'd never have to see her again.

Another flush and he moved into the second to last stall. We worked quietly, both engrossed in our tasks. I wiped down the mirrors before grabbing the mop, starting in the back. The silence was killing me. KILLING me. But do you know what sound was killing me even more? The sound of Duke scrubbing the toilets.

"Can we please talk about something else, if you insist on helping me? This is so weird."

"Sure." He waited a moment and then added, "The other day I found this weird abscess on my—"

"STOP."

I turned in time to see him step out of the stall, his tie askew and a teasing smile on his face. For a moment I just blinked at him, taking in the devastating pull of Duke Webber. I wanted another hug, dang it.

"Ok. Can we talk about how you were sitting on the men's urinal when I first walked in here?"

"It was clean, okay! I scrubbed the whole thing. Please don't make me cry again."

Silence fell between us. I could feel him staring at me, though I couldn't meet his eyes.

"Hey," he said, and even across the room, the sound of his voice brushed across my skin like a feather. I turned from him and made a noise to indicate that I'd heard. His voice sounded soft and tender, and I couldn't do soft and tender at the moment. I was one shot of tender away from—

A hand at my arm startled me. I reluctantly lifted my gaze up to his.

"I would never want to make you cry. Ever."

Instantly, my eyes were a running faucet, my features morphing into my ugly cry face. It's like that moment when you've been having a bad day and you keep telling everyone that you're fine. You're fine. You're fine. Then someone looks you in the eye and asks how you're doing, and you completely break down. I whirled back around, dropping the handle of the mop to hide my face behind my hands.

"Well, that's ironic," I sobbed.

He took a few steps toward me, but I held him off with a hand. I was now a horrifying mix of laughter and tears.

"I'm okay! Really. I'm just on a roll now and can't stop."

"Yeah. You seem okay." For his part, Duke looked miserable, running his hand through his hair.

"I promise I won't do any better if you come near me." I held my hand out to him once more when he looked as though he was debating another rescue in the form of a hug.

We both stood there awkwardly while I wiped my tears and jabbed my fingernails into my hand to give my pain sensors something else to focus on besides my eyes.

Slowly, Duke picked up the toilet brush he must have dropped and stepped back into a stall. I picked up the mop once more.

"Well, this is going to be horrifying tomorrow," I reflected, my sorry attempt to lighten the mood.

"Don't worry about it. If I had a dime for every time I cried in the women's bathroom…" Duke said.

In spite of myself, a laugh bubbled out of me. I waited a moment before adding, "Thanks for the Dr. Pepper."

"Sure. Sorry about the tires."

"Thanks."

"Was the drink better having fallen? I had to walk down to the gas station on the corner for that."

My heart fluttered at the thought. "I'm surprised you remembered."

"I did take a tiny swig, and it tasted exactly the same to me, but what do I know?"

"You can't be trusted. You drink Coke from a can."

"When you start out with perfection, it's hard to settle for anything less."

I plunged my mop into the brown, soapy water. The sound of scrubbing and flushing became the only noise in the bathroom—until he spoke again.

"And by the way, I remember everything about that night."

I paused in my mopping for a moment at his words before forcing my limbs to start up again, to keep moving. Taking a big breath, I searched for something else to occupy our minds. "What's your favorite candy bar?"

"Thinking of getting me a treat?"

"No. Just conversation to drown out the sound of you scrubbing my toilets."

"Snickers," he said firmly.

"Wow. You just skipped past Twix without a word?"

"Sub par."

"What? No way. It's a cookie, chocolate, and soft caramel. It's culinary perfection." I had almost made it with my mop to where he was cleaning.

"Wrong. That can't keep you alive in a desert. A candy bar needs some protein."

"Wait. Why am I in the desert?"

We went on like this for a few more minutes, mindless chatter and teasing occupying our thoughts as we finished our parts of the bathroom. He held the door open for me as I moved the cleaning cart out into the hallway.

"What's left?" he asked. "And don't lie to me."

"I always save the men's bathroom for last. It's like a special little treat for me."

"Gross. Okay, then can you wait here for a sec?"

I paused, glancing up at him. "Why?"

"Because I really have to pee, but I don't want you to run away."

A laugh bubbled out of me, suddenly mortified at this knowledge. "Have you had to pee this whole time?"

"That's why I went in there. I usually don't have company this late."

"That's a long time to wait. I'd be dancing like crazy by now."

"I'm about five seconds away from crossing my legs—in a very manly way." His eyes shone with laughter, a smirk on his face.

"Go. I'll wait for you."

He turned and strode into the clean men's bathroom while I waited, surprising myself with the fact that I didn't have the urge to run away, though I probably should have.

"Why were you here so late?" I asked a minute later, as we walked toward the cleaning closet.

He glanced at me. "Once a week, I have a meeting in the evening with a company from Japan. I have to stay late."

"A meeting in Japan?" I asked incredulously.

"Yep."

"Once a week, you say?"

He smiled. "Yep."

I waited a beat. "Every Tuesday?" My mind needed to know specifics, and he seemed bent on giving me as little as possible. We arrived at the cleaning closet. He opened the door and ushered me and the squeaky cart inside.

"We'll probably wrap things up in the next couple of weeks."

I parked the cart in its spot by the corner and turned to face him. I must have visibly sighed because his mouth quirked upward the slightest fraction. He leaned against the doorframe, hands in his pockets, looking very much like he had all the time in the world to be here.

"But there are a lot of other reasons a guy could stay late. Right now, it's Tuesdays. Tomorrow, I might need to take advantage of the quiet hours at night."

"Your home is quiet!" I protested.

"Yeah, but there are so many distractions."

I pointed at my chest. "I'm a distraction here!"

A full-blown grin appeared, but before he could say anything, I added, "Not that kind." I pointed at the vacuum. "A plane taking off is less noisy than that thing."

He laughed softly. "It's great white noise."

"What are you doing?" I asked, leaning back against the sterile white wall of the closet.

He looked mildly surprised. "What do you mean?"

I motioned in the direction of RDM's office. "Why did you help me in there tonight? Why'd you get me this internship? Why are you here right now?"

"Can't a guy just enjoy cleaning?"

"A public bathroom? No."

He held my gaze for a long moment. "I helped you tonight because it's late, and you needed to go home. I didn't *get* you the internship. I told you about it. You applied and got accepted all on your own. And I'm here now because I'm planning to be a gentleman and see you to your car so you don't walk alone in the dark. How's that?"

"Solid reasonings," I said, folding my arms and ignoring the wild amount of fluttering inside my stomach. "Except, I didn't apply for the internship. I got an acceptance email."

The tiniest dimple formed in the corner of his mouth. "Huh. That's weird."

"Duke," I warned. "Why are you here helping me when you have a girlfriend?"

He straightened. "You didn't hear?"

"What?"

"We broke up. I figured Anita or somebody would have spread it all over the office by now."

"You…you broke up?"

"A few days ago."

I stared at him, stunned. My head had a hard time computing his words. Should I hug him? Offer condolences? Or maybe congratulations?

At my long and awkward pause he cleared his throat. "I should probably warn you, Kiss Cam, that RDM has a very strict no-dating-the-interns rule."

Was mental whiplash a thing? Because I definitely had it. Shouldn't this man be drowning his sorrows in a bar, or buying a puppy, or booking a cruise after breaking up with a girl he had dated for almost three years? Not staring at me like something was amusing him. Something wasn't adding up, but he was moving the conversation too fast. I'd have to circle back to over-thinking at a later date.

"So, anyway, I'm going to need to make sure you can handle being in the office and not flirting with me. Especially now that I'm back on the market." He twirled his keys lazily on his fingers.

"You're worried about *me* flirting with you?" I tilted my head, and raised one eyebrow. It was quite possible he was prowling for a rebound. Why not start with the girl he had already gotten to kiss him once before? Ew. Prowling wasn't a word that fit Duke Webber, but three years and no tears?

"Yeah, see"—he pointed to my face—"that smile right there. The one you're trying to hide. What am I supposed to think with that?"

I could feel the flush rising on my face, unable to help the delicious heat glowing everywhere inside my body. I bit my lip to attempt to rein in the smile growing wider once I realized what he was doing.

He groaned. "Don't bite your lip."

Immediately, my teeth dropped my lip, but I made the mistake of looking into his sweet, smiling eyes, and my hands flew to my cheeks, where an unfamiliar heat bloomed. I needed to stop this. It wasn't just the fact that I was in a slightly sweaty shirt and stained work pants while he wore a suit and tie. That *shouldn't* matter. In a perfect world, that didn't matter. The real problem was that I could get fired. He could not. He was my boss. I needed this job. Correction: I needed to WIN this job. I'd have to be careful before he weaseled his way into my life and, more importantly, my thoughts. Things had changed for me in the three years since I'd seen him—and not for the better. He was officially off limits. If there was anything I loved to follow, it was rules, so I ignored the forearms and his crinkly brown eyes and assured him flirting wouldn't be a problem.

"Great. One more thing. The elephant in the room," Duke said, folding his arms. "Since you still owe me, I need to know if you can handle doing the lift without trying anything inappropriate."

"I'm not doing the lift." I crossed my arms now, gaining a little of my edge back.

"You worried about making me uncomfortable?"

I laughed, in spite of myself. Duke loved to tease. That was all this was. I gathered my purse and made my way closer, lightly elbowing him in the stomach while he opened the door for me. He then proceeded to ride the elevator down to the parking garage with me, telling me a funny story about him and Ryan back in high school, before walking me to my car, two rows down from his Toyota.

He inspected my new tires, kicking them once or twice for good measure.

"Easy. Those cost me a pretty penny," I said, pleased I was now able to joke about the tires to some degree.

"They've got good tread," he determined. "You'll be glad you have them in the winter."

"My car will probably give out before they do."

Duke's eyes left mine to rake in my gold, rusted Civic in all its glory.

"Nah. It's a Honda. It will last forever—or 300,000 miles, whichever comes first."

My heart lightened at his approval for some reason, which was strange. I didn't need his approval, nor did I seek it out, but…it felt nice all the same. It was only a Civic, but I'd gotten it for a steal years ago. The car was one good windstorm away from demise, but his eyes were kind when he said it, giving me the space, once more, to feel completely at ease in his company.

Our eyes held a minute too long before I unlocked my car and opened my door. "Well, thanks again. See you tomorrow."

"Are you sure you'll be able to resist me?" he called, a teasing smile on his face.

"Try me," I replied brazenly before my eyes popped, and I thought about what I was doing. "No! Wait. Don't try me. No flirting."

"You said it."

Something about the way his smile turned into a full-blown grin made my heart pound deliciously as I drove away.

15

Mom: Thank you, Nora!! I just got notice from the storage unit company. I really appreciate your help. I know it was a sacrifice. Kip gets paid in two weeks, and then we'll be sending you some money. You're the best. Hope your new job is going okay.

I COULDN'T BRING MYSELF TO REPLY.

THE NEXT FEW weeks at the office slowly picked up speed. I began working closely with Tenisha as she gave me a few menial tasks to lighten her load. Not to say I didn't do my fair share of coffee runs, take-out orders, and wading through client emails; but beyond the basic intern tasks, she taught me the latest design programs she used for her graphics, her favorite places to find unique fonts, website design tips, and the ins and outs of her job.

I ate it up.

The late hours in my bedroom from ten until midnight were used to practice my growing skills in the programs. I took careful notes and studied trends on the internet. I could feel my ability improving, and for the first time ever, it felt like I was finally making a significant degree of progress on something that actually had the potential to move me forward in life.

Duke seemed bent on flirting with me constantly while keeping up the pretense of *not* flirting with me, which was very confusing, in all actuality. But ignoring a large Dr. Pepper on my desk with beads of sweat dripping slowly down the side of the cup when I'd been forced to listen to Anita talk about her dad's new cabin in Park City was a slow form of torture. Actually, Shawn mentioned his buddy's cabin in Park City, and then Anita had to talk about her dad's bigger and better cabin. Then, when Shawn mentioned he liked a certain restaurant downtown, Anita had to share another restaurant she knew of that blew Shawn's recommendation out of the water. And so on and so on.

I deserved a drink. Anybody would crack under these conditions. But every time I reached toward the bubbly nectar, curious to see if I'd find another note underneath, I stopped myself. It was exactly what that conniving flirt wanted. And what I was trying to avoid. Whenever he happened to pass by my desk, I'd take a big swig of my water bottle, waving to his laughing frame as I did so.

"Isn't it crazy that Duke is single now?" Anita's voice was a low purr in my ear later that day. With some regret, I turned to face her as she slid my drink over so she could plop onto my desk. Luckily, Duke's note remained hidden. I mean, *if* there even was a note under there.

"I guess," I said, taking in Anita's bold zebra-print top. Compare that with her striking black hair and chilling demeanor, and my Cruella De Vil assessment seemed spot on.

Feeling quite at home, Anita picked up a bottle of hand lotion I had sitting on my desk. She opened it and took a sniff, making a face before setting it back down. My fingernails dug into my hands.

"He's so hot. Do you think he's upset by the breakup? I haven't noticed him acting any different. Three years and now he's just fine?" Her eyes moved past my cubicle and toward Duke's office. "Look, he's laughing at something with Mike and Ryan."

I didn't admit that I had thought the same thing, because under no circumstances ever would I be gossiping about Duke's private life with this woman. And what did I know? Maybe men grieve differently. I had been surrounded by estrogen my entire life.

"Maybe he's sad at home," I offered.

My contribution to our conversation clearly wasn't the vibe Anita was after. She kept her eyes trained on Duke's office door as she leaned in, whispering conspiratorially, "He's probably one of those guys who keeps it all locked inside. Maybe work is just a distraction to him?"

I swallowed. Distraction could come in many forms. It would be smart to remember that, I thought, as my eye followed a bead of water dripping down the Dr. Pepper cup.

Anita leaned back on my desk to stare at me, and if that wasn't disconcerting enough, her hand was now mere centimeters away from my Dr. Pepper. If she spilled it, I'd never know what it said.

"Well, I've got to send some emails out," I said, watching her clueless hand as she checked her nails on the other.

After an awkward pause, she stood up, tapping my drink with her long nail. "You really shouldn't drink so much soda, Nora. I promise you'll notice a difference in your skin if you cut back."

And then she was off, strolling back to her desk, completely oblivious to how close I was to getting fired for attacking a fellow employee.

I grabbed the Dr. Pepper and guzzled. Let me be clear: it wasn't DUKE I was giving in to. It was my need for caffeine therapy.

I refrained from reading the note for thirty whole seconds before grabbing it, knowing full well I wouldn't be able to concentrate on a thing today if I didn't read it. Even though I tried hard not to, I couldn't help but smile at the scrawl of his hand.

I knew you wouldn't be able to resist.

THIS WAS TROUBLE. That's what it was. As much as my body seemed to enjoy his attention, I had to disengage. Shut him down. But first, I needed to nobly inform him that I would be taking the high road and not participating in whatever he thought *this* was.

During my next break, I strode toward the break room and bought a can of Coke. Sneaking it into his office without being seen was a bit trickier, but I got it done. I placed a tiny rolled-up note under the can and set it on his desk.

This is NOT flirting. I am just letting you know a very factual fact. I will not be buying you another Coke.

I DIDN'T SEE him find the can. In fact, I hardly saw him at all for the rest of the day, which led me to believe he might have taken the hint—but when I arrived at my desk the next morning, a fresh Dr. Pepper sat waiting for me, shining like a beacon. I didn't even try to resist checking the note.

*A factual fact? How interesting. Now you won't have to buy me
a Coke.*

HIS MESSAGE PUZZLED me most of the morning, until I opened
my bottom drawer to grab a new pen and found it stacked full of
Coke cans. I couldn't help but glance behind me toward his
office and was startled to see him leaning against the doorframe,
taking a swig of his Coke. He lifted the can to me in a cheers
before slipping back into his office.

That dirty, rotten flirt.

OVER THE PAST FEW DAYS, the pile of work on my desk had
grown taller as Tenisha slowly became more comfortable giving
me assignments. Anita and I had settled into a one-sided relationship where she would sit at my desk and talk *at* me
throughout the day before Shawn would say or do something to
run her off in a huff. I almost started to enjoy our daily chats, as
long as Shawn was nearby.

I had also been denying myself the drink and resisting the
man who had the audacity to sit on my desk and proceed to tell
Anita over the partition how much he loved a cold Coke on a
hot day.

To my surprise, rather than berate him for his unhealthy
habits, Anita smiled coyly and agreed that she'd occasionally
allow herself a Diet Coke as a little treat.

"What about you, Nora? I always see you with a cold drink
on your desk. What's your favorite?" Duke kept his face earnest
as I shot him an exasperated look.

"I'm actually trying to cut back."

"How noble of you."

"*That's* cutting back?!" Anita scoffed from her desk.

Before I could respond, we were interrupted by an arrival in the office.

"Duke!"

Duke's head shot up, and I thought I saw his shoulders droop slightly as he took in his guests. The expression on his face was unreadable but he stood, moving around our desks to greet an older couple striding into the office.

"Hey, Mom. Dad." His jaw twitched the tiniest bit. "What are you guys doing here?"

The layout of the main office was open, with cubicles in the middle, so it wasn't exactly eavesdropping when they were literally stepping into everybody's office.

"Just thought we'd drop in and say hi." His mom wore light-colored jeans over her slender figure and a relaxed white button-down shirt with sunglasses hanging on the top button. Her light-brown hair touched the tops of her shoulders. Bright red, perfectly pedicured toes peeked out of gold sandals. She had a mega-watt smile that seemed instantly charming.

"Looks like you've hired on a few more people," his dad said, looking around, his perceptive eyes taking in every detail. With the exception of a few wrinkles lining his face and his salt-and-pepper hair, he was the spitting image of his son, down to the suit and tie.

"How long have you been back?" Duke asked as he led them toward his office.

Their replies were muffled as the door closed.

Sometime later, I was working on a logo when the door to Duke's office burst open, and he stormed out, yanking open Ryan's office door.

"Meet me in Mike's office," he said. "Now."

A moment later, the three owners were holed up in Mike's office, and Duke's parents wandered out, with his dad looking annoyed as the two of them left the office.

The rest of the day, things seemed tense. The camaraderie between Duke, Ryan, and Mike felt off, though the other two tried to put up a good front. Duke mainly kept to himself, but in the few glances I snuck, he seemed to be in a different world. The teasing glances had stopped.

None of what was happening was any of my business, and I didn't want to flirt with him. That was not why I did what I did. It was the look of defeat on his face that pushed me over the edge. He'd been hurt by something, and that knowledge weighed on me. I hadn't realized how much fun he brought into the office until it was gone—his sunshine hidden away by clouds.

There was a perfect storm later that day, when Duke was in the boardroom with clients and Anita was in the bathroom, so I took the opportunity to sneak a Coke into his office. To cheer up a friend, nothing more. With shaking fingers, I placed it on his desk, tucking the note underneath.

It's no Dr. Pepper, but I'll bet even a can of Coke can help a day go better.

I DIDN'T SEE him again that day, but the next morning, a fresh Dr. Pepper sat glistening on my desk.

The Coke was just okay. But your note worked wonders.

THROUGHOUT THE NEXT couple of weeks, I broke.

I started small, allowing myself to give him ONE Coke a week. That wasn't much of a breach. One day in five. But then slowly (i.e. two days later) that turned into twice a week. Okay, it was three. I almost couldn't keep up. To be honest, I wasn't much of a soda person. It had always been more of a treat for me. An every-once-in-a-while thing. But the amount of sugared liquid filtering on and out of my desk the next few weeks could have set a world record.

Much to my irritation, this quickly became something I looked forward to each day, sometimes ending with three or four notes passed between us in a single day. The amount of soda must have been too much for Duke as well because our drinks began lasting us a couple days or more, just moving to different spots across our desks—our only clue there had been another drop.

Sometimes our notes would be random. Friendly. Things like:

Duke: *Do you think Kiss Cam Jason ever cut his mullet?*

Me: *No. I think he was in a relationship with his mullet.*

Or

Me: *Do you think Sandy remembers all the times she touched you inappropriately?*

Duke: *Honestly, I hope at least one of us got some enjoyment out of that.*

Or

Duke: *When should we do the lift?*

Me: *Last time we attempted the lift, I ended up in the hospital.*

Duke: *Eh. It was only a sprain.*

Me: *Thank you for paying that bill, by the way. You didn't have to. I owe you.*

Duke: *YES. Exactly. You owe me the lift. Nothing else. I MADE you go to the ER.*

AND THEN THERE were notes that definitely didn't feel like they took place anywhere near the friend zone.

Duke: *Okay. No more curling your hair. My productivity level is at a big fat zero today.*

Me: *Fine. No more wearing your blue suit.*

Duke: *That's my favorite.*

Me: *Kiss it goodbye.*

TWO DAYS LATER.

Me: *HEY. No more wearing that suit.*

Duke: *This old thing?*

WE SHOULD HAVE STOPPED. But strangely, my heart wasn't up for stopping. We were friends, and I loved the feeling of having a friend again. Mira had been there my whole life, but since her engagement, our relationship had shifted, a man now occupying the space where I used to be. My sisters were both busy with their lives, and I was finding truth in the idea that the workaholic woman in all the romantic comedies was indeed...lonely. At least I was.

For the most part, these little soda messages were our only way of communicating during the day beyond polite nods and private smirks, which worked out well with Anita seeming to watch my every move. It was all fun and games. Privately.

Which was great.

It was exactly what I wanted, so...good for me.

Thank you, Duke.

Of course...that was during the day. I was learning that Duke seemed to feel differently about the night shift.

ONE NIGHT, almost two months into my training, all three owners stayed late on Friday night, holed up in Ryan's office until after eight. The tension between the three had seemed to fade more each day after the visit from his parents. Now there was a big potential client they were hoping to win, and they'd been working together to draft a proposal. I had steered clear of his office, hearing the voices, and was trying my hardest to be done and gone by the time they all came out. I'd gotten used to Duke being around on occasion in the evenings, but I really didn't want Ryan and Mike to see my evening transformation to janitor.

It was my day for vacuuming. There had apparently been a disaster in the reception area involving a three-hole punch, and the whole space looked like the crime scene of a murdered piñata. I couldn't recall vacuuming up confetti paper in recent history, and I must say, it was the absolute worst. When I finally switched off the vacuum and rolled up the cord, I turned to see my cleaning cart missing a few things—or a lot of things.

I strode past the lobby area and stopped short when I saw Ryan washing windows I'd already cleaned and Mike gathering the trash I hadn't gotten to yet. Duke was nowhere to be found, but I had a sinking suspicion I knew exactly where he was. I wanted to curl up in a ball on the couch in the lobby and pretend this wasn't happening. I didn't want their help. I wanted them to go home at a reasonable hour so I could clean in peace. Mike and Ryan had wives and kids at home. They shouldn't be here. Watching people do MY job was too much. And now, it wasn't just Duke, it was his friends too. My BOSSES.

Marching over to an unsuspecting Ryan, I schooled myself to keep things light so the mortification I felt didn't come out in ungrateful whining.

"Hey!" I grabbed the squeegee from his grip. "You guys don't need to do that! Go home. Right now!"

Ryan held up his hands. "Whoa. Duke said you'd be testy. He wasn't kidding."

"Listen, guys." I waited until Mike turned from gathering trash and grinned at me. "I don't need any help. I promise. It's so nice of you guys, but seriously, go home. Your families are probably wondering where you are."

"Our Zoom meeting was expected to run late," Ryan said, checking his watch. "My kids are already in bed, and my wife is probably watching a *Bachelor* re-run right now."

"What'd you think of last week's episode?" Mike asked,

carrying an extra-large black garbage sack over his right shoulder like a below-average version of Santa Claus.

Ryan busted out a laugh. "On the beach?"

"Yeah."

While they were talking, I walked over to Mike and attempted to nonchalantly grab his garbage sack.

He smiled kindly, holding it out of my reach. "Actually, I'm on my way out, I'll just drop it in the dumpster by the cars. Is that okay?"

My heart sank. I looked at both men, my hands in a prayer pose. "Alright, thank you. Really. This was very kind of you both. But this is a one-time thing. Next time, if you're still here when I'm cleaning, just smile and wave. That's all I want, I promise."

Ryan dropped the window cleaner back into my cart. "We know. But we had some extra time. And Duke in NO WAY whatsoever put us up to this."

"No way whatsoever," Mike agreed, nodding definitively.

A smile crossed my face at that, my heart soothed the tiniest fraction at their sweet nature. "Glad to hear it."

"We'll go back to our normal sloppy selves tomorrow."

"I appreciate that."

"Alright," Mike said, readjusting the garbage sack as he and Ryan returned their equipment to my cart and gave me a quick high-five. "Windows are done, garbage cans are done. No idea what Duke is doing, but he took off that way." He motioned toward the hallway before they moved toward the exit. I waited until the door closed before making my move.

"Duke!" I yelled, storming down the hallway, my cleaning cart struggling to keep up. "We need to talk."

I found him just stepping out of the men's bathroom, holding the toilet brush and cleaner.

"A talk? That sounds fun."

"It's not a fun talk. It's a boundary talk." I immediately

began taking everything out of his hands and placing them back onto my cart.

He reached for the mop handle, but I slapped his hand away.

"I thought we had rules, but apparently, after hours, this place is mad chaos," I said.

"Mad chaos?" he repeated, smiling at me.

"I didn't want to have to do this, but you've left me no choice." I motioned around the office. "After six pm, this place is mine. Your shift is over. It's my office now."

He cocked his head to one side. "Are you doing this so you can flirt with me? Now that we're technically out of the office?" He looked like he was about to keep going, but I leveled him with my stare.

"Rule number one," I interrupted, jabbing my finger into his chest. "You have to stop helping me. It's embarrassing. I hate that Ryan and Mike—my BOSSES—were doing my work tonight."

He held up his hands. "In my defense, they weren't supposed to be here. They joined my meeting at the last minute."

"And they just happened to both want to clean some windows when they were done?"

"Looks like it."

"I don't need the help." His face settled into an expression that I took to mean he was listening. "It's nice of you, but please just let me do my job. You've got other places you need to be. You don't need to be here."

He nodded, this time his voice soft. "What if I want to be here?" I started shaking my head, panic filling my insides, but he went on with his eyes dark, and sweet, and slowly dripping an IV full of honey into my veins. "I go home to an empty fridge and a TV. There's never anything good on. But the nights here are wild."

I laughed, in spite of myself. "No, they're not."

"They are. During the day, there are so many rules. I have to wear a tie and be polite all the time. It's exhausting."

"There are still rules here at night."

"You just told me my shift was over. There's a new girl running this place now." His hands were in his pockets, easily countering my remarks, looking sexy and confident and dangerous all at once.

"This new girl loves rules. Now shut up and let me finish. Rule number two is—"

"Did somebody here order a DoorDash?"

We looked toward the doorway, where a tall, thin high schooler with chains on his pants and a beanie on his head held two large black plastic bags bursting at the seams.

I was about to tell him no, when Duke said, "Right here."

If Duke noticed my suspicious glare pointed his way as he sauntered over to accept the bags of what smelled like some really delicious, sweet and garlicky Chinese food, he didn't acknowledge it. When the delivery boy had gone, Duke finally met my gaze, a hint of a smirk teasing the corners of his mouth.

"Well, shoot. Looks like they gave me way too much food for just one person."

16

It was an art form, really, how Duke could talk me into doing things outside of my tidy existence. Out of my comfort zone. My only defense was that sometimes a girl gets tired of trying to resist Duke's charms.

Also, the smell of Chinese food was irresistible. Nobody in their right mind would say no. That was a fact.

The office building had a rooftop I had no idea about. I'd never gone higher than the fifteenth floor. As I followed Duke into the elevator, allowing him to lead me farther and farther away from my cleaning cart, the more my fingers clawed at my palms.

"Actually, I don't have time for this," I said while we both watched the numbers tick higher toward twenty-four, the top floor of the building.

He turned his gaze on me. "You don't have time for dinner?"

"I always have time for dinner," I protested.

"Great." He went back to watching the number creep higher and higher.

"But my dinner can be a bowl of cereal scarfed down in two seconds standing over the kitchen sink." I threw him a pleading

149

glance when the elevator dinged and the door opened. "I don't have time for this. I'm going back down."

Duke blocked the door with his foot and turned to face me. "Nora." He waited until my panicked eyes met his. "We can take as much time as you want up here. If it's two minutes"—he shrugged—"it's two minutes. If it's two hours, that's fine with me too. It would just be a shame to miss this view."

Even as my heart rate slowed at his words, I couldn't help but be wary. Those eyes were a bit too deliberately casual. "That's your only reason for bringing us up here? Because this girl still has a lot to do downstairs."

"I know." He nodded, and I watched with growing alarm as a lazy grin appeared on his face. "But every once in a while, this girl blows off the rules, and I love having a front-row seat when it happens."

I sighed, feeling myself cave at his warm brown eyes. "Five minutes."

He removed his leg blocking the exit and motioned for me to go in front of him. "After you."

There was a stairwell to the left of the elevator that led us to the rooftop. Duke opened the door, and the warm summer air hitting my face had me taking in a deep breath. In an instant, I could almost feel the day melting away. Purple and orange clouds streaked across the Salt Lake skyline. A breeze blew at the wisps of hair along my cheeks as Duke led me toward two metal folding chairs facing the west that looked like they'd seen a few years—and windstorms.

He plopped down in one of the chairs. "Welcome to my thinking spot."

I pulled the other chair a few inches away from his before sitting down next to him. "So, those times when Mike and Ryan are looking everywhere for you, this is where you're hiding out?"

He opened the bag and handed me a white square takeout

box. "You are now the only one who knows my secret, so if it gets out, I'm coming for you."

"What is this?" I asked, holding up the box.

He shrugged. "I told the guy to give me his two-person special. I have no idea what's in here."

My eyes widened. "You'd do that at a Chinese restaurant? Their menu is bigger than the Bible." Before I could open my box, something else hit me. "Wait. Two person?"

Duke had been about to take a drink from his can of Coke but stopped just before his lips touched, a hint of a smile playing across his mouth. "Did I say two person?"

"Duke Webber. You are my boss. And might I add, very newly single."

"Technically, you just said you were my boss now. You can do whatever you want with me."

I pushed his arm while he laughed, grabbing another box from the bag at our feet. He motioned toward my food. "What'd you get?"

Giving him a side-eye, I opened the flaps and inspected the contents. "Looks like beef and broccoli."

"Ugh. That's yours."

"You don't like it?"

"I'll eat the beef, but my mom is the only person who can get me to eat broccoli. And she's not here."

He handed me a fork before he opened his box. "Fried rice." Leaning down, he rummaged through the rest of the plastic sack. "Jackpot. Sweet-and-sour chicken."

Before I knew what he was doing, he leaned down and grabbed the leg of my chair, dragging me back until I sat next to him, shoulder to shoulder. "So we can share," he said almost shyly when I looked at him in question.

For the next few minutes, we looked out over our kingdom of lights, snatching bites from each other's containers and feasting on the most delicious and filling meal I'd had in weeks. Through all my financial troubles of late, I'd been surviving on peanut butter and jelly. If I felt super fancy, sometimes I'd boil some noodles and throw on a jar of spaghetti sauce. Though, most nights, it was a bowl of cereal before dropping off to bed.

This had all the makings of a rom-com moment, but I kept reminding myself that this was not a date. Not a date. Even though the press of his shoulder against mine began to consume my thoughts. A person moves their arms a surprising amount when they're watching the sunset and eating dinner. Too much, really. Every time he settled back in his chair, the heat from his arm brushing against mine would send a jolt of awareness throughout my entire body. I casually inched away and attempted to redirect my thoughts.

"Why do you hide out here?"

He shrugged. "It's a good place to clear my head. I work with my best friends every day. It's good for me to step out now and then."

I leaned closer to jab a piece of his chicken and pop it into my mouth, the crunchy, gooey sweetness doing a delicious number on my taste buds.

"It seems like you all get along well."

He nodded. "We do, for the most part."

I played with the oversized chunks of broccoli in front of me. "For the most part," I mimicked. "That's an interesting phrase."

A crooked smile parted his lips. "It's true."

The honk of a car horn from somewhere down below sounded, bringing me back to myself, and I was about to make my exit when he spoke.

"We get along well with all the day-to-day stuff. We have things divided out really well. The bigger we get, I'm sure we'll have to re-adjust. But we all have different ideas for the business. Where to take it. How big we want it to grow. If we should sell it eventually. Things like that."

"Sell it?" I asked. "Who wants to do that?"

He paused. "Ryan's got a few other business ideas he wants to spend time on. He's been working with a snowboard company to manufacture a new style of board. He's thinking of selling his portion of the business to pursue that."

"What does Mike think?"

"He's in it for the long haul, but he wants me by his side."

"What do you think?"

He laughed. "That's why I've been up here a lot lately."

"Do you enjoy the work?"

"Yeah. More than I ever thought I would. I'm proud of everything we've done so far. We started in my garage. I always thought I'd like starting up a new company every few years and then selling it like my dad, but I don't know. I've really loved running the business. The day to day stuff. Getting new clients. Getting to know all the employees. I guess I'm not sure where to go from here when I always figured I'd sell and move on. I wasn't expecting to love the business so much."

"Did your parents have any advice?"

"They'd be all over this company if I'd let them," he said almost bitterly. "But"—he nudged my shoulder—"thanks to a date I went on a while back with a brazen woman who kissed me within an hour of meeting her, I decided not to involve them in this business."

Warmth spread across my body at his words, even as I palmed my forehead into my hand. "I've regretted that moment for the past three years. Telling you that when I had no idea what I was talking about."

He raised his eyebrows in mild surprise. "Yeah, you did."

I scoffed. "I knew nothing about business when I gave you that advice. I'm sorry."

"Well, your advice is probably the reason I'm actually enjoying what I'm doing." When I could only look at him in shock, he continued. "I hadn't realized how much I'd been depending on my parents to back me up. I'd had at least three other companies or money-making ideas I let them help me with, and they all fell through. That kind of borrowing gets complicated, mixing business and family like that. But I always thought it would be stupid to go through a bank when my parents were more than happy to lend support. My dad was always itching to give me his two cents. But you were right. The businesses always felt like theirs, not mine. Like I needed their approval or had to run things by them all the time. After talking to you that night, I told Ryan and Mike I wanted to try it all on our own. It took longer, but the end result was so much better than it would have been." He nudged me. "So thank you."

I took a bite while a warm glow filtered through me at his words.

"Can I ask you something?" he asked.

"No."

"I'll eat a piece of broccoli," he baited.

I should have been heading back to work. It was close to ten. I'd pay for this extra time in the morning, but for some reason, I couldn't find it in me to end the night. A small part of my soul seemed to be able to breathe for the first time in months. Maybe years. So I'd bargain away more time at the cost of a question.

"Just one piece?" I asked.

His nose wrinkled. "I think that's more than fair."

"Two pieces. Final offer."

Before I could blink, he reached across me and stabbed a piece of broccoli on his fork and began chewing. With some alarm, I held the container away from him, trying to block his access to the second piece, but he cheated, holding my arm and pulling me closer toward him before acquiring his second piece. At the sudden close proximity, I gave up the broccoli. Within seconds, his mouth was empty.

"I'm starting to think you actually like broccoli and I just got played."

"I hate broccoli. That's how bad I wanted to get an answer to this question."

I sank lower in my seat. "What is it?"

"Why were you crying in the men's bathroom a few weeks ago?"

I should have left while I had the chance. My eyes moved over to the skyline. The sun had set, making the city come alive in glowing lights, street noise, and moving cars that looked like ants down below. The yellow lights on top of the building left a cozy campfire-like glow to the rooftop. The five-minute dinner break I'd promised myself was on track to turn into hours.

"Nora," Duke whispered. I turned to face him and was startled by the way his eyes trailed gently across my face. "It's just me."

It's just me. Those simple words blasted a sweet awareness throughout my body that I wasn't sure what to do with. His words spoke of friendship. Of kindness. Of…trust. Which terrified me more than any other sensation. But to not speak at all would end our night on a weird note. Not only that but it would end our night. Period.

"I'd had a string of bad luck," I said. "That was me dealing with it."

"Meaning?" he prodded, lounging in his chair, his long legs stretched out in front of him.

"It probably won't make sense without some backstory, and I'm not sure we have time for that."

"We have time."

I wondered what to tell him. How much to tell him. There was so much to unpack at the root, and even though I would much rather cut it off at the head than meander through the years, something about the easy way he leaned back in his seat, his hands resting on his stomach and his full attention on me, spoke peace to my cautious heart. He wasn't my boss in this moment. He was my friend, Duke. I cleared my throat.

"My time with my grandma didn't go like I thought it would. She had offered to pay for me to go to school and give me a free place to live in exchange for helping her out in her home. I knew she'd get progressively worse, but we must have made all the arrangements on a day when she'd been very lucid. By the time I got there, months later, she'd fallen for an email scam, which had taken most of her savings, and her cupboards were almost completely bare. She'd been surviving on bread and water. Her social security check came every week, but most of that went to paying down gambling debts I also had no idea she had. When she died, her estate couldn't even pay them all off."

I glanced at Duke and was surprised to see his gaze intent on my face. I forced myself to keep going.

"Anyway, I had been so set on going to school, so I enrolled at a community college in Fargo and took out a student loan, which was something I've always tried to avoid, but by this time, I was so desperate for something to work out. I didn't want three years to go by and not be going to school. Anyway, the loan paid for the first year of college, but halfway through, my grandma had gotten a lot worse, so I could only make it to class half the time. I ended up flunking out. If you remember how I retook a test because I'd gotten a B, you can probably imagine how that affected me. But she needed full-time help, and there was no one else, so I had to." I took a shaky breath. Part of me died inside telling him this, but I kept going. "I paid back some of the loan with my savings, but I also had to use some to pay for groceries. And to keep her car running. So by the time my grandma had passed and I made it back to Utah, I was in crazy debt with literally nothing to show for it."

Duke sat frozen, staring at me with such an intense expression of disbelief on his face that I immediately regretted my words.

"Does your grandma have any other kids to help out? Why was this falling on you and not your mom? Or another sibling?"

I gave him a wan smile. "This is my dad's mom." Might as well paint him the whole picture. "My sisters and I all have different dads. I never knew mine, and he took off when I was really young. Nobody was able to track him down when she passed away. My grandma reached out to me when I was young, and we grew somewhat close throughout my teenage years. But by the time she passed away, I was the only living relative she had."

The more I spoke, the more I wanted this all to end.

"So, anyway. It's okay. Lots of people have student loans. But that day, I had also gotten notice that my rent was raising in a couple months. Combined with the fact that, an hour later, my tire blew and what little I had in savings was now almost all gone. It was a big morning."

Other than his hand moving up to cover his mouth while I spoke, Duke still hadn't moved.

I had to kill the awkward silence. This was why I kept things locked inside. "I'm sorry. I shouldn't have said all that. It's fine, I promise. I'll figure it out. I'm glad I was there with her in the end, no matter all of that...she was so lonely and—"

"Nora—" he broke off, seeming lost for words. I desperately wanted more words to change this awful subject.

"Duke. It will be fine. I shouldn't have said anything. Money talk always makes things weird, but you asked." I stood to go, laughing nervously. "See, *this* is why I should have only stayed for five minutes."

Before I could move, his hand reached out, locking onto my forearm. I made the mistake of meeting his eyes as he eventually pulled me back down beside him.

"What bothers you the most?" I looked at him, confused, before he continued. "About all of that. Your student loan? Your rent?"

That answer came easily. "It's the fact that I can't ever seem to get ahead. The student loan eats at me, but it's so much more than that. I've dedicated my entire life to working and saving, but something always happens, and I end up worse off than I was before. I have no social life. I rarely date. I work two jobs. Every time I get some money saved, without fail, something will happen that takes it all. This time, it was tires. Last time, it was my mom's storage unit bill. She's in Florida, with a new husband, and I'm stuck being the adult, paying for things I shouldn't be but feeling guilty when I try to put my foot down. I keep trying to let her fall, like we talked about, but I can't ever seem to do it." I risked a glance at Duke, already regretting my loose tongue. "*That's* why I was crying. Because I started the weekend proud of having a measly eight hundred dollars saved up, and by the end of Monday morning, I had no money, but I had four new tires and my mom still had her storage unit."

I stopped almost as abruptly as I began. Instant regret filled my body, the weight of my words leaving a strange energy between us.

Duke leaned forward, his elbows on his knees and his hands clasped together. "That sucks, Nora. Can I—"

"No. I don't need help." I stopped him before he could ask the question. "That's not why all of that came flying out of my mouth." I slunk back in my chair. "You're the worst, by the way. Asking me a question like that."

He actually looked like he had more questions to ask, but I cut him short, desperate to change the subject. I had planned to leave, go back downstairs and finish cleaning, but another thought came to me instead. One I liked much better. "You owe me a question now."

He took a moment to respond, probably jarred at the change. "What?"

I reached for the broccoli container. "I'll eat my two pieces of broccoli, and then you owe me a question."

He held the container away from me, his eyes narrowing. "That's not fair. You like broccoli."

"Not my problem."

He set the container down on his side and, instead, reached for his open can of Coke and handed it to me. "Two big swigs or no deal."

Grumbling, I took the can, which was now half full, and held it in front of me. "You're forcing me to climb Mount Everest."

"Stall all you want. I could stay up here all night."

I plugged my nose and took a drink. And then another. My face contoured to weird expressions as the carbonation sliding down my throat delivered a disgusting taste in my mouth that took forever to subside. "Oh, that's so bad."

"I'm sad for your taste buds. What's your question?"

Now that my moment was upon me, I chickened out. My first thought went to Rachel, but I couldn't find it in me to ask him about her so directly. I might as well carry a flashing neon sign that said *I'm jealous*. So I took the roundabout way, hoping we'd arrive at the same place.

"Unless it's business stuff you can't tell me, what happened when your parents were here? What made you so upset?"

He sighed, bringing his ankle to rest on his knee. He rubbed the sole of his shoe absently, and to my relief, the air between us shifted in balance as I watched him struggle with what exactly to say.

"Since we started this company without my parents' help or money, they've been a little…antsy. They've always had a hand in everything I've done, and it bothered them when I cut them off. They dropped by on the pretense of seeing me, but really, it was so my dad could check out how big the company was getting, which isn't growing as fast as he thinks it should be. I was annoyed because, apparently, they'd met with Ryan and Mike behind my back a few weeks earlier and tried to get them to talk me into accepting money from them to grow the business faster."

That would explain Duke storming out of his office and meeting with Mike and Ryan in private.

"They turned my parents down, but they never told me about the offer. And it ticked me off."

He leaned back in his seat again, his shoulder coming to rest against mine, where I kept it, though it became a struggle trying to focus on what he was saying.

"Do you think they wanted to take the money?"

He shrugged. "I don't know. It's my parents, so they aren't in a position to accept without my approval. And they wouldn't. I just...this is the first thing I've been a part of without them holding my hand. I didn't realize how much I needed something of my own until I didn't have their voices in my head anymore. They've been trying to control me for my whole life, you know? They're always nice about it, but it's still a manipulative move. It's almost like they're so concerned with making sure I'm successful that they don't trust me to do it on my own."

"A lawnmower parent? Isn't that what it's called?"

His brow furrowed. "A what?"

"A lawnmower parent. Where they potentially mow down any obstacle in their child's life so they'll succeed. They try to block every problem their kids might face."

He seemed moderately stunned by this information, but I could feel the wheels turning in his head. "You might be right. How'd you know that?"

"I've heard of parents like that. I've always wanted one," I teased.

His soft, rich chuckle settled between us. Bringing up Rachel was halfway on my tongue, but the longer we sat lost in our thoughts, staring out into the night, the more it felt like the moment had passed.

"My five minutes are up, Boss." I stood, collecting the empty containers at my feet to throw away. The night had grown chilly in the absence of the sun. I rubbed my hands against my arms.

He hesitated only a minute before picking up the rest of our garbage and walking with me toward the trash can next to the door.

Once inside the elevator, all of the things I had told him began filtering loudly through my mind. On repeat. I'd given him something I couldn't take back. Those words would always be between us and it felt vulnerable in a way that had me sucking in a breath.

Duke punched the button before he turned to face me, leaning against the wall of the elevator with his hands in his pockets. I swallowed, feeling the pull of him even while I resisted.

"You felt like a friend. You know that, right? That's why I told you all of that."

His eyes shot up to mine curiously. "I am your friend."

He stood so close. The sweet scent of his cologne tickled my nose. His gaze wandered across my face, down to my lips before roaming back up to my eyes. My breath caught. How easy it would be to take a step closer. But I didn't. I did what I always did.

Built walls.

"You *are* my friend," my words came out in a breathy whisper. "But you're also my boss. It's confusing who I'm talking to at any given moment. Tonight, you felt like a friend, but now I'm worried I said too much."

"Nora. You're safe with me. You know that right?" When I could only look at him in response, he added, " You don't have to do everything on your own. You can let people help you, you know."

"No. That's my whole point. I don't want your help, and if you think I do, I'm going to cry again."

Duke grew quiet after that, though he insisted on helping me finish my cleaning for the night. It was ten-thirty, and I didn't have the energy to argue. We said little as we finished up, and then he walked me to my car. He waited until I was in my car driving away before striding toward his truck.

Maybe there was something internally wrong with me. Anita's face came to my mind. Not many girls would deny themselves a chance at a man like Duke—if that was even what he was offering.

There are moments in our lives that can shape us. Define us. Make us who we are. My entire childhood had been a series of naively extending trust only to have it broken. Time and time again. My mom had been married and divorced three times before I was fifteen with countless boyfriends in between. I thought of how dangerous those years had been—so many strangers, men from all backgrounds, wandering in and out of our lives. Thankfully, my sisters and I had come out of it physically unscathed, but each time, we had been left a little more emotionally scarred. Tentatively growing attached to the *idea* of someone, a new husband or a new boyfriend, only to be let down again and again. Until one day we stopped growing attached. Stopped caring. No longer trusting my mom to put our best interests above the shiny lure of a new relationship.

Being the oldest, the self-appointed burden of responsibility fell onto my shoulders, and I vowed to give my sisters the childhood lost to me. While my mom showed up to as many basketball games and dances as she could to support her daughters, it was me who paid for their uniforms. It was me who paid for their spot on the club teams and dance competitions. I sent them to school with lunch money. At thirteen, I had begun paying a few hundred dollars a month toward rent, but as I grew older and my work hours grew longer, that amount more than doubled by the time I graduated. By some silent agreement, my mom and I fell into a pattern more suited for a married couple than mother and daughter. Though now I wondered what might have happened if I had put up a fuss, made some noise.

Either way, it was through those experiences that I began to craft a meticulous plan for my life. I wouldn't be afraid of love, but I'd only take part when I was sure I'd never leave myself or my future children vulnerable in that way. They deserved a life where they could be kids and never worry about providing for the family. For so long my meticulous plan for my life had included depending on only one person.

Me.

Unburdening myself on Duke left me tense with immediate regret, like I'd severed myself wide open. In my experience, knowledge was power, and having power could hurt people. Intimate knowledge of someone meant a sharper sword to yield in the divorce proceedings. It meant a harsher tongue to wound and inflict acute pain in an argument.

But tonight had also left me with another feeling. Hope. Something I'd felt often as a child, but the feeling had slowly disappeared as I gained more experience in my world. Maybe it was the soft way he looked at me, the understanding in his eyes, and the sweetness of his words that left me lighter. A bit more free. As I readied myself for bed in the quiet of my apartment, I found that the word hope had a melody, and ever so softly, it sung me into the sweetest sleep.

17

THAT NEXT MONDAY, I DIDN'T SEE DUKE ALL MORNING.

Our dinner on the rooftop had been full of secrets and melodramatic angst. After a weekend of overthinking and overanalyzing until I finally pretended indifference for my sanity, I was ready for friendly, flirty Duke again. For some reason, that side of him seemed safer. Untouchable, even. The side of him that knew my secrets and weaseled information out of me while stuffing me full of sweet-and-sour chicken and MSG was by far the most dangerous Duke of all.

Today was the day the interns would be meeting with our managers and the owners regarding the marketing project they had ready for us. The competition would soon be starting. We'd all heard bits and pieces of the project throughout our two months of initiation, but today we'd finally be getting our assignments. If what Tenisha said was true, I'd be working closer with Duke during this last month.

"Hey." Anita slid into my space, parking her pert rump on her beloved spot at the edge of my desk. Her bold red dress clearly meant business, and so did she. Her posture was faux friendly, with a hint of toxic undercurrent. "Are you excited to be working with Duke on your project?"

I guess we're getting right after it today.

"Sure." I gave her a smile as real as her own before typing nonsense into my computer. "I hadn't really thought about it much."

"Oh, really?" Her head cocked to the side, her eyes big and inquiring. "You guys seem pretty chummy."

I rubbed at my temples. Unless she'd been spying on us in the evenings while I was vacuuming up her fingernail clippings, Duke and I hardly interacted at all at the office, beyond our soda can notes. Even then, I'd been ultra-careful, only sneaking those in at lunch time or whenever those I was most concerned about—i.e. Anita—were in meetings or on a phone call. Which meant she was baiting me with catlike purrs and claws that stung and retracted.

"I don't really know him very well," I stated blankly. Very well was one of those relative terms. It all depended on context.

"Then if you don't care, would you mind if I asked to work with him on the project instead?"

A bolt of jealousy shot through my stomach, surprising even me with its intensity. I had worked hard to be intentionally obtuse about working with Duke, simply to keep Anita believing I was nonchalant about the whole thing. Not because I actually *was* nonchalant.

"*Can* we switch? I thought they already had them assigned," I managed, clicking into my email to give my fingers something to do.

"They are," Shawn's dry voice filtered loudly between our cubicles. I hid a smile.

Anita rolled her eyes and looked toward me for commiseration, but I pretended to pull a hair off my shirt.

"Duke brought in a big skincare company client for RDM last year. I'm really hoping to be able to do a marketing package for a friend of mine who's starting a new all-natural make-up line. I just think he'd be the best one to help me."

Liar.

Before I could say anything, Shawn said, "You won't even know if a makeup company is an option. The owners said they'd have three picks for each of us to choose between."

Anita sighed impatiently, her voice so slow and full of barely bridled hatred that I almost shivered. "I'm aware of that, Shawn. Thank you so much for your help. But I'm going to ask if I can pull in my own client instead of being assigned."

"I'm guessing they have their specific picks for a reason," Shawn said again cheerfully.

I leaned back in my chair, suddenly craving popcorn.

Anita made a strangled cry, looked again to me for understanding, and found none. "Never mind. You two are impossible." She slipped off my desk and stalked away in the direction of the women's restroom.

Using my hands, I lifted myself up out of my chair enough to see Shawn's eyes over the partition. He winked at me. I laughed and settled myself back down at my desk, working through some client emails Tenisha had asked me to respond to.

SHAWN, Anita, Tenisha and the two other designers, April and Susan, were already seated at the conference table by the time I arrived at the meeting that afternoon. I took my seat next to Tenisha.

My chair was pointed directly toward the front door, but the energy of the room completely changed when Duke came striding in. He was wearing gray dress pants and a fitted, white button-down shirt, rolled at the sleeves. A light-blue tie rounded out the attractive ensemble. I looked away before I started drooling.

His eyes were on me for a long moment before he scanned the room, smiling at us all.

"Morning. Looks like I beat Ryan and Mike here. I'd like everyone to take note."

Tenisha and the two other designers in the room laughed at that, while the rest of us looked on, slightly confused.

"Ryan and Mike like to think they beat me here every meeting, but obviously, we know they don't." He turned to the white board and made a tiny mark in the upper right-hand corner. Squinting, I could see a chart with the names of all the owners and tally marks below. Duke made a notch under his name proudly.

He was sitting down in a seat next to mine when Mike and Ryan came barreling into the room, red-faced and panting.

Mike pointed at Duke. "You!"

Duke's face was a mask of innocence.

"Yes?"

"You locked us in the men's bathroom."

He sat back down, rubbing at an invisible spot on his shirt, as though bored. "Why in the world would I do that?"

Ryan looked at all of us, asking, "Did he mark it?" before whirling toward the tally marks.

"How many did he have yesterday?"

"It could NOT have been that many," Mike said.

"Should we start the meeting?" Duke asked innocently, smiling at all of us at the end of the table. No one seemed to have any trouble smiling back at him.

"Remind me not to go into business with my friends next time," Ryan quipped. He and Mike slammed into Duke's shoulder good-naturedly as they slunk into their seats, bragging about finding a way out of the locked bathroom door.

Once the meeting started the trio was all business. First, Duke dumped a handful of swag onto the table. Everything from backpacks and t-shirts to mirror compacts, chapstick, pens, and water bottles, all made with the RDM logo.

"You guys are welcome to grab anything you want," Duke said. "We bought some of this stuff to hand out at conferences, but we're going to make a couple changes to our logo before the next event, so these will be out of date soon."

The big items were snatched up quickly, but I snagged a t-shirt probably two sizes too big and some chapstick.

Duke began the meeting with a speech about how thankful they were to have us all here. While he spoke, I opened my new chapstick and slowly applied it to my lips, low-key impressed at the quality. It glided on smooth. I pressed my lips together before applying another coat.

"Anyway...we've really appreciated the, uh...the... Um. We've really appreciated the..."

I looked up at Duke as he stalled in his speech and was startled to see his eyes trained on me. As was the rest of the group, looking from Duke to me in confusion. He blinked and looked away, though he still couldn't seem to get his focus together.

"Sorry." He ran a hand through his hair. "I lost my train of... We really appreciate the...uh..."

"Help," Mike supplied, flitting his gaze toward me while hiding a sardonic smile behind his hand.

"Help. There we go. You interns have been invaluable to us. So thank you."

I looked at Duke. Then to Mike and Ryan, both trying not to laugh and glancing at me from the corner of their eyes. To Anita, furiously applying chapstick on her lips. Was that...was that about me? Was Duke flustered because of—

Duke quickly ended his speech and passed the rest of the time over to Ryan before returning to his seat next to me. He settled in, leaning back in his chair. Though my cheeks were warm and my hands suddenly felt like two left feet, I had to address this. It wasn't often that I had the upper hand with Duke and I wasn't going to waste this opportunity. I waited until I made sure the focus of the group was solely on Ryan before I dared a glance his way. Out of reflex, he met my gaze, taking in my expectant raised eyebrows before he shook his head slightly and looked away, fighting an embarrassed smile.

While Ryan continued on, it was my turn to fight focus. Duke seemed to be coming back to himself. For that matter, was Duke somehow closer than before? Our chairs suddenly seemed mere inches apart when, before, it had been at least a foot. Unless I imagined it all. He had to have noticed that I was staring at him since I wasn't the slightest bit discreet, but other than the tiniest twitch of his mouth, he kept his gaze intently focused on Ryan.

Heat from his shoulder at my left arm had me biting my lip even as my heart rate spiked. I wasn't completely crazy. The chairs were definitely getting closer together.

While Ryan continued on, I fought to focus. The enticing odor of Duke's cologne caused my mind to swirl. I really needed to pay attention. This was a meeting for the interns. It was MY meeting. Just because Duke was sitting next to me, didn't mean I had to freak out. It was fine. We were friends. He was my boss.

My arm fell off the armrest.

No. It was pushed.

As much as I tried to school it, my lips took on a life of their own. I bowed my head, trying to hide my reaction as Duke brought out an entire Pandora's box worth of emotions with this one action–emotions I had tried very hard to keep at bay. The warm memory of the night of the kiss cam had taken weeks to fully dim. Maybe years. And apparently, it hadn't ever gone away. When I made certain nobody was looking our way, I reclaimed my dominance over the armrest.

Duke relented and leaned forward, his elbows resting on the table as I watched him hide his own smile with his hand. My heart burned with a rush of excitement. We needed to stop. *He* needed to stop.

I lifted my chin and committed to concentrating on what was being said in the meeting, which I discovered, when the entire room grew silent, staring at me, was a question Ryan must have asked…me.

I sat up taller in my seat. "I'm sorry. What was that?"

Anita huffed out a laugh. "I can go first if you'd like. I think our little Nora is tired today."

Our little Nora. If there were ever words that made me want to punch another person in the face, those might be three of them.

Ryan shrugged and motioned to Mike, who looked less than thrilled at who he'd be working with. He passed a sheet of paper to her. "There are three companies I've looked into that could use some help with a marketing package. Pick the one that sounds most interesting to you, and we'll go from there."

Anita glanced over the paper, her nose wrinkling slightly.

"Here are your businesses to pick from, Shawn." Ryan leaned forward and handed Shawn his own paper to look at.

Duke opened his folder on the desk and pulled out a sheet of paper, sliding it toward me.

A throat cleared. "Actually, um…Duke. Nora and I were wondering if we could trade owners for our projects."

All eyes at the table zoomed in on Anita. I froze.

"What do you mean?" Duke asked, his low voice a mumble.

She laughed, a high-pitched twinkly sound that made my skin crawl. "I was hoping I could pick my own assignment. I have a friend starting up a makeup company, and I wondered if you'd be able to help me, since you're the expert." When she was getting no reaction, she kept going, though with more blinking and twitchy movements with her hands. "Since you worked so well with that skincare company last year. I figured you might be the best person to help me."

An awkward silence fell across the room, shifting eyes taking in both me and Anita as though we'd been in some sort of cahoots.

Some people just weren't meant to be friends.

Ryan shook his head. "The businesses on everyone's papers have all been vetted specifically for this program. We intend to work closely with the owners to take into account how they've been treated and make sure there's been steady and professional communication throughout the process. We're not taking on the company of friends. You're more than welcome to do that on your own, but not for this internship program."

Anita's face fell, and she shot a glance at Duke.

Duke turned toward me, his brown eyes holding mine steady. "Would you prefer working with Mike?"

I shifted. A pin drop at the table would have sounded like an explosion. The attention of the entire room was on me. He was giving me a choice. I couldn't detect any hurt or anger in his tone, so either he was good at hiding it, or he honestly didn't care if he worked with me or not. Maybe I'd blown everything up in my head. But as I stared longer, I added one more option, the one that felt the most true to Duke. He genuinely wanted me to feel comfortable, and he'd sacrifice his own wants to make that happen.

Too bad I was a glutton for punishment, because I was quickly discovering that I wanted all the sweet discomfort that came from being too close to Duke Webber.

"No. It was her idea. I'm fine to work with Duke."

"Rude," Mike shouted good naturedly. "I'm a delight to work with." The whole room chuckled and when I mouthed a 'Sorry' to him, Mike gave me a wink.

I didn't look at Anita, but I could feel volts of her anger threatening to burn me to the ground. Duke's gaze was also burning me but for a different reason.

"Oh, you're fine to work with Duke? I'm so relieved." His soft voice in my ear was brimming with amusement.

I shook my head slightly, clamping my mouth shut. With trembling fingers, I slid his paper in front of me to concentrate on the letters that I assumed made up words of some kind.

"Are you nervous?" Again, his whispers were not helping my very noble cause of settling my heart the heck down. I ignored him, studying the paper for ten whole seconds before my twitter-pated brain computed what it said.

"Why is your foot shaking?"

Ignore him, brain.

"You still owe me the lift."

I turned to him and gave him my best stare, communicating my intense need for him to shut up. He grinned and sat back in his chair, his hands folded on the table, finally giving me space to concentrate.

After a long moment, my mind began to compute. On the paper were three business names and a tiny blurb about each one. I scanned through the first two. One was a makeup company, which the petty part of me secretly wanted to pick just to watch Anita's reaction. The second was a bagel shop looking to ship and sell homemade bagels across the country. It was the third business idea that caught my eye.

Birdie's Bird Houses and Furniture (Company name is up for a change)

A woodworking couple is looking for help designing a marketing package for their furniture business. It used to be exclusively birdhouses sold locally, but the business has since expanded to furniture and is looking to sell nationwide. They would need pictures taken of each item for their website, a logo, and a social media package. Must love the sweet and slightly eccentric elderly. You will probably be fed chicken pot pie and be forced to play card games upon meeting.

Ryan cleared his throat. "Okay, interns. Have you all had enough time to pick your company?"

Shawn raised his hand. "I've got mine. Malta Snowboard Company. I'd love to build them an awesome website. Maybe they'd let me test a few of their products."

"Nice," Ryan said. "I think you'll be awesome for the job."

"Are these all of my choices?" Anita asked, looking at Mike.

"Yup," Mike said, smiling at her.

"Then I guess I choose the dermatology office."

"Nora?" Ryan looked at me.

I glanced down at my paper again, curious to see if I'd be drawn to the same business. It certainly wasn't what I imagined I'd be creating a design package for, but I couldn't deny the pull. I think it was the eccentric elderly that reeled me in like a fish caught on a lure. Memories of my own grandma before the end tugged at my heartstrings. If there was one type of person I fell in love with while working at the cafe, it was the sweet and eccentric elderly.

"Birdie's Woodworking and Furniture."

Ryan's eyes flicked to Duke's before landing back on mine. "Really?"

I shrugged. "Yeah, I think it sounds fun."

Anita laughed. "Suddenly mine doesn't sound as lame."

Nobody laughed. Shawn leaned over and high-fived me. "I like it."

"Thank you."

"Okay, now that everybody has your assignments, you have less than one month to create a killer design package." He passed around another paper to the three interns. This tells you what each package must include and how to pay for the website host and company, etc. The last day will be August 30th. We'll have a meeting that day where we present our packages to our three biggest clients and their offices, who will be deciding the winner.

And unfortunately, there can be only one winner. Everybody clear on the rules?"

We all nodded.

"Great. Managers, they can still help you with a few things around the office, but make sure you give them ample time to work on their projects. Let me, Mike, or Duke know if any problems come up."

The meeting adjourned.

Tenisha turned to me and Duke. "I don't know much about woodworking. Do you know the company well, Duke?"

Duke was leaning back in his chair, his elbow on the armrest. He looked at Tenisha. "Yeah, I know the owners. I can help her get started." His eyes flicked over to mine. "I'll call and arrange for a meeting this week. Sound okay?"

Tenisha and I nodded, and when it seemed like the designers and the owners were going to meet together for a few minutes, I headed back toward my desk.

I was halfway down the hallway when Anita popped out in front of me, blocking my pathway.

"It looks like you got what you wanted. For hardly knowing Duke, he sure has taken to helping you."

Oh my gosh. Make it stop.

"Yeah. He's nice."

It felt like we were negotiating our place here. The hierarchy of our roles as interns. There was no question she thought Shawn was beneath her, which meant in her mind it was down to me and her, which felt crazy because I'd seen some of Shawn's designs. He was a genius.

And then she went in for the kill. "Oh, I almost forgot. It was the strangest thing. A couple weeks ago, I had forgotten my purse at my desk, so I came back to grab it, and I thought I saw you and Duke in his office together. At first, I was like, there's no way they would be doing anything inappropriate…" She leaned forward conspiratorially, her hand on my shoulder as though telling a secret to a friend. "But you never know. *Was* it you?" Her voice dripped with fake curiosity.

"Well, this has been lovely. Have a nice day," I said, moving to go around her when her arm shot out, holding me in front of her. I looked down at my arm and then back up at her.

"Listen," she said sweetly. "I've been dying to work in an office like this for a long time. I wouldn't want to find out you're screwing around with the boss to get a leg up. I just want to make sure we're all playing fair. In case you need a reminder, there's no dating within the company while you're an intern. I'd hate to have to go to HR."

"There's nothing going on. Besides, none of the owners are voting."

She moved in closer. "But what were you doing here that late?"

Okay. Here goes. I hated telling her this, but I hated her thinking she had something on me and Duke even more. "I work for the cleaning service next door in the evenings. I was cleaning. Duke must have been here late for a meeting that night."

She blinked, taking it all in. "You...were cleaning the office?"

"Yes."

"After everybody goes home?"

"Yup."

Her hand covered her face, failing miserably as she pretended to hold back her smile.

I moved to leave, when she asked, "If that's actually what you were doing, can I make a request?"

My eyes narrowed. "What?"

"The carpeted floor is disgusting. I'm assuming you're not vacuuming every night, but maybe you need to?"

"Oh, do you mean the section of carpet by your desk that's always covered in fingernail clippings? You're right. It is SO disgusting. I'll try to remember to take care of that." I turned and walked back to my desk, proud I hadn't caved to her level. Well, maybe I'd caved a tiny bit. Even though it was the lesser of the evils I could have told her, I knew she would now be making my life a living nightmare.

One more month.

I could make it one more month.

18

On Thursday afternoon, near the end of the day, Duke called me into his office. Since the intern meeting on Monday, he had been in and out of meetings, trying to secure a big client. I'd seen so little of him that I was beginning to worry he might have forgotten about our project. With only three and a half weeks left, the clock was ticking, and I wanted to be sure I had plenty of time to create without pressure. The one time I had caught him today, he said he was still working out a few details and would go over it with me before the day was finished.

I stood from my desk, stretching my back as I did so, ignoring Anita's frank stare. At the cafe and the cleaning service, I was used to movement in my job. Sitting all day seemed like a luxury, but it was taking some getting used to. I minimized the spreadsheet Tenisha had me working on for the day and walked into his office and closed the door.

For the record, he still looked handsome. His hair seemed longer today, rumpled casually over his forehead, giving him a boyish sort of charm that wrung me inside out.

"Hey, Kiss Cam."

"Hey." I folded my arms in an attempt at being casual, unable to help the glow of warmth swelling inside me at his mere smile. It was disconcerting to know that the minute he got me alone, all it took was one smile and his knowing eyes on me and my body quite literally melted.

"Are you ready to talk about my project? Or did you want me for something else?"

A curious expression crossed his face. "Are you flirting with me?"

"No."

He leaned back in his chair, the squeak filling the room. "Oh, good. Cause…it almost sounded like you were." He gave me a meaningful glance that was completely full of crap. My body relaxed as our back and forth felt normal again. This was Friend Duke today with a side of flirting.

"Nope. I was just wondering about my project. Are you done finalizing the details?" Something about it all seemed fishy, but I couldn't place my finger on it.

"Yeah." He pointed toward the chair on the other side of this desk. "Have a seat."

I sat down and braced myself for something. I was already a bit apprehensive. In all actuality, I knew absolutely nothing about making things out of wood, and I was worried that might come across when building the website.

"Bart and Birdie can meet with you on Saturday morning. Would that work?"

"Their names are Bart and Birdie?"

His eyes crinkled. "Yup. Kind of catchy, right?"

"What's the story? How do you know them?"

He shook his head. "It's best to get into all that in person. I'll drive us down. You can meet them and get whatever you need."

My eyes narrowed. "Together?"

"Yup. On a very professional business trip." If it wasn't for the slight twinkle in his eye, I'd almost believe him. The way he leaned back in his chair, so relaxed in his tailored suit, his hands resting on his stomach and his leg crossed at the knee, felt very dangerous in the most innocent way possible.

"Is Tenisha able to come?"

He blinked. He clearly hadn't been expecting that. "I'll ask her," he said.

I wasn't disappointed by that in the least. I needed professionalism. I needed to get this job.

"You sure Saturday will work? You don't have a hot date or something?"

He gave me a pointed look. "I wouldn't say that."

A thrill raced up my spine, but I tamped it down, determined to re-establish our barriers. Anita's threat to go to HR still weighed heavily on my mind. I knew Duke was the boss, but I'm sure he could still get into some sort of trouble and I certainly didn't want to do anything that might put my chance at this position in jeopardy.

"Duke. Stop it."

To my relief, a hint of chagrin crossed his face. I mean, it wasn't *that* much, but it was something. "Sorry."

"Does that day work for you?" he asked again.

I was still getting used to the idea of having Saturdays off, since I was no longer picking up shifts at the cafe and my cleaning job was only Monday through Friday.

"Yeah."

"Great. What's your address? I'll come pick you up."

I swallowed. "I can meet you there. Where do they live?"

"Malad."

My eyebrows raised in surprise. "Malad? Malad, Idaho?"

"We'd better carpool. Better for the environment and all."

"Duke…" I began, slowly putting a few puzzle pieces on the board. "Is this your family?"

"Nora. They're new clients. It's a business trip. If you promise you'll be on your best behavior, we shouldn't have any problems."

That brought on a little smile. "It's not that I don't trust you. It's just that I really don't trust you." Not verbally, anyway. Though my heart was beginning to think otherwise. My brain, however, was a different story.

He only grinned and slid a piece of paper my way. "Address please."

———

I OPENED the door on Saturday morning to a Duke wearing very attractive jeans, a gray shirt, and a gray baseball hat on his head. His earthy cologne trickled into my nose, the scent of sweet pine warm and inviting. A flood of swear words entered my mind at the physical attractiveness that was Duke Webber.

Before I could back out of our *business trip,* citing irreconcilable differences, he brushed past me and entered my apartment, committing a humongous breach of our rules. Maybe we hadn't specifically spelled them out, but obviously the apartment was a safe space. A no-boss space. Everyone knew that.

"Is your hot boss here ye—" Mira rounded the corner of our apartment, stopping suddenly as her eyes grew wide as saucers. "Whoa."

Duke seemed to enjoy that, but before he could say anything, I glared daggers at my friend while attempting to push Duke back toward the front door. "Nope, he's not here yet."

He stepped out of my grasp, holding out his hand toward my roommate, who shook his with stars bouncing around in her eyes —which was interesting because according to our gab-fest the night before, she was still very much happily engaged.

"I'm Duke."

"Mira."

"Got anything good on Nora?" Duke asked, acting very pleased with himself.

She folded her arms, her eyes twinkling. "Oh, I've got stories."

"Okay, bye." Grabbing his arm, I physically pushed him toward the door. "Good chat."

"We'll talk more later, Mira," Duke called cheerfully as I closed the door behind us. I dropped his arm so I could lock the door. Okay, I hadn't fully prepared for Duke to be in my space and conversing with my people. There had to be something work-related I could say to bring us back on safe ground.

"Is Tenisha here?" I asked as we walked toward the stairs to head to the parking level one floor down. I scanned the parking lot for his white truck and found it, but I couldn't tell if anyone was sitting inside.

"She couldn't make it."

"Did you ask her?" I asked, eyeing him with suspicion.

A hint of a smile touched his lips and vanished before I could point it out.

"Duke..."

We got to the stairs, and he motioned for me to step down ahead of him. "I didn't want to make her work on a Saturday. She's got a family."

My heart begrudgingly thawed. "Don't think that being all considerate and nice is going to make me think any better of you."

He laughed. "Good to know."

I tried not to stare as we walked toward his truck in the back of the lot. I hadn't been expecting Casual Duke. In fact, I'd almost completely forgotten about that side of him. The Duke of the basketball game. Of long legs clad in denim and deep-set eyes underneath a baseball hat. I'd been surrounded by sexy Office Duke in a business suit, and like any red-blooded female, I enjoyed seeing a handsome man with a crisp white shirt and tie. Of course I did. But his clothes today spoke more to my soul than all the ties and dress shoes ever could. Casual Duke erased physical barriers between us. Instead of my boss, he became a hot guy I could have met on the street or in the cafe.

Or at a basketball game.

Casual Duke felt attainable and close enough to touch, which he was still very much…not.

Just before we reached his truck, his low voice reached my ears.

"Pretty ballsy move to wear the hair curly today, Kiss Cam."

In an instant, a wave of tingles, excitement, rapture–and anxiety–began coursing through me. I made the mistake of looking over at him, his dark eyes blazing into mine. My cheeks flamed, and I fought for control. I wanted to hide my face away and let my blush go unfurled, but this was a business trip, and he was my boss—even when wearing jeans.

"I didn't do it for you." My hands grasped self-consciously at my strands, silky and brushing against my shoulders.

"Never said you did."

"I like to change it up every now and then."

"Sure."

"I'm meeting clients. I wanted to look nice."

"You look beautiful."

By the time we arrived at his old white Tacoma, the amount of butterflies in my stomach were at an all-time high. It was going to be a long day if I allowed Duke full flirtation power. I needed to keep us focused and on track. This was a business trip.

Should I say it a little louder for the people in the back?

He opened the passenger door for me, and I climbed inside, transported all at once to the night when this truck first became familiar to me. The smell of mint and pine that was inherently Duke wrapped me up like a blanket. He slammed the door shut and walked around to his side while I took in the state of the interior. It had been recently vacuumed, and I smiled to think of Duke taking the time to do so. A pack of mint gum had been flung onto the dash. The backseat was clean, except for a gym bag tucked in the back corner. And in my cup holder was a brown drink, clearly fresh from the gas station, with ice and bubbles fizzing deliciously.

Duke settled himself behind the wheel, his presence already making this small truck feel even smaller.

I pointed to the cup closest to me. "Dr. Pepper?"

He smiled. "I hear it's better when it falls."

"Any secret notes under here?" I picked it up and checked the bottom of the cup but found nothing.

"No secrets today."

I tried keeping the flutters in my belly at bay by taking a big swig. After swallowing, I motioned to the Coke can in his seat. "Have you checked to see if a Coke tastes better when it falls?"

"I don't think I'd care either way. I just like the sound it makes when I open it from a can. I feel like I'm in a Coke commercial, dancing somewhere on a beach."

I laughed at the image as he pulled onto the road.

He rustled around in a bag in the middle console and pulled out a Twix. "It pained me buying this."

I tucked back a piece of my hair before reaching to take the bar from his hand. My fingers brushed against his and I felt my face flush. "Thank you. I didn't know we were getting snacks."

"Sure. You all ready for this?"

"I think so." I nudged at my laptop bag sitting at my feet. "I wasn't sure what to bring or do, but I was thinking I'd take notes about what exactly they're wanting and go from there."

Duke nodded, pulling us onto the freeway. When he didn't say anything else, I continued. "So, how do you know Bart and Birdie? Please tell me they're not your family."

He smiled. "They're my grandparents."

My hand covered my face. "I knew it! Why didn't you tell me?"

He flipped his hat around backward. "I didn't say at the

meeting because I didn't want you to feel weird in front of everybody, and then I kind of…forgot."

I gave him a look.

"I *mostly* forgot. My grandpa's the coolest guy you'll ever meet, though. He and my grandma live on a little ranch, although they've sold off most of the cows now. I grew up coming here for weeks at a time every summer. I'd pretend to be a cowboy. My grandpa used to have this old mechanical bull he'd let us ride, like the ones at the fair. Me and my brother would ride that thing all day."

I surprised myself when a memory of the kiss cam night came back to me. "Are these the grandparents you were sent to after you blew up the mailboxes?"

"Yeah. You'll love them."

"I didn't know you had a brother," I said.

"Two of them, actually. They're both married with kids. One lives in Logan, and one down south in Cedar City."

"Kind of funny you have two brothers and I have two sisters."

He adjusted his hat, pulling it low over his ears as he watched the road. "Where are your sisters at? Do they live at home still?"

"They've both moved out. One is in college in Logan, and my middle sister moved to New York a couple years ago."

"New York?"

"She got a job as a nanny for a family there. She's the one who had the hardest time with my mom."

He nodded. "So, how's your mom doing now?"

I looked out the window, watching the city pass in a blur. I caught sight of our gray office before the crowd of buildings blocked its view.

"She got married again. With all her kids graduated, she didn't feel like she needed to stick around this time. She and her husband, Kip, have been road-tripping all over the country in an RV. She moved out of her apartment, and he sold his house."

"What does he do?"

"Something online, I think. To be honest, I haven't chatted with him much. I'm just counting it a win that he has a job."

He nodded, readjusting in his seat slightly. "How many marriages is this for her?"

"Number four. Countless relationships before that and in between. Four have cheated on her, one scammed her and stole quite a bit of money, and one was not a very nice drunk."

His hands gripped tighter on the steering wheel. "Did you or your sisters ever get hurt? Or your mom?"

"No, he didn't hurt any of us. He just destroyed our living room."

He shook his head slightly. "Do you think this marriage will last?"

I shrugged, playing with the strap on my purse. "Granted, I've spent a grand total of about three hours in his company, but he seemed like all of the others. She loves to date the same person, just a different face. But I guess you never know. I hope, for her sake, she's happy. And mine."

We drove in silence for a bit before Duke rubbed his hands together. "Okay, I've got a plan."

"Should I be scared?"

"We're headed to Idaho. Land of possibility."

"And cows," I added.

"What do you say about finishing out our bucket list?"

Some part of me had known he was going to say that. That same part was cautiously thrilled. The other part was hearing Anita's dumb threat of going to HR on repeat in my head.

"It just doesn't seem like something a person would do on a very professional business trip."

Duke rubbed his face. "What are you talking about? Bucket lists are vital to the structure of our company. We have meetings reporting our progress. And more importantly, you owe me." He had me there, and he knew it.

"I know."

"My grandpa has a pond."

"I didn't bring my swimsuit."

He grinned and motioned with his head to the gym bag sitting in his backseat. "I've got two options for you."

A smile found its way across my face at the memory of a cozy night shared together in the ER.

My first instinct was to say no. It was always no. Fun meant idleness when I should be working. But I *was* working today. I was driving with my boss to Idaho to meet with clients. *My* clients. No matter that they were my boss's grandparents and that he had probably spoon-fed me this job, it was mine. Today, I was going to claim it. Today, I wasn't stuck at home, worrying about my dwindling bank account. I was driving to a farm, and there was a pond, and I was with Duke Webber. It felt so reminiscent of our night three years earlier that I couldn't deny myself this chance even if I wanted to. Which I didn't.

"Okay."

"Okay?" Duke's questioning gaze found mine. He looked like he thought I'd promised to buy him a puppy but wasn't sure I meant it.

"Yeah," I supplied, my excitement growing. "If you think your Idaho muscles can handle it."

"Oh, they can handle it. You just make sure *you* can handle it."

His words were rimmed with something I couldn't quite place. Teasing and laughter were still at the core, but something else lined the edges. It was more than excitement. More than determination, even. It took a while into our drive before I put my finger on it. It came to me as he was explaining a stretch of our drive. I had told him I rarely had reason to venture this far north of Salt Lake. I was almost embarrassed by how little of my own state I'd seen. Instead of making me feel awkward about it, he began telling me about the sights we were passing.

He pointed to a town at our right, nestled up against the base of a small mountain chain. "Brigham City has a stretch of road that's lined with orchards and fruit stands every summer. You like peaches, right?"

His question caught me off guard, and I assured him that I did.

"I'll take you back here in August, then. Next month. We'll get us a box. Best peaches in the state."

I blinked as it clicked. *We'll get us a box.*

Promise. His earlier words had been lined with promise. Just like his promise to get a box of peaches. One tangible and the other much more open-ended. Maybe it was the strangeness of the day, or being with Duke like this again, but I found myself growing excited about both.

19

We pulled up to a cheerful yellow farmhouse in the middle of a hay field, tucked down a short lane. Despite the proximity, I had only been to Idaho one other time. One weekend, during our summer with one of my mom's more stable husbands, Bill, he had driven us all to Lava Hot Springs, an hour north of the Idaho border. I remember staying in his run-down camper and spending a glorious two days swimming and tubing with my giggly sisters down the windy Portneuf River that ran through the charming eclectic town. Despite the fact that Bill happened to be an occasional drunk who stole our TV and my mom's credit cards when he left, even he couldn't taint those precious memories of my childhood. I'd had so few carefree days in my life, the few happy moments I did have stayed close to my heart.

Hopping down from the truck and onto a gravel driveway, I breathed in the smell of hay and freshly mowed grass. The backdrop of the farm was a picturesque mountain chain, flanked by a dotted pattern of houses and fields. The sounds of cattle in a corral behind the house caused a stir of excitement in my veins. I remembered visiting a small farm for a field trip in elementary school. I wasn't even sure what age I'd been, but I thought that was the last time I'd stepped foot anywhere near a cow.

The squeak of a screen door alerted us as we made our way toward the house.

"Is that my long-lost grandkid? Did you have to buy a map at the gas station to find yer way?"

Duke grinned, striding toward a small, gray-haired man in baggy jeans and suspenders, stooped with age but lively in countenance. "Maps are for old guys now, Gramps."

I watched the man embrace his grandson, his thick, knotty fingers clutching Duke's arms, gathering him close to his chest. He came up to Duke's shoulders. It was so strange seeing people in a different light. With a different lens on the glasses. Duke's strong frame had always stood tall when he led meetings and greeted clients. His voice rang out confident and capable. His handshake was sharp. Here, Duke's impressive frame grew soft and pliable as he bent down and wrapped his arms around his grandpa. The organic sweetness of the moment both startled and melted me to the point where I felt like I was intruding.

Duke stepped back, motioning toward me, his voice extra loud. "Grandpa, this is my friend, Nora. She was hoping to help you with your website."

His sharp blue eyes landed on me, appraising me with a twinkle in them. "Just a friend, you say?" He looked back at Duke incredulously. "Boy, you'd better get yer head checked. That girl needs to be more than just a friend." He motioned me forward with an impatient flick of his hand. "Come here, Laura. We're huggers in this house."

Before I could blush or correct him on the name, I found myself being squeezed in a hug that nearly crushed my shoulders as I leaned down into his bony body. I met Duke's eye and found him grinning broadly.

He pulled back. "I'm Bart, and this is my—" He turned his

head both ways but didn't seem to find what he was looking for. "Birdie?! Where are you? The kids are here!"

A muffled voice from behind the screen door was slowly becoming louder. "I'm coming! The oven went off at the same time Duke pulled up." The door opened, and out stepped a frail, matted, white-haired woman wearing a purple cardigan and holding a cane.

Her cherry-stained lips opened wide with excitement upon seeing her grandson, and she held open her arms. Duke hugged her tenderly before kissing her on the cheek. He motioned toward me. "Grandma, this is my friend, Nora. Nora, this is my grandma. Her real name is Roberta, but her favorite grandkids call her Grandma Birdie."

"Nora, so nice to meet you."

I went in for a handshake but received another hug. A pleasant floral scent mixed with a little homemade bread met my nose. Though frail, her arms squeezed me tight.

"Nice to meet you," I said.

"Goodness, you're a pretty thing," Birdie said to me, her cloudy blue eyes taking my measure. "I always wanted red hair like that, but mine was just plain old dirty-dishwater blonde. And now"—she pointed dejectedly at her white hair—"none of it matters."

My eyes flicked to Duke's in question. My hair was quite visibly dark brown. Not red.

Bart cleared his throat and motioned us all into the house.

"Birdie's made some homemade bread and jam for you kids. Come on in."

Duke opened the door for his grandparents to enter, and before I could cross the threshold, he leaned down, whispering, "Grandma's almost blind in one of her eyes, and the other one is getting worse. She's a saint, but I'd be wary of anything you're about to put in your mouth."

"Is that why she thought I was pretty?" I quipped. "Cause she couldn't see my face?"

Duke's face lifted in a silent laugh. "I guarantee that's not the reason."

His words warmed me as we followed his grandparents into the house, the smell of vintage furniture and mothballs greeting our noses. The decor was a mishmash of generations. Gold-rimmed mirrors and popcorn ceilings. And I smiled at a plastic cover over the long, gold couch in the small room to the right of the front door.

"That's the company room." Duke motioned to me. I had slowed down to take in every gold and crystal-infused detail. "Reserved for important guests."

I laughed. "Can I go sit in there now, or do I need to wait to be invited?"

"Invitation only." He stepped in closer to me. "And I should warn you that if you try to sneak in there and eat a plate of spaghetti on the squeaky couch, you will have to sit facing the corner for a good twenty minutes."

I laughed, imagining a childlike version of Duke with a spaghetti sauce smear over his face, trying to eat on the couch. "No eating in the company room. Got it."

We walked down a hallway that opened up into a medium-sized family room. The pink and blue floral couches that greeted us were at least a couple of decades more modern. Before I could soak it all in, Duke ushered me through a doorway and into the kitchen and dining room. His hand pressed lightly against the small of my back and caused my breath to hitch.

"Sit down, you two," Bart said to us, walking toward the stove to stand by his wife, who was attempting to extract the loaves from their pans. "It's nice to see Duke bringing a girl home, Laura."

"It's Nora, Grandpa," Duke said loudly as he pulled out a chair for me at the small round table surrounded by windows.

Bart cocked a hand over his ear. "What?"

"NORA," Birdie supplied. "With an N. NORA. Like that receptionist you like at the dentist."

"Oh. Is her name Nora?"

The two bantered back and forth while Duke and I sat chuckling under our breath.

It took Birdie two times trying to grab the butter knife on the counter before she actually took hold of it. Bart held the loaf pan steady as she dragged the knife gently along the edges, breaking the bread away. The movements were fluid, as though she'd done it a thousand times before. She turned the pan upside down, and a steaming fresh loaf of bread fell to the cutting board.

A few moments later, they sat down next to us at the table, uneven cuts of bread dripping with butter and homemade jam on the plates in front of us. Duke's warning about his grandma's cooking held no ground with the warm piece of heaven sliding down my throat right then. The chatter going on between Duke and his grandparents was muffled in my pleasure. When I finally came up for air, the laughter had lulled.

"I was telling Nora about eating the spaghetti in the company room, Grandma," Duke said, reaching for a second slice of bread.

Birdie growled good-naturedly at her grandson. "Oh, you little impish stink." She looked at me in camaraderie. "He was always trying to push my buttons. If I said he couldn't be in that room, he spent every second of every day trying to sneak in there."

I leaned forward. "You wouldn't happen to have any pictures of him here would you? Old photo albums?"

Her eyes lit up. "Do I? Don't leave without me showing you a few things about him. He's got two more brothers just like him." She clasped his hand on the table. "But he could always pull a smile out of me faster than any of my grandchildren."

Bart's ears perked up. "You kids staying the night?"

Duke shook his head. "Not tonight, Gramps. This is just a day trip."

His face fell. "Oh, just stay the night. You don't have anything to be back for tomorrow, do you? It's not a workday."

Duke smiled. "We work together, Grandpa. If I let Nora see how badly I get skunked in rummy, she'd never take me seriously again."

Bart looked over at me. "So what are your plans today? If you're too scared to play us in cards tonight. What all do you need from us?"

I held Bart's gaze as he cupped his ears toward me. I made a conscious effort to speak a little louder. "I wanted to get to know your story. I'd love to ask you both some questions about your business and maybe see some of the things you're wanting to sell so I can take pictures and put them on the website. Is that okay?"

Bart motioned toward his wife. "You tell it, Birdie."

Birdie had just taken a bite of bread, a lone bit of raspberry jam stuck to the upper corner of her mouth. When she swallowed, she began speaking. "It was my business. Bart was busy farming his whole life. My dad used to be a carpenter. He taught me a lot as a kid. I inherited some of his tools when he passed. At first, I picked up the hobby when all my kids were in school, making picture frames and a really bad dining room chair." She and Bart laughed at the shared memory. "But slowly, I got better. Started selling some local pieces to friends and neighbors. The word spread. I never went crazy with it. I mostly liked to build things for fun. But now..." She motioned to her and Bart. "We're just here all day, doing nothing. Bart rents out the land, and we've sold most of our cattle. It's good for us to keep busy."

"Birdie's been teaching me a few things," Bart said, "but it's her company." Suddenly, he stood up and pointed out the window. "Bald Eagle!"

Duke and I abruptly stood up, startled, and turned to where he was pointing. My eyes peered through the window and into the trees for a sign of the nation's bird. I was guessing this was something that happened often in this house on the farm. There was a slight breeze out today, ruffling the leaves on the maple tree, but no sign of an eagle.

Duke turned back around and sat down. "You sure you saw one, Gramps?"

Bart sat back down in his chair, this time snuggled next to his wife and nodded. "Oh, I'm sure. He shows his face here every so often."

When I looked back to Birdie to ask her a few more questions, the bit of jam on her face was gone.

AFTER A LUNCH of homemade white bread and jam, Bart and Birdie walked us outside to their shop. He pulled up the sliding metal door on the building where they kept all their tools and wood-working equipment. I took a step inside, and my mouth fell open in astonishment. On the right side of the dusty metal shop sat dozens and dozens, if not nearly a hundred, different wood items. Benches and tables, chairs, wooden frames, barn doors, and coat racks lined every crack and crevice of the room. I didn't know much about wood, but each item was unique and made with different shades and cuts.

"Wow, you two." Duke rolled an impressive eye to his grandparents, standing proudly together in the doorway. "You've been busy."

"Can I take some pictures of you both working together? For the website?" I asked. Duke handed me his phone. It was about four years ahead of mine in camera technology. I smiled at him gratefully.

"What can we make you?" Birdie turned to me, taking my hand in hers. "A little picture frame? You can keep it. As a thank you."

I couldn't remember the last time I'd gotten a picture off my computer or camera to display. And all of a sudden, I was saddened by that thought.

"I'd love that. Thank you."

The two of them got to work, Bart bringing the wood to the saw. I noticed him helping Birdie to line it up for him. When he asked her to go grab the broom, he quickly readjusted the wood once more before making his cut. Birdie swept the wood chips over to a large vacuum that sucked everything up into a pipe on the wall and out of the building. I became entranced with their work. Not only the work itself, but the way they worked. Confident Birdie setting things up, capable Bart adjusting and readjusting when Birdie's back was turned. A dance of love and loss and gentleness. And I found I could not get enough.

Of course, there was exasperation at times too, like when Birdie brought the cut pieces closer to her face and realized Bart had brought over the wrong wood. But Bart's pleading look toward me had me reassuring Birdie that I'd much rather have a picture frame made from pine than oak. They glued the pieces together and presented it to me. After I promised them I'd stain it any color I wanted, I had them pose together with several intricate birdhouses Birdie had made.

"Give her a kiss, Gramps," Duke said. He was leaning against a workbench with his arms folded.

Bart turned to both of us and said, "You don't have to ask me twice," before he leaned forward and kissed his wife sweetly on her cherry-stained lips while I snapped a quick picture.

Bart and Birdie wandered back toward the house while Duke and I spent much of the next few hours pulling out each piece of furniture and placing it in front of the metal shop to take a picture. Neither of us were professionals, but with the natural light, the simple background, and Duke's good camera phone, we cobbled together some pictures decent enough for the website.

"How'd you do?" Bart asked after he and Birdie came back out to check on us. They stood with their arms entwined after we closed up the shop.

"I think you'll be happy," I told them both. "You have the most beautiful furniture. I'm so impressed."

A dash of pleasure stained both of their cheeks.

Duke reached for me, putting his arm around my shoulder and squeezing me in close. "Do you mind if we use your pond real quick? I promised Nora we could take a quick dip."

Birdie's face scrunched together. "The pond?"

Instantly, I was on guard, looking at Duke in question. "What's wrong with the pond?"

"Nothing. You'll love it."

Half an hour later, I found myself wearing Duke's baggy gym clothes as he led me to the unattached garage just off the house. Then he proceeded to wheel out a motorcycle that looked more fitting for a kid than a grown adult, much less two.

"Are you kidding me?"

He looked up, grinning. "Do I look like I'm kidding?"

I motioned toward the bike with my head. "We can't both fit on there."

He shrugged, amusement lighting his features. "I think we'd regret not giving it our best shot."

My teeth tugged at my bottom lip as I contemplated my next move. I was Fun Nora today. And Fun Nora would probably say yes to sitting on Duke's lap while we rode on the potential death trap to the pond Birdie looked nervous we were headed toward.

"I'm determined to be Fun Nora today," I told him, suddenly needing him to be aware of my plan.

His amusement faded. "You're always fun, Nora."

I scoffed, looking down to stare at the dirt bike, trying to imagine myself with my arms wrapped around Duke as he drove us through the fields. It wasn't the worst image I'd ever conjured up in—

"Hey." Duke's hand reached out and touched my chin, gently tugging my face upward to look at him. "If you're not fun, then explain to me why you make me laugh more than anyone else," he said as he released my face to grab my hand instead, leading me to the motorcycle. He held me steady as I climbed onto the machine, scooting as high onto the seat as I could go. Duke settled on behind me, somehow the two of us barely fitting, with me sitting halfway on his lap.

I sucked in a breath as his arms came around me. "Your friends are even lamer than me?" His response was to squeeze me tighter until I squealed.

"Nope." His voice was gravelly in my ears, and I wondered if Fun Nora was going to get her fill today.

"You want to drive, Bucket List Lady?" Duke asked before he stomped on the kickstart a dozen times, revving the throttle and patiently waiting until the engine sputtered to life. For a moment, I sat mesmerized at how sexy and capable his hands looked starting a motorcycle.

"You driving?" he asked again, turning toward me with a knowing look, and my fate became irrevocably sealed to his. With a deep breath and a nod to all the romantic comedies I'd watched that included a motorcycle ride with the hot guy, I put my hand on the throttle and rotated it toward me.

The bike surged to life in both a forward and upward motion, the front wheel leaving the ground. I dropped my grip on the handle and screamed while Duke swore, took control of the handles, and quickly planted his feet on the ground, somehow stopping us from flipping over.

We sat there in shock for a long moment, the mortification falling off me in waves.

"See? I told you you were fun."

I squeezed his thigh with my shaking hands, trying to settle my pounding heartbeat.

"How about I get us going and you take over when you're ready?" he said.

"Deal."

I wasn't sure I was going to like riding the motorcycle. I had only said my bucket list item on a whim, after all. But it took about two whole seconds for me to realize I loved the carefree way the wind blew against my face, taking my hair with it. The smell of dirt and hay breezed past as Duke flew us down the trail. It took ten seconds before I regretted that my entire life so far had been missing this experience. There was a beautiful weightlessness about the ride that I hadn't been expecting. Of course, Duke's arm wrapped tightly around my waist could also have had something to do with that.

"You ready?" Duke asked as he slowed the bike down to a meandering pace.

"I think the question is, are *you* ready?"

"Been ready for a while."

Before I could dissect his words, he brought my hand to the throttle, covering it gently with his, giving me time to get a feel for the movement and speed. Once he felt certain I was ready, he removed his hand and allowed mine full control. I sunk back into his chest, our proximity a definite highlight of the ride for me. The bike wobbled a bit but straightened out as I drove us through small hills and bumps, testing my newfound skills as a biker. Turning became the hardest part for me, knowing I had to lean into the turn but never completely trusting the bike to hold us up.

"Gotta trust the bike," Duke said in my ear, his hands at my waist. "Lean into it. You won't fall."

As we rode down the dirt pathway carved off the side of a hay field on a warm summer night with Duke's arms wrapped around me, falling seemed...inevitable.

20

I WASN'T SURE WHAT I WAS EXPECTING THE POND TO LOOK LIKE, but it wasn't this. A small crop of willow trees surrounded a glimmering pool of water, their branches dipping softly along the surface. Across the way, a small dock stretched over the water. The years had weathered the wood, and some of the planks looked uneven. On each side of the dock stood two imposing willows with entwined branches acting like an umbrella across the edge of the dock where a long rope swing hung, swinging lightly with the breeze. For a moment, we both stared at the scene before us, where patches of sunlight cast their glow through the trees, setting the pond aglow.

"This is not real life," I said. "Nobody has places like this in their family."

Duke pointed toward a haphazard picnic table on the left side of the pond. "That's where I saw my brother sneaking a kiss with the farmer's daughter from next door." Then he motioned toward the rope swing. "That's where I broke my arm when I was seven."

He stood up, lending me his arm to balance myself as I

gingerly climbed off the motorcycle, my legs feeling stiff and unnatural for the first few steps.

We walked toward the pond, the sound of birds chirping through the trees and the smell of mud and hay setting our scene. A thrill of anticipation began trickling through me as we picked our way between weeds and wild sunflowers toward the outer bank.

My steps slowed as I examined the entire dock stretching out a few yards into the water, the lonely swing swaying in the breeze and the weeping willows surrounding.

Duke had walked a few paces ahead of me when he realized I was no longer beside him, and he turned to see what I was looking at. I didn't really want to swing in. Did I? Things were confusing when I was with Duke. I was beginning to remember that now. Who I thought I was and who I thought I wasn't always seemed to clash.

"You want to swing in?"

His eyes were patient as I looked from the swing to him and back again. My heart pounded, but I couldn't keep the smile from forming on my face.

"It just feels like a romantic-comedy moment that shouldn't be missed."

"A *romantic* comedy, huh? Interesting."

I pretended not to hear his comment and turned from him, picking my way through the weeds. He caught up to me easily.

"Care to make this interesting, Kiss Cam?" His hand brushed against mine as we walked, while his low voice sent tingles shooting down my spine. One glance at his mischievous face and alarm bells began to sound.

"I'm about to jump in a pond with you to reenact a question-able scene from a movie. I feel like that's pretty interesting."

His eyebrows raised. "Eh, but is it something we'll remember in five years?"

I shook my head, attempting to hide the thrill coursing

through me, trying to stay strong, even when I knew he already had me. He had me the second he said *farm in Idaho*.

"Something to write home about?" I said.

"Exactly."

"What do you have in mind?"

He held out a hand and stopped our walk around the bank. We were about twenty yards of weed and mud patches away until we reached our goal.

"First one to the swing on the dock wins something from the other person."

I swallowed. "Wins what?"

A crooked grin began to form on his face, his eyes darting to my lips. No. It wasn't a dart. I would know because heat burning on my face followed the trail. The luxurious journey began at my eyes, before venturing to the freckles scattered across my nose that came out every summer, until they finally reached my lips.

"Whatever you want," he said, low and hot, before his gaze flitted back up to mine.

I begged my brain to stay with me. My heart was probably a lost cause, but I was toast without my head. "So, if I tell you to clean the men's bathroom for a whole week, you have to do it?"

He smiled. "Yup. And one more thing."

"What?"

"We live in the moment. We're here now. No worrying about anything else. Just have fun."

We locked gazes for a long moment while I felt myself being pulled in opposite directions. But he was right. I had said yes to this moment and I didn't want to be anywhere else.

"Deal?"

"Yeah." The words came out so soft, but they seemed to be enough for Duke.

My pounding heart went into overdrive as he leaned forward, into my space, my breath catching. A light breeze could have toppled me. He opened his mouth, and my eyes dropped to his lips.

"GO!" He took off like a rocket, leaving me in the dust.

Dang it, brain. You had ONE job!

I followed him, a mixture of panic and laughter, already paces behind and working my way through a mud patch. Ahead of me, Duke slipped in the mud, one knee hitting the ground for a few seconds, but it was enough for me to gain some decent traction. Just as I was about to pass him, his hand reached out, pulling my gigantic shirt backward.

"Cheater!" I yelled, fighting off his hands. Squealing, my foot skidded through the mud, and I began to flail. His hands were on me fast, holding me up so I didn't fall. Then it was an all-out war, laughing and shouting as we each pulled each other's shirts, trying to gain the advantage. He slipped again, and I broke free, running as fast as I dared, careful to make sure that I wouldn't end up needing another emergency room visit today. After putting some necessary space between us, I glanced back to make sure he was okay in time to see him dive gracefully into the pond. I squealed, moving myself farther away from the bank to hopefully avoid the mud patches. It cost me some time, but it didn't matter anyway. Before I reached the dock, Duke had pulled himself up onto it, with arms full of muscles and sexiness.

"It was a pleasure doing business with you," Duke called cheerfully, watching me approach.

"I didn't realize you were a big fat cheater," I said, breathing heavily as I came to stand in front of him.

He laughed. "I guess next time you'll have to establish all your rules up front."

"What do you win?" I threw my hands on my hips as I regained control of my breathing.

His eyes trailed down my body, sending shivers leaping chaotically down my spine. "I'm still deciding. But I'll keep you posted."

I stilled.

Okay.

One of us needed to take control here because right now, he seemed as far away from Boss Duke as I'd ever seen him before. My body was going to combust if he kept doing...whatever it was he was doing.

With a voice that sounded in more control than I felt, I said, "No unnecessary touching. And nothing we wouldn't do at work."

His lips curved into a smile. "You're greatly underestimating the things I would do at work."

Holy crap. "DUKE!"

He laughed, his face lighting up with boyish charm. "Next time you should really establish those rules before we start the bet."

My nose wrinkled. "Double or nothing?"

"Nope."

I gave a laughing Duke a light push before moving to stand shoulder to shoulder with him.

"Fine. You go first," I said, peering down into the cloudy water with some degree of apprehension.

He sat down on the swing and pushed off. "For the record, if I break my arm again, you're in big trouble."

I made a face. "Please don't break your arm again. Then I'd feel bad."

He sighed and turned to face me. "This is for you, Kiss Cam."

A smile broke out across my face as he saluted me before pouring his concentration into gaining momentum, his weight and movement causing the tree branch holding the swing to sway dangerously. I moved out of his way and prayed he cleared the dock. At the peak height, he swung out over the water, readied his hands, leaned back, and flipped. I let out a breath when he cleared the dock, landing in the water with a large splash.

I walked to the edge, waiting for him to resurface, hoping that whatever lived in there didn't eat him. Finally, he emerged from the water, like Colin Firth in Pemberley. He had forgotten to take off his white shirt before he jumped, and I watched as he did so now, seemingly in slow motion, before tossing it to the edge of the bank. Then he sunk back into the water, but not before flashing me a clear shot of abs and muscles. I swallowed, second-guessing this whole plan.

"You're up!" he called out. When I hesitated, he added, "What's that look on your face?"

"It's not nerves, that's for sure," I yelled. "Because I'm not scared to get in the water with you. Not one bit."

"Stop thinking. We have rules here, remember?"

Rules. That's right. I had to live in the moment with a scorching hot Duke in the water, staring up at me like I was definitely *not* his employee. I'd lived my entire life trying not to get attached to guys and here I was, about to offer myself up to one on a silver platter—or more like a rickety swing with splinters. I sat down and pushed off gently, taking my time going higher, enjoying the view. It really was beautiful up here. Duke liked to tease, but he was a gentleman. I knew that. I wasn't nervous to get in the water with him for any safety concerns. But I seemed to be all heart here, and I'd have to face that sooner or later. I had a feeling the water meant sooner. Duke seemed much smaller and less intimidating from this distance. And hey, feeling shy was also living in the moment. I kept swinging.

"Get in here, chicken! Quit stalling."

"I guess you should have waited to jump in until after I did."

A dangerous gleam crossed his face as he made a sudden beeline toward me, his arms slicing effortlessly through the water. Before I realized what was happening, he was hoisting himself up onto the dock. I squealed, legs kicking and waiting until the swing was at its peak height before launching myself off and into the murky depths.

Cool water enveloped me as I landed, surprised when I lightly touched the bottom of the pond. Ferns and weeds swished around my body, brushing against my skin in such a creepy way that I burst out of the water, shuddering deeply.

Duke resurfaced next to me, drops of water covering his face, the light from the sun highlighting his strong jaw and cheekbones.

Something swished against my leg again, and I yelped, slapping at the water and shooting a pleading look at Duke.

"Come here." Duke moved toward me, and in a series of movements, he pulled me onto his back, my arms around his neck and his hands clutching my thighs at his waist as he moved us toward the bank.

"We need to be able to touch the ground to do the lift," he said, his hands on my legs making me forget about anything unpleasant in the water. Even now, his body radiated warmth. Heat. Which was a total unfair advantage, with my lips now quivering.

We moved exactly four more feet before he released his hold on me and stood, the water reaching the height of my collarbone and the bottom of his ribs. My eyes drifted down from his face to the droplets of water now scattering over his chest.

Boundaries, my brain spat out. We needed a reminder of the boundaries. The amount of touching this little bucket list item would require of us demanded it. Duke's baggy gym shirt floated around me in the water, and his shorts felt like they weighed a ton of bricks. Maybe I could lead with that. It would take a miracle for him to be able to lift me out of the water and over his head, let alone with me acting like some graceful nymph from the sea.

"It's not too late to change your mind, you know," I said kindly, tying my shirt in a knot at my waist. "These shorts alone are going to weigh a ton."

"No backing out now, Kiss Cam," Duke said, his hands

coming to rest on my arms. "If you bend at your knees, I'll put my hands on your hips, and we'll count it off."

Romantic comedies were full of skinny dipping and swimming in ponds and lakes. It never seemed like that big of a deal on the big screen. Duke's hands fell to my hips and I sucked in a ragged breath. He counted us off.

"Go!"

Without thinking, I bent down and made my best effort to jump up while he tried lifting my hips above water. Our first attempt gave the impression of a sick dolphin, getting halfway out of the water before losing its energy and collapsing back down again.

I landed on top of Duke as we both went under. When we came up, he was laughing, wiping the water from his eyes. As for me, the water had shot up my nose, and I came up sputtering. We moved into position again. This time, I tried to be more focused, but we had the same result. We only made it halfway up before we tumbled once more.

Duke's laughter when we surfaced failed to calm me.

"You need to trust me," he said.

"Maybe your Idaho muscles have grown soft," I retorted.

Did I not trust him? Why did those words ring both true and false?

"The balance of our lift comes from you. I can support you, but you're the one who has to let go of my shoulders and let yourself fly. Without that, we're going to fall every time."

Duke released me and moved my body into position once more. We tried again. The first time, I ignored his advice, and it backfired immediately—to my utter annoyance. The second time, I did try to remove my hands from his shoulders but began internally freaking out, and we dropped yet again.

"This is a really stupid thing for a bucket list," I said, defeat lacing my words with frustration. His hands were on my hips again, feeling much more at home there now.

He scoffed in jest. "You can't judge what's on somebody else's list."

"It wasn't really on your list and you know it." I yelped again as another weed brushed my calf. "Things are touching my legs right now. Consider yourself judged."

"It's probably just the snakes," he said calmly.

Welp.

That was the wrong thing to say.

I didn't wait for the countdown. I didn't bend my knees. But I did fully launch myself at Duke. If I had been jumping upward instead of outward, we might have pulled the whole thing off—that is, if he'd had any sort of warning. My arms clung to his neck while my legs encircled his waist.

Duke fell back into the water. His hands held me fast as I screamed the whole way down until the water silenced my cries. Duke came up, laughing and wheezing, while I continued using him as my own personal ladder. Whatever issues I may have had with touching and boundaries had suddenly vanished.

It took a while for our laughter to die down. And when it did, Duke held me cradled in his arms, the water hitting him at his chest and cocooning me in an embrace of safety and Idaho muscles.

"Probably a good time to tell you that I hate snakes," I whispered. "Like a completely irrational fear of them."

"So I gathered."

He was so close. His jaw clenched, and water droplets fell in a haphazard line down his face. His eyes scanned my face, coming to a stop at my lips before he swallowed. My breathing came out in a deep, panting breath that refused to slow. I needed to get down, though with his tight hold, it would take a joint effort to release me.

"This goes against everything inside of me right now," he mumbled, "but I've actually never seen snakes here, and it was probably just a weed."

Relief poured into my nerves but also something else. Disappointment flared as he helped me down, the splash of water spraying my already soaked shirt once more.

"If you're wrong, you'll regret it."

He took my arm and led me into position. My shorts felt heavy again, and I took a second to tighten the cinch.

"Alright," Duke began. "I have a good feeling about this one."

It was sweet of him to think so. But as we fell time and time again, our laughs were fewer and fewer as determination began etching its way onto our faces. The problem was me. Duke was right—once he got me past his shoulders, I was the one in control. I had to hold out my arms in a Superman position, locking my body to keep it as stiff and as still as possible, while he held me over his head. Even though the water was there to catch me, something inside of me panicked each time I passed his shoulders. Instead of straightening and locking my body, I'd curl, sending us both backward into the water.

"Should we just count it?" I begged after the fifteenth attempt, spitting out another mouthful of water, no doubt infested with parasites. "You got me up pretty high."

A water-logged Duke stood before me, hands on his hips, breathing heavily. I followed the motion of his stomach and chest for a long moment before recollecting myself.

"Nora." He bent down to my eye level. "We can do this. I promise I can hold you up there. Is it really that scary letting go?"

"Um. Yeah. It is. Hella scary." My hands were at my hips now, annoyed that his dumb bucket list required so much of me.

Amusement lit his face but I held my ground and tried my best to look stern.

His gaze softened as he took me in, sweeping over every detail.

"Close your eyes," he said.

I froze. "Why?"

"Because I want to try something."

There was something so vulnerable about closing your eyes for a person. I wanted to fight it, but I was already here, sopping wet, in Duke's clothes, attempting a lift from a movie. He'd get me to cave eventually.

I closed my eyes.

"First time I asked? I'm shocked."

"Don't let it go to your he—"

My words slowed when I felt his body before me, the water between us lapping farther up my sides at his movement.

"What are you doing?" My words came out in a breathless whisper.

"I need you to trust me," he said. "I'm not going to let you fall—at least, not without me."

A small gasp escaped my lips as his hands found their way to my hair, his palms lightly gripping the sides of my head. They didn't stay for long but traveled softly down the side of my neck and stopped on my shoulders, his fingers twirling the strands of hair that had escaped my ponytail. Each touch heightened without sight. Ever so slowly, I felt his hands on my arms, moving them back past my waist.

"We're going to bypass my shoulders," Duke whispered, his breath a puff of heat next to my ear. "Keep them back here."

Ever so slowly, his hands were back on my arms, making their way back up to my neck. A sigh escaped me just before Duke's mouth landed on my cheek, as soft as a whisper, before making his way down my jawline.

"I'm calling in your debt," he whispered.

I was too far gone to resist—not that resistance was anywhere near my thoughts. My breath hitched as I felt his lips on the corner of my mouth, taking his time, teasing me. But I didn't want to be teased anymore. I was antsy and restless. When his mouth finally found my bottom lip, tugging and tasting, I closed the gap, kissing him with a sigh.

In the foggy recesses of mind outside of Duke's kiss, I felt the slide of his hands down the side of my body, stopping at my hips. I didn't have time to miss the loss of them from my hair because before I could blink or protest the absence of his lips, I was being lifted into the air. With my eyes still closed, my hands reached out for balance as my body tightened, falling into the movement. After a second or two of intense concentration of stillness, I opened my eyes in wonder.

The feeling of flying was similar to what I felt whenever I was with Duke, the absence of gravity creating a moment without limit. Endless possibilities. A weightlessness when I should have been grounded. But I was grounded. I had always been grounded. Duke held me up—the gravity to my flight. We held the position for a record-breaking seven seconds before we started to fall.

We came out of the water laughing and spitting out water. Cresting the wave of our high. We had finally done it. My body felt as light as air. Physically, gravity had done its job bringing me back down to earth, but mentally, emotionally, spiritually, I was somewhere else. My soul was in the clouds. The pounding of my heart felt like it would burst out of my chest. A part of me hated that we were back down to earth, our moment gone. Or was it?

Duke was wiping the water from his eyes when his low chuckle met my ears. He hadn't opened his eyes yet and I couldn't look away.

Live in the moment, he'd said.

It did sound dreamy. My own slice of heaven. Because in this moment was a world where Duke wasn't my boss and there was no HR. There was no competition for a job or my need for a career. In this moment, there were no thoughts of ex-girlfriends of three years taking up space in my brain. It was just us. The

Nora and Duke of the basketball game. Impulsive and free. And we had finally checked off the most obnoxious bucket list item known to man. Surely that was cause for…celebration.

Right?

I didn't let myself think. Instead my body took over. Ever so slowly, I made my way toward him. Duke's eyes were open now. His hair had been brushed impatiently off of his forehead and his face was covered in drops of water. The laughter so ready in his eyes and on his lips faded as my hands found their way to his cheeks. And before I could over-think, I rose up to meet his lips.

His mouth was hot against mine, dipping and taking everything I offered. The splash of water between us was the only sound as his arms wound their way against my waist, pulling me closer. The light bristles from his face marked my skin, causing my breath to catch and my footing to stumble. This moment felt like coming home in a way that didn't quite make sense. He held me with such sweetness and care it almost made me ache.

I was beginning to think Duke was a liar.

I won't let you fall.

This felt very much like falling. My seven seconds being airborne couldn't hold a candle to the ecstasy I was feeling now.

Not without me.

Was he falling too?

It felt risky…this living in the moment business.

And then, he stopped, pulling his lips back from mine a fraction of an inch.

My eyes opened, meeting his wild gaze with confusion. His chest dipped up and down in the water, breathing heavily.

"Interesting," he said, his voice gravelly. "I don't remember you winning a kiss."

Disappointment laced through me at his words. Until amusement flared in his eyes. I splashed water on him in outrage and turned away with a short laugh, intent on hiding my heart if he was only going to turn it into a joke.

I made it half of a step before his hand was at my arm, pulling me back to him. My hands landed at his chest, and then he was kissing me again. His hands held my face as his mouth moved over mine. Hard, fast, slow, sweet…it was all-consuming.

"Looks like I forgot to read the fine print," he mumbled some time later.

"Oh yeah?"

"Yeah. It says that you can kiss me anytime you want."

I swallowed, adjusting my grip on his shoulders. "That's pretty open-ended fine print."

"I don't make the rules."

My eyes trailed down to his lips. Every moment we stalled it brought me one step closer to remembering myself. There was a time for everything. A time to live in the moment and a time to live in the real world. The real world was calling now.

"We better get back," I said. "Your grandparents might be worried."

"They're not," he said.

A laugh bubbled out of me. I tipped my head down to escape his gaze.

When I finally gathered the courage to meet his eyes, I said, "I think our Idaho moment is about over."

"There's an interesting word in that sentence."

I shook my head, trying desperately to keep the smile off of my face. I failed.

"What word is that?"

He leaned forward, his mouth a whisper away from mine. "About."

He caught my smile with his lips until ever so slowly our mouths began to soften and our lips began a dance. A tango of longing and sweetness, perfect for the moment. Our moment.

All too soon, Duke pulled back, as though he sensed my own hesitation. His brown eyes were sweet and kind as he rose up and pressed a kiss to my forehead.

Before I knew what he was doing, he bent down and picked me up like a sack of flour, ignoring my elated squeals, and threw me over his shoulder as he picked his way out of the water.

I had been right. Whatever came next, I knew this had been a moment not to be missed.

21

It was a chilly motorcycle ride back to the house. I leaned into Duke, my arms wrapped tightly around his waist. Duke wanted me to get the most out of my riding-a-motorcycle bucket list item and proceeded to take every turn and hill possible on the way back. By the end of the ride, sinking into the turns instead of pulling away had become second nature.

I could no longer deny the pull I felt toward Duke. My feelings were vast and deeper than anything I'd ever experienced. From the time we met, three years earlier, there had been something between us. Something I'd tried to push aside for so long, first thinking I'd never see him again, but then again when I did. He had wrapped me up in a bundle of flirting and friendship so unexpected that I didn't know what to feel. I'd held my heart so guarded for so long, and his surprise attack had been quick and efficient, disarming me so gently with toilet brushes and squeegees, flirtatious notes, and countless smiles.

We each took one of the two bathrooms to shower. I opted for the main guest bathroom, with the sea-green carpet and rose-pink walls, while Duke showered in his grandparents' bathroom. Being in a place brimming with love and a cozy sense of family began pricking at emotions inside of me that were long-since dormant. I didn't allow myself to dwell. Instead, I got dressed and twisted my hair up into a messy wet bun, not wanting to take the time to dry it. It was close to six in the evening, and we had to get on the road. I opened the door and nearly ran into Duke in the hallway. He wore his sexy jeans again and smelled like a delicious kind of manly soap. His tousled hair glistened, looking like he'd just run his fingers through instead of a comb.

"You smell good," I said like an idiot before thinking that statement through.

"Thanks," he said, pulling me into his arms. "Better get closer, then."

I laughed and tried to wiggle free as we bounded down the stairs, but as we rounded a bend in the staircase, I swore, stopping abruptly.

Duke stiffened, looking to see what had caused my reaction.

A light-cream ceramic cat with big disturbing blue eyes stood probably four feet tall on a table opposite the stairs. His mouth was open, with his tongue painted a soft pink, and his head cocked at just the right angle to be disturbingly creepy.

"What, Fluffy?" Duke asked, motioning to the devil incarnate.

"What is that thing?"

"That's their pet cat."

"Holy crap."

"Do you need another shower?" Duke asked.

I elbowed him.

"How dare you. My sweet grandmother made that thing out of love for all of her family to enjoy."

"You do not enjoy that thing. Look at its eyes."

"Before she turned into a wood master, my grandma made dolls and scary cats out of porcelain."

My hands flew to my mouth. "She has dolls?"

"Cabinets full of them," he whispered, eyes big and serious.

I smacked his shoulder and moved past him, giving the cat a wide berth as I passed, ignoring the deep sound of Duke's chuckle.

"You KIDS SEE any snakes out there?" Bart's voice from the rocking chair on the front porch greeted us as we stepped outside, my purse and laptop bag in hand, along with a slew of ideas for creating a logo, business name, and website for Bart and Birdie.

At his statement, I sent a scathing look Duke's way. "What?"

He just smiled and continued on toward the truck. "Nora thinks she felt one, but we never saw any."

"You told me there weren't snakes in the pond."

Bart chuckled in his rocker. He was eating an ice cream bar in his overalls, the squeak of his rocker creating a picture I'd never forget in a million years.

Birdie rocked next to him, an ice cream sandwich in her hand. "There are snakes all over that pond. Consider yourself lucky if you didn't see one."

Before I could scold Duke, he leaned down and gave his grandma a big hug goodbye, melting my heart into a puddle. She squeezed him tight, giving him a kiss on his cheek and leaving the faintest smudge of lipstick across his skin. I hugged Bart, surprised when I felt his whiskery lips on my cheek in a sweet kiss.

"It was a pleasure to meet you. Next time, come here as Duke's girlfriend." He nudged my arm. "Or at least make it official." Duke's low chuckle gave me the confidence to laugh off my embarrassment. "And will you make sure Duke comes and visits us more than every six months?" he added.

"You came down to visit my parents three weeks ago. I saw

you then, old man." Duke leaned down to hug his grandpa affectionately.

"Well, it feels like a long time ago."

I leaned down to embrace Birdie, taking one last whiff of her floral scent. "I wish I could have chatted more with you," I told her honestly.

She patted my cheeks affectionately. "Same, dear. You come on back with Dukie next time."

"I'll bring her," Duke said. I ignored the tiny shiver that ran down my spine at those words.

"Dukie?" I whispered as he nudged me toward his truck.

"You are never to repeat that."

"I'm going to be honest. I don't know if that will be possible."

"She's a sweet old woman who doesn't know what it means."

"She's my favorite."

Duke's grandparents watched as we trudged toward the truck. They watched Duke open my door, Bart shouting his approval at Duke's good manners.

"I must have taught that boy well."

"Grandma taught me that," Duke teased, slamming my door shut and making his way around to the other side.

They watched calmly as Duke climbed in on the driver's side, setting the plastic bag of his wet clothes on the seat between us. They watched as Duke tried to start the truck.

They watched as he tried to start the truck again.

They watched as he tried to start the truck one more time, confusion etched on his face.

They watched as Duke yanked open the door and popped open the hood, jiggling some things around before hopping inside and trying again.

And again.

"Looks like yer truck's not starting," Bart commented, taking a bite out of his ice cream bar.

Duke took the keys out of the ignition and got out of the truck, an exasperated look growing on his face. I followed him out.

"Hey, Grandpa, do you know of any mechanics who could come out and look at it tonight?"

Bart checked his watch and made a face. "Oh, it's after six now. Nobody in Malad is working that late. I've got a friend I could check with in the morning, and I'm sure he'd be happy to take a look."

He frowned, running a hand through his hair. "I should really get Nora home tonight, if possible. So if you know of anybody else I could call—"

"Oh, what's one night? It's Sunday tomorrow. You're not working, are ya?"

"No, but—"

"Stay, then. You and Nora were just saying you wished you could stay longer." He took another bite and continued rocking.

"I was fixing to make some fried chicken and mashed pota-toes tonight. I know it's your favorite. We'll just throw another couple of pieces of chicken on the stove." Birdie rocked as she talked, her voice sounding a bit too casual to feel authentic. "It's not any big deal. We've got the beds all made up for guests."

Duke turned to me, a hint of humor in his gaze. "We could rent something if you need to be home tonight."

"Oh, no need to do that," Bart spoke up. "I'm sure my friend would be happy to come look at it. Tomorrow," he added decidedly.

"Right." He nodded at Bart before looking at me, lowering his voice. "Or I could tackle my grandpa and search all his pockets to find whatever wire he stole from my truck to make it stop working."

By this time, a grin had spread across my face. "They love you so much."

"Would you be okay staying the night? I'm not sure we have

another option since my truck is mysteriously not working," he raised his voice a little louder for the hard-of-hearing couple casually rocking in their chairs.

"Happens all the time," came the commentary from the porch. "That's an old truck."

A small chuckle from Duke. "What do you say?"

I couldn't hide the thrill of pleasure that shot through me at the thought of not leaving. Of having Duke all to myself for one more day. Of spending time with this unique and eclectic couple with fake cats and plastic couch covers who loved their grandson so much they'd personally break down his truck to keep him around another day. I didn't even try to hide my excitement.

"Only if we can play cards after dinner."

IT TURNED out that in the middle of the unassuming home full of sweet rose-pink hues, plush, shag carpets, and the faint smell of Bengay, Duke's grandparents were delightful cheats who'd do just about anything to win at cards. Producing aces from under the table and sly underhanded dealing was bad enough, but then they'd stuff you full of ice cream and homemade blackberry cobbler until you were having too much fun and were much too sugar-drunk to care.

We played for hours. I believe that I yawned more than his grandparents, who seemed completely energized by our extended stay.

"I won!" Birdie screamed, pumping her arms into the air. It was after eleven, and she had just laid down her entire hand in rummy, a sea of blacks and reds categorized in runs and sets.

We all leaned forward a bit, squinting at the black ten of spades mostly hidden in a run of black clubs.

"That's my girl!" Bart pounded on the table excitedly. He

stood, placing his hand directly over the fake run and looking Duke and me both in the eye. "More cobbler?"

A grin stretched across Duke's face as he leaned back in his chair. "The two bowls I already had are probably going to do me, Gramps. That's quite a winning streak you both have there."

Bart stood up, stretching. "Well, when you got it, you got it." Turning to Birdie, he said, "My dear, let's get to bed."

"What time do you need my help in the morning, Grandpa?" Duke asked.

"Six." He looked at me. "And if Nora wouldn't mind helping Birdie with breakfast…"

"I'd love to," I said as we all stood from the table.

"I can do it," Birdie stated, clutching her husband's arm as they walked toward the stairs, "but I'd love the company."

"I would leave you lovebirds downstairs, but I don't want any hanky-panky going on in this house. I saw the eyes you made at each other during dinner. I'm not leaving you two down here unattended," Bart said, a twinkle in his eye but seemingly very serious when he motioned Duke and me up the stairs before him.

I bit my lip to stifle a horrified giggle.

"Birdie has a couple rooms ready for you," Bart said once more.

I gave the ceramic cat the side-eye as we all trudged up the stairs, following Birdie down the hall to my room. The pink carpet from downstairs graced the floors. The window had been opened, and the curtain billowed softly in the evening breeze. A bouquet of freshly cut wildflowers sat on the nightstand. The double bed had a homemade quilt on top, made with a splash of colors. There were doilies hung decoratively on the wall along with old family pictures.

"I put one of my nightgowns on your bed for you to sleep in, dear." Birdie patted my arm.

My eyes widened as they landed where she indicated. There

was indeed a nightgown on the bed. The rose-pink material had been well-loved, worn and washed many times. The high collar and ruffled sleeves at the wrist was the icing on the cake.

"I know it's not the fashion nowadays to wear these, but it's all I have," she said hesitantly, as if she was unsure I'd accept the garment. Any reservations I had were gone in an instant.

"It's perfect. Thank you," I said, giving her a squeeze. "I've always wanted to try sleeping in a nightgown. Are they comfortable?"

Birdie's eyes lit up. "Oh yes! You won't go back to anything else." She leaned in closer, whispering conspiratorially, a twinkle in her eye, "And I will say this...Bart has always loved me in this nightgown—if you know what I mean."

She patted my cheeks before turning from my frozen smile and padded in her slippers toward the door. "I'll let you get some rest now. There's a toothbrush for you on the bathroom counter. I always keep a few extra around in case someone has car trouble." With a wink she closed my door and was gone. I took another look at the nightgown flung across my bed, hid my face in my hands, and laughed.

Twenty minutes later, I had just turned off the lamp next to my bed when my phone buzzed with a text.

Unknown Number: Sorry there couldn't be any hanky-panky tonight.

Me: How did you get this number?!

Duke: You really shouldn't leave your phone unattended.

Me: Does your room have pink carpet too?

Duke: Blue. This was my uncle's room. You're in my mom's old room.

Me: There's a picture on the wall with a tiny Duke dressed like a superhero and being kissed by four women at one time.

Duke: You jealous?

Me: I've always loved a man in Spiderman pajamas.

Duke: Are you flirting with me? Cause that's exactly what I'm wearing right now.

Me: Apparently our office rules don't mean anything here.

Duke: In that case, I'll meet you downstairs in two minutes.

Me: You heard your grandpa. No hanky-panky.

Duke: Question…did I hear my grandma say she had a nightgown for you to wear tonight? Can I get a picture?

Me: What happens in the pink room stays in the pink room.

Me: By the way…I love your grandparents.

Duke: Guess I'm going to have to bring you back for another visit. Sweet dreams, Nora.

FULL DISCLOSURE: I was all set to wear the nightgown from Duke's sweet grandma—until she said that bit about Bart loving her in said nightgown. So I put it aside to definitely NOT wear it. I then proceeded to go back and forth for two miserable hours from being too cold and way too exposed in my shirt and underwear, to wearing my jeans and being too uncomfortable to sleep, before finally woman-ing up and yanking on the nightgown.

Perfect temperature the rest of the night.

22

AFTER A BREAKFAST OF SAUSAGE, SCRAMBLED EGGS, AND TOAST, Bart stole Duke to help him outside. Something about moving some dirt around in the tractor and needing a gate operator, which Duke explained to me just meant he would stand by the gate to keep any cows from getting out of the corral while his grandpa went back and forth moving dirt inside the pen.

"He doesn't let you drive the tractor?"

A chagrined look crossed his face. "When I was a kid, I ran into the side of his shed with a tractor one summer. He's never trusted me since," he explained, making me smile before he followed his grandpa out the door.

Birdie and I cleaned up the kitchen table before we washed and dried the dishes by hand. She wore a loose pair of jeans, a blouse, and haphazard curlers strewn all about her hair. I kept myself near her in an attempt to be available to help if necessary, but she moved about the kitchen with the ease of a woman who had spent fifty years doing the same routine. Standing next to Birdie and drying the vintage casserole dishes she handed me felt sweet and nostalgic in a way that filled my soul up with goodness.

Once the kitchen was cleaned to Birdie's satisfaction, we sat down at the table. Birdie slid a stack of photo albums in front of me.

"Bart helped me find some pictures to show you."

I mentally girded up my loins to see pictures of Duke as a child. I would in no way whatsoever imagine what our children could potentially look like. That thought had my mother's vibe all over it.

Birdie turned onto a page. Colorful pictures of Duke and his two brothers appeared. He looked to be about seven or eight if the freckles and adorably boyish face told me anything. The album was filled with images of them scaling the haystacks, shooting guns, playing with bows and arrows, and swimming in the ditch. I had to remember to tease Duke about his chipped front tooth and how he was shirtless in ninety percent of the photos in the book.

"This was after Elaine's family had just moved back from school in Washington. Elaine is Duke's mom and my daughter. They lived with us for four months until they found a house in Utah."

Several pictures caught my eye as I thumbed through the next few images. A shot of all the boys lined up in a row, each of them holding a bow and arrow. Swimming in the ditch and flexing their muscles with his dad and brothers. Duke's mom, Elaine, jumping on the trampoline. And one of the entire family posing together on the front porch. Each picture held big smiles and the bright excitement of childhood on their faces.

A surge of sadness wove over me as I wondered what my life would have looked like in pictures if I'd had a dad. What would my mom have been like? Maybe we would have had a house? A photo of all of us on a fishing or camping trip? Maybe she would have had the time to take part in the PTA or help out in my elementary school classrooms. Maybe I'd have photo albums with my sisters wearing wide smiles and summer tan lines. This void I'd carried regarding my absentee father had never been a huge crushing blow because I'd never known any different. My mom's boyfriends were like characters in my life, not real people. My dad's absence became a punchline pushing away any heavy grief. Even though I knew Duke's family life hadn't been all stars and rainbows, it had been good, and looking at this beautiful family unit caused me to ache for something I'd never known to ache for.

"Brings back some fun memories of childhood, doesn't it?"

I laughed politely, even though she couldn't have been more wrong. "These make Duke's childhood seem very idyllic."

She tapped the book with her crooked finger. "We had a great time that summer, but don't let the highlight reel fool you. I also remember lots of crying and whining and plenty of attitude." She laughed. "And I would know because they left those kids with me quite a lot while they were trying to find a house. I had to find ways to keep them busy, or we all went crazy."

I smiled, tucking the hair behind my ear, grateful for her splash of realism in our conversation, and turned another page. I leaned forward, squinting at something that caught my eye.

"Is that the truck Duke drives now?"

Birdie leaned closer to examine the picture. "Yes. It was Bart's town truck for a lot of years. Duke used to drive it when he lived with us during the summers. When Bart mentioned putting it up for sale, he jumped all over it."

"Town truck?"

She smiled. "It's just farmer talk, hon. We have a truck for work, full of all kinds of random tools and dirt from the farm, and another truck we take to town and church."

"Didn't Duke's parents buy him a car?"

Birdie rolled her eyes. "A car way too expensive for any kid to be driving. Yes." A soft look came over her face. "But our Dukie never cared much about that kind of thing. He had a lot of good memories with Bart in that truck. A lot of good talks in there over the years. Bart sold it to him when Duke was in high school."

I could only nod, putting a few of Duke's puzzle pieces into place at her words.

"Tell me about your family."

It was almost like I had expected this question from her, a natural progression of our conversation. Birdie seemed different here, without Bart, who was so insistent on taking care of her. Though one of her eyes was especially cloudy, a sweet wisdom showed on her face. She would have sensed me holding back my answers, so I didn't. "It was just my mom and two sisters. I'm the oldest."

She nodded. "And you live in Salt Lake?"

"Yeah, in an apartment downtown."

"And what about your dad?"

"According to my mom, he was around a bit for my first year of life, until he turned eighteen, then he left." My mom had kept a blurry photo of him and her from high school for me, but that was all he'd been to me. A blurry picture.

She gasped lightly, indignant of my past. I smiled, if only to reassure her that it wasn't a big deal. I had never known the man, so how could I miss someone I never had? I glanced down at the photo album and swallowed.

"Do you have any memories of him?"

Why did I suddenly feel like crying? It wasn't like I ever thought of him. "No. I don't remember him at all, but I knew my grandma, and she used to tell me a few stories."

"I don't understand how people can leave their children like that."

I could. That was more real to me than the photos I saw of Duke's childhood. Those pictures looked like something out of a children's magazine I'd find in a doctor's office—full of sunshine and happiness.

"Well, Nora with an N…" Birdie smiled, her voice cracking

in the most pleasant way. "What are your intentions with our Duke?"

She sensed my deer-in-the-headlights reaction and added, "He'll never tell us, so I thought I might get a few answers from you." Her crooked fingers pressed lightly on my arm. "Woman to woman."

I breathed out an awkward laugh, my fingers twisting together underneath the table. "He's my boss, so…"

"Wrong answer. That man drools over you."

I drew my hands up to my cheeks to cover the flush. Her chuckle was deep and rich and warmed my soul.

"How did you two meet? In the office?"

Duke was going to kill me, but I wasn't about to lie to his grandmother. "We actually met a few years earlier at a basketball game."

Her eyes widened with excitement. "Wait. Are you the girl from the kiss cam?!"

An embarrassed smile lit my face as I ducked my head, surprised Duke would have told his grandparents. "Yes."

She stared at me in slight disbelief. "His friends teased him a great deal about you, you know that?"

My cheeks warmed at her confession, and I immediately tried to push past the feeling. "It was quite the night."

"So I heard." She nodded, a shine in her eyes. "So what are your intentions?"

My heart dropped. I had hoped we'd moved on from the awful question.

"He's my boss. We're just friends."

Birdie shook her head. "Sweetie, I may be almost blind, but you are not just friends."

My foot began to twitch uncontrollably at her knowing stare. "The thing is, I don't usually date."

Her brow furrowed. "What?"

I wanted to stop there, but saying I couldn't date her amazing grandson was something a girl had to explain. "It's just… I grew up watching my mom go through a lot of relationships when I was younger. And every divorce or breakup would leave us worse off than before. It would take us a long time to get back on our feet, and by then, she'd be dating another guy, and the whole cycle would start all over again." I tucked my hair behind my ear. I wasn't sure why Duke's grandmother was the person I decided to bare my soul to, but here we were. "I've always avoided relationships so I wouldn't get involved with anyone before I was ready. I need to be sure my family has a different life."

She blinked at me, a soft tsking noise coming from her throat. "I'm so sorry that happened to you."

I shifted nervously. I'd never really spoken this out loud. I wasn't sure why I felt compelled to do so here, but something in me had been craving a moment like this. With a woman with kind eyes and a soothing touch, just like Birdie.

"I've dated a few times, here and there, thinking I would be different than my mom, but I always ended up picking guys similar to my mom's relationships, even though I didn't think so at first." I braved a timid glance at her face and was relieved to find compassion in their depths. "I just…always wanted to be able to take care of myself first. And make sure I have a good job."

"Understandable." Her eyebrows lifted a fraction. She opened her mouth as if to speak but hesitated again before she asked, "What do you want out of this life, then?"

I desperately wanted to give her an easy answer, brush her off, but the earnest way she was looking at me told me she wasn't looking for brush-off answers. "A good job. Kids. A family."

"What does that look like to you?"

I smiled, happy I had an image I could convey. "I've always had this image of waking up in the morning in a nice house and making my kids breakfast before getting them off to school. I'd spend the day working at home, hopefully in graphic design, in my pajamas. That way, I could still be there for my kids, you know? Be around when they get home from school, join the PTA if I want to. I just want to be completely dependent on myself."

Memories of getting sick at school and having to go to a neighbor's house one door down from us to be watched until my mom got home from work had branded itself like something sour in my mind. She had been mean and grouchy and spent the whole time yelling at me while watching her soap operas.

"Seems very smart of you. Your future kids will be so grateful that you thought of them so much in that way."

I breathed a sigh of relief, grateful for her words. "I hope so."

Her fingers played with the frayed yellow tablecloth. "Can I ask you a question, then?"

"Sure."

"Do you want love?"

Though I feared it was a trick question, I answered honestly. "Yes."

"Where does a man fit into that scene you just described?"

I opened my mouth to say something, but the words ran dry. I thought again about my mental image of happiness. The nice house, loving kids, a job where I could provide for my children with everything I never had. I had always assumed there was a man. A husband. Somewhere. But where was he?

"I don't..." I started, but everything running through my mind felt hollow. With gentle eyes, she watched me start and stop my answer several times.

"You know, my experience is different, but you remind me a little of myself. Bart had to ask me three times to marry him before I finally said yes."

"You didn't want to marry him?" I asked, floored at this revelation.

"Heavens no." She squared her shoulders. "He wanted to be

a farmer. No, thank you. I had spent my whole life on a pig farm. I wasn't about to chain myself up to that for life."

"So how…" I trailed off.

"Well…" she began with a twinkle in her cloudy eyes. "He promised me it wouldn't be a pig farm."

I held on to her words, waiting for more, but nothing came. "That's it?" I asked, a teasing smile brimming my face. "You caved that easily?"

"Oh, honey, I was in love with Bart Bensen. There was no getting around it. Him promising there'd be no pigs was just the sprinkles on a cake already frosted. I was a goner, and to deny that would have destroyed me."

Her hands gently patted mine on the table. "Hope and fear like to think they can occupy the same space, but there is only room for one. It's up to you to decide. I picked Bart. Nobody can predict the future. We can only do the best we can. While you can certainly find happiness alone, if it's love you want, that partnership is codependent. You have to give some and take some, but overall, it's about trust. There are people who break trust and people who earn trust. I'm guessing most of your experience has been with the former."

One light breeze would break me, so I sat stiff as a board, willing the sudden wetness in my eyes to retreat.

"I had a sister who gave her kids a life similar to what I imagine your life might have been with your mother. She never had a particular idea of what she wanted in a boyfriend, so she took anyone who looked at her twice."

My eyes widened, feeling less alone with her words. "That sounds familiar."

"I thought so. But do you know what? My sister and I were related by blood. We shared a room. We were raised in the same house, had the same parents. But I never had that problem. Because I wasn't her. Just like you're not your mom. Even if you're scared you might be."

I sucked in a breath, wondering if everything I feared was written across my face for everyone to read.

Her gaze held mine in a trance for a long moment before she clasped my arm with her frail hand. "The point is, reward takes risk. Life is messy. People are messy. Nothing is ever going to be perfect, but oftentimes, it can be even better than perfect."

"Well, hell's bells! It's a summer miracle!"

Bart's exuberant shouting caused me to jump, breaking me out of my trance. We both looked over to see Bart and Duke striding in from the back door. My heart stopped for a moment, seeing what I had missed earlier. If you looked past the wrinkles, the white hair, and the frail body, Duke was the spitting image of his grandpa. It was the teasing expression and a sweet, almost earnest look in both of their faces. Now, I was suddenly curious to see if he could also pull off overalls and a plaid button-down shirt. The baseball hat I already knew he could pull off just fine.

"We got Duke's truck running!" Bart clapped his grinning grandson on his back.

"Yeah. Apparently it makes a big difference to have *all* the truck parts inside the truck when you try to start it," Duke said, looking at me in amusement.

After "one more *quick* game of rummy" that turned into four more *quick* games of rummy, a *quick* snack of Birdie's homemade banana bread she defrosted real *quick* from the freezer, a promise to call and update them on the website, and a mountain of hugs from the two charming and lonely rascals that I wished I could call my own, Duke and I climbed in his truck and began driving south.

We started the trip laughing over funny things his grandparents had said, but eventually, we grew quiet, both of us lost in thought.

"Idaho looks good on you," Duke finally said, as we eased onto the freeway.

"It felt good," I admitted, wondering if he was mourning the end of our time here as well.

"Which parts?" he asked, his dark eyes watching me under his baseball hat.

"Every single bit of it," I told him honestly.

I felt him consider me, but I kept my eyes locked on the road in front of us.

"It doesn't have to end, you know," his soft voice ventured between us, almost hesitantly.

"Do you worry we were just in a bubble here?"

He said nothing, but I watched the veins in his arm move as he flexed his hands on the wheel.

He cleared his throat. "Are you talking about when you made a move on me in the pond?"

A smile escaped me even as I tried to hold it in. "Yup. When you forced me to do the lift and then I proceeded to—" I stopped, suddenly realizing we probably didn't need a play by play. At least I didn't. I had re-lived every kiss and touch between us like a movie in my head before falling asleep last night.

"Don't stop there. What did you do to me?"

I reached out to give him a light push on his arm. In retaliation, he grabbed my hand and pulled, barely giving me time to unbuckle my seatbelt before he forced me to scoot next to him on the bench seat. I mean…I put up a really big fuss.

My new seat had significantly less leg room with the gear stick in the middle, which meant my left leg was pressed quite firmly against Duke's leg, which meant I felt his movement every time he pressed on the gas or the brake.

We had just pulled onto the freeway when his hand dropped lightly on my knee. I threw him a questioning glance, but he only grinned. "It's just easier this way, for when I need to shift."

We drove for a while in the quiet, his hand on my knee and my heart on my sleeve.

"What was it you were worried about?" Duke asked, his hat slung low across his forehead. "Something about being in a bubble?"

That word brought me back to earth. Bubble. Yes. Boundaries. All things usually so second-nature to me finally reawakened and began edging their way past Duke's warm hand palming my knee. I forced myself to think of words to say.

I swallowed. "You're my boss," I said, in case he had forgotten. "And I'm not sure what we do with this." I motioned to my being practically in his lap and his hand now moving upward a few inches on my leg. "I need to focus these next few weeks on my project. I just..." My voice trailed off as Birdie's words began to make mine sound shallow to my ears. "You just got out of a big relationship, and I need to figure out my life and job stuff," I said, as excuses began pouring off my lips. "I'm a mess, Duke. You don't really want a mess. You shouldn't even be thinking about...and maybe you're not. And that's fine. Great, even. I just..."

My words trailed off as Duke pressed on the brake and pulled to a stop on the shoulder of the freeway. I whipped around, looking for the reason we were stopping. Maybe there was a lookout? But I saw nothing, except the *Welcome to Utah* sign sitting directly in front of us.

"What are you doing?"

He parked the truck and unbuckled his seatbelt before reaching across me to do the same with mine. Before I knew what was happening, he was pulling me from the truck, his hand in mine, and walking me to the other side, out of the immediate view of traffic. He pressed me lightly back against the passenger side door.

I was still trying to catch up as cars whirred past.

"What are you doing?" I asked again. His face held a range of emotions, some I couldn't read, but there was fire in his eyes.

"You need some space? Fine. You want us quiet at work?

Fine. You want to work on your project? Great. It would make it a lot easier if you won the whole thing. But don't put yourself down. And don't put words in my mouth."

I sucked in a breath as the heat from his eyes scattered across every part of my face.

"I'm your boss in Utah." He motioned to the Utah sign. "There are rules there and things we can't do. Things I can't say. But we're not in Utah right now and I'm not ready to play by the rules just yet."

Before I could think or blink or build walls, his hands were at my neck, pulling me close, and his mouth was on mine. I breathed him in—as his lips became words spilling secrets I hadn't even dared to hope for. Some things he told me slowly—achingly soft—like the tenderness of a whisper and the lightness of a feather. Over and over, he brushed the words against my skin until I was a breath away from curling up in his arms. Some parts spilled out in a rush, fast and furious, with hands in my hair, tugging and tasting and boiling over with heat and haze.

I told him things too.

Secret things.

Worries and wounds camouflaged and concealed deep inside of my heart.

They came out in gasps and sighs as his lips made a trail along my jawline. It wasn't thoughts of being like my mother that had me pulling away and demanding space before nestling closer, resenting the distance. Birdie had been right. I wasn't my mom. I would never be her. Instead, I let my fingertips trail across the line of his jaw and the stubble at his cheeks, and I begged him to be gentle with me. To be patient while I figured out what to do with all the wants and needs and fears threatening to drown me. Then he cradled my face and pressed a kiss to my forehead, and the fear began to quiet once more as hope burrowed its way through my chest. A dichotomy of light and dark, dancing and swirling until I was left dizzy with emotion.

I broke from his lips, breathing heavily and fighting against the part of myself that wanted to still be kissing him.

"You know you're still my boss here too, right?"

"Shut up." His mouth was smiling as it took over mine again.

Sometime later he pulled back, his dark gaze taking in my face while his finger brushed a strand of hair off my cheek. A soft smile played across his lips, as if he liked what he saw, which was probably a very dazed expression.

I blinked, coming back to myself, and the breeze in the air, and the fact that cars still flew past us on the freeway. I looked around trying to find something to recenter my brain around. I had quite possibly had the best kiss of my entire life on the side of this freeway and I needed to shake up the thoughts that were seriously considering pulling his face back to mine again. I blew out a shaky breath as my eye caught on something that made me smile. And no, it wasn't Duke this time. We were still in Idaho after all, and I had just thought of one more thing.

"Are you up for checking another thing off the bucket list?"

"Huh?"

I laughed, feeling lighter than air, for some reason. "I've always wanted to be in two places at once, like in *A Walk to Remember*."

He followed my finger pointing toward the *Welcome to Utah* sign and smiled.

"Well, you're in luck. I've always wanted to kiss you in two places at once."

And so we did.

Amid the noise and honks of every car that passed, Duke grabbed my hand and we waded through weeds and sagebrush before coming to a stop on the other side of the sign, where we proceeded to check one more thing off the old bucket list.

23

THE NEXT THREE WEEKS IN UTAH FLEW BY IN A RUSH OF HIGHS and lows.

One of the highs happened a few days after we returned from our trip to Idaho. Maybe high wasn't quite the right word. But low wasn't right either. Either way, Duke had stayed late for a meeting with his company from Japan. We were the only two left in the office. Since I knew Duke was still around, I made sure to clean the bathrooms first, so he wouldn't try to do it with me. Having his help cleaning the windows and taking out the trash somehow felt less of an imposition, since he was so insistent on lending a hand. I was cleaning the windows in the main office when Duke found me.

"Still here, Kiss Cam?"

I turned at the bridled excitement lacing his voice. He looked handsome in his gray suit, which was a bit wrinkled after a full day of work. His hair was disheveled on top, like he'd been running his hands through it. But his eyes sparkled like a kid on Christmas morning.

"What's going on?" I asked, turning to face him as he approached.

He stopped a few paces away, a smile breaking free at my question. Then he moved again, back and forth, pacing excitedly.

"You know that company I've been working with? The one in Japan?"

"Yeah."

"They hired us."

"I thought they had already?"

"They hired us for a small project on a trial basis—to see how they liked working with us. Tenisha and I did a few websites for them and designed a couple small marketing packages. But they just told me they want us to put together some huge marketing campaigns for them. And their *five* other businesses in the US."

My mouth fell open as I beamed at him. "Are you serious? That's amazing. So all this time, you weren't lying about meeting with Japan?"

He laughed. "Nope."

"What are they having you do for them?"

"TV spots, interviews, websites, radio, everything. It's a huge win for our company."

"I'm so proud of you. That's awesome."

"Thanks."

We both went for a hug at the same time. It was only natural, right? To give someone a hug when they accomplished something amazing. I was proud of Duke. I still held the bottle of cleaner in one hand and my squeegee in another during the hug, so it made it a little awkward, but nothing we couldn't work through. His cheek was warm as it pressed against mine. I breathed him in, appreciating that he still wore the same cologne as he did the night of the basketball game.

A throat cleared.

"Knock, knock."

We broke apart as we turned at the sound of a man's voice. Duke's parents stood there by the entrance, watching us with raised eyebrows. Looking closely, I could see the resemblance to the young father in Birdie's pictures, but the man staring at us now, wearing a fancy polo shirt and dress pants, was a far cry from one I'd seen playing with his sons and flexing his muscles. At my side, Duke stiffened.

It was his mom who spoke first, her quiet eyes taking in every detail, from the way Duke's shoulder pressed against mine to the cleaning supplies in my hands. She was dressed in jeans and a t-shirt and looking more casual than her husband. She held up a Tupperware container.

"Dad told me you weren't going to make it to our family dinner tonight because you had to work late again. We thought we'd come say hi and bring you some dinner."

Duke blinked and stepped forward, remembering himself. He gave his mom a hug and took the container from her hand. "I just got out of my meeting. Thanks."

His parent's eyes flitted over to me once more and I might as well have been an elephant standing in the room for as out of place as I felt.

"Who's this?" Duke's dad asked, nodding toward me.

We all waited, myself included, to see what Duke would say. He didn't disappoint. At least, he didn't disappoint…*me*.

He walked back over to me and put his arm around my shoulder. "This is Nora. She works for us and is a good friend of mine. Nora," he motioned toward his parents, "these are my parents, Roger and Elaine."

"Nora?" A puzzle came over Elaine's face. "Grandma and Grandpa told us you brought a girl named Nora to their house over the weekend."

I smiled, pushing aside my nerves to speak like a human person to these people. "Hi." Duke's arm was still currently around my shoulder and something about his touch grounded me in this moment, so instead of walking forward, I gave them a little wave. "For one of my projects with RDM, I'm creating a website and logo for Bart and Birdie's company. Duke came with me this weekend to introduce me to them so I could get started."

"So, do you work at RDM?" Roger's eyes drifted over to my cleaning cart.

"I'm an intern," I supplied, brushing a strand of hair behind my ear.

"Nora's the hardest worker you'll ever meet," Duke added with a smile. "By day she's an intern, at night she cleans our office building and another upstairs."

Elaine looked thoughtful, processing this news, but Roger began getting fidgety. With jerky movements and sharp huffs of breath, I felt my nerves rising. Though Duke didn't make any big movements, he seemed to be waiting for something.

Roger didn't make us wait long.

"For hell's sake, Duke. Is this your meeting?" He threw his hand out and motioned toward us both. "Cleaning the office? You've been at this company for three years. In three years I had already expanded the car wash into a franchise and was working on building up another business. You have to think bigger. How many more times will it take for this to sink in? You have to use money to make money. Please take our loan and get going. You're wasting so much time." At this point, he was pacing, using his flailing hands to emphasize his tone and drive home the message. And he wasn't done. "As an owner, you shouldn't be concerned about some of these businesses you're putting your time into. I know you love your grandparents. We all do. But their little wood carving business isn't going to change a thing for your company. Send the intern to take care of that. I was ticked when I found out you went there this weekend to help someone do it, though," he motioned toward me, "now I under-stand why you wanted to."

"Roger," Elaine warned, pulling on his arm.

"Just a sec, hun." He took a breath before sending one more pleading look toward Duke. "As the owner of a company, you can't spend your time making five dollar decisions. That's someone else's job. It's your job to make the million dollar decisions. Or else this isn't going anywhere. You have people working under you that depend on you to make this company a success. You might make a living, but if you keep things up this way, you're never going to make a life."

Elaine sighed, as though she'd heard this same argument many times between these two men she loved. Duke had remained rigid by my side, his arms folded and almost pulling off a passive air, if not for the twitch of his jaw. But he didn't say anything. He looked beaten down by his father's words and seeing it made my blood begin to heat.

I had many emotions when they suddenly showed up here. At first, I was embarrassed to be caught hugging their son. When their eyes took in my dirt-stained clothes and my cleaning cart, I wanted to hide. I didn't want to make Duke look bad in front of his parents. That thought shamed me now. Duke hadn't looked or acted embarrassed by me, so why should I be? My cleaning job wasn't something to be embarrassed about. I was suddenly so proud of working. Of this job. Of making sure this office was spotless each night. Even when I could hardly keep my eyes open and my limbs felt like they weighed a thousand pounds, I came here, I did my job, and then I came back to do it again the next day. There was something satisfying in that. There was something satisfying about getting my hands dirty and the lessons I learned every time I did. And while I appreciated Roger's insight about million dollar decisions, there was a place for both. Because both were necessary.

There were so many things to be proud of in Duke. If his own father didn't see that, then someone would have to tell him.

"I've got something to say." My voice sounded stronger than it did in my head and for that, I was grateful. I put my cleaning supplies back in my cart and turned to face them.

His mom watched me curiously, his dad in disbelief.

Here goes nothing.

"You guys should feel so proud of your son. He and his friends made this company from nothing. In three years they outgrew their garage, hired over fifteen employees, and just tonight won a huge client. Duke was bouncing off the walls before you walked in and ruined that." I reached over to clutch Duke's arm but I didn't look at him. I was scared he'd tell me to stop, but I was just getting started.

"Duke is here working hard every day. He's laughing with all his employees, he's making this office a fun, comfortable space where people *want* to be here. Everyone loves him. But you know what he also does? He pays attention to the little things. If he finds me still here cleaning, he picks up a brush and helps. Even when I beg him to stop, he still does it. Because he appreciates every aspect of every job that runs a business."

Roger snorted, "With all due respect, Nora, I don't think that's why he's—"

"It is," I said, arms folded, blocking hits and taking down names. "Because he's got the best heart of anybody I've ever known."

I couldn't believe I'd interrupted Duke's father, but I couldn't stop even if I wanted to, the words were spilling out of me. I could feel Duke looking at me.

"I have no doubt that you're a brilliant businessman. There are probably lots of things Duke would love to learn from you, but if he told you he doesn't want your money, you need to respect that."

"There aren't too many people in this world who would refuse free money to help grow their business," Roger said slowly, exasperation rimmed on every word he spat.

"I don't want it, Dad," Duke said quietly, his hands disappearing into his pockets. "I appreciate the offer, I really do, but I want to do this my own way."

Roger stared at his son in disbelief. Elaine bounced back and forth from me to Duke and then to Roger. He blew a heated blast of air from his nose and let out a dry laugh and held his hand out toward his wife. "Well, Elaine, I guess we'd better go. We can't fix crazy."

Duke ran a hand through his hair and made a noise as though he'd heard that phrase a hundred times.

One time was enough for me.

"Maybe you could learn a few things from him? Did you ever think of that?" Roger's annoyed eyes landed on mine like I was a bug he'd like to squash. My stomach clenched inside, but on the outside I was a force to be reckoned with. "There are so many things you miss in life when you pass off everything you deem not worth your time. Things too small for you. But the five dollar decisions are where the people are. Where humanity is. That's where the real lessons are learned. Even you had to start somewhere, and shame on you if you've forgotten that. You were mad that he wasted a whole Saturday to come work on a five dollar business. But if you could have seen the look on Bart and Birdie's faces when he showed up, I don't think anyone would have called that a waste. They broke down his truck so he wouldn't leave. That's the kind of stuff that fuels the world. He's got an office of employees he genuinely cares about and is creating a company they'd want to spend a lifetime working for. So yeah, this business could probably explode with your help, but I'd say he's doing just fine growing it on his own."

The well of words building inside of me had finally run dry, leaving me a panting, sweaty ball of rapidly diminishing fire. I braved a glance at Duke. I would have laughed if it wasn't so sweet. He was looking at me with a stunned expression, his eyebrows furrowed as though he was trying to compute everything that just happened. But there was another expression on his face, one that made it all worth it. Relief. After a moment, he smiled at me.

I turned back to his parents. Elaine looked the most

approachable. Roger had his arms folded and looked like he had more to say, but his wife's hand on his arms seemed enough to keep him from speaking.

Clearing my throat, I said, "I apologize if I overstepped, but—"

"No apology necessary." Elaine said, smiling at me ever so slightly. "I think you made some excellent points. We're going to get out of your hair, but Nora, I hope we see you again."

I knew Roger had more to say, but Elaine coaxed him out the door, with a promise to come visit another day. And then they were gone.

After a long moment of standing together in a sort of shocked silence, Duke looked over at me.

"What. Was. That?" Duke spoke the words slowly, incredulously.

My hands covered my face. I didn't regret the words, but I'd hate myself if Duke regretted me saying them. Maybe I should have asked. Maybe yelling at his dad made him feel less like a man. Oh my gosh, I yelled at his dad. His big business, high profile dad. I didn't just yell at him, I gave him *advice*. I assumed so many things about him, I—

I slowly felt myself being pulled into Duke's arms. His touch released a sigh and a smile from me at the same time. My head fell against his chest.

"I don't think I would have ever had the guts to say all of those things to his face like that."

"I don't know what came over me. I hated the way he spoke to you and I couldn't help it. I'm sorry if I shouldn't have—"

His arms around me squeezed gently. "That was amazing. Thank you. I've never had anybody stick up for me like that."

He held me close for a long moment, my head tucked below his chin, before I felt a brush of his lips on my forehead, making the fact that his dad probably now hated me, worth it.

A FEW DAYS LATER, Cathy acquired another office suite in the building to clean, and I asked her to add it to my schedule. She'd been concerned at how late that would have me leaving the building at night, but all I could see were dollar signs. The weight of my student loan wore so heavily on my mind, and I wanted nothing more than to be rid of it. My weekend in Idaho had been like a fuzzy dream, giving me a taste of what life could be, until I stepped back into my reality in Salt Lake. Now, I wanted nothing more than to be rid of the debt and the physical reminder of how far I still had to go to achieve my dreams. If I didn't get the position at RDM, I'd have to save up for tuition again, but saving and paying for both at the same time would take too long. If I could dedicate myself and pay the whole thing off in less than a year, I could put it behind me and not think of it ever again. In fact, I'd pretend the whole thing never happened.

I didn't want Duke to find out about me adding a new floor to my shift, because I knew he'd insist on helping me. And more than that, it was hard to concentrate on my goals in life when I had Duke's full attention. He had a way of scrambling my head and altering my brain chemistry. Too much time spent in close proximity and his gaze would turn heated, and I'd start reminiscing about the pond and the way his lips had trailed up my neck and kissed just under my ear.

Yes. A little separation was responsible. And I told him so. We both had jobs to do and with Anita's eyes trailing me everywhere, I didn't want anything to jeopardize Duke's credibility or my chance at this job.

He granted me space, but an ice-cold Dr. Pepper began showing up on my desk every morning. And some days, that was everything. That is, until he began to get suspicious.

"Nora. Can I see you in my office, please?"

I hesitated until I felt Anita's eyes on me. Duke had tried

texting me several times, but I always found a way to ignore his pressing question. I had no interest in explaining myself, but he called my name loud enough that the entire office heard him. He was my boss, and I had to go.

He wasted no time when I closed the door to his office.

"Why haven't I seen you cleaning after work? Did you switch offices?" His intense gaze settled on me. Sexy, smoldering Duke in a suit at his desk was back, and he was almost hard to look at.

"No."

"Where are you, then? I stayed late the past couple nights—" when I started to say something, he lifted his hands up in a pacifying gesture and continued, "for *meetings,* and you were nowhere around. But the office is always clean the next day."

It wasn't his business. Boss Duke couldn't make me tell him anything. But Friend Duke would pull it out of me eventually.

"I added another office to my routine. I do RDM last, and it puts me here an hour or so later."

"What?" Duke nearly exploded. "You can't do that. You're already working until after nine most nights as it is. Can't they ask someone else?"

"I wanted to take it."

His gaze grew incredulous. "Why?"

I waited a long moment, trying to decide how to answer. "Are you my boss right now, Duke, or my friend?" I asked.

He sighed, running a hand through his hair. "I'm just Duke."

I fidgeted under his stare. "I'm hoping to work really hard and throw everything I make toward my loan to get it paid off in a year. If I try saving for tuition while I'm still paying the loan, it will take too long." My eyes shifted, unable to watch the range of emotions crossing his face.

"You can't keep up that schedule. You're working yourself into exhaustion."

"I'll be fine."

"I'm coming to help you every night."

"No, you're not." I marched forward to his desk, shaking my finger at him. "Duke, that's not why I told you. Lots of people have two jobs. It's only for a year. I can do this, and I don't want your help."

His jaw clenched, and his fists tightened, but ultimately, he sighed and nodded slowly. I walked out of his office not really knowing if I'd won the argument.

As I got closer to finishing the website, I'd had a few lovely phone calls with Bart and Birdie. It was always on speaker phone, usually going something like this:

Me (trying my best to project my voice without yelling directly into the phone): "Is there anything you'd like different on the About Us page?"

Bart: "What'd she say?"

Birdie (louder): "She asked about the page with our pictures on it."

Bart: "Oh, the one where they snuck a picture of me necking my woman? That's my favorite page."

Birdie: "Oh, Bart! Go do your chores. I'll talk with Nora alone."

Me (laughing by this point): "Wait! Don't go yet! Did you both have a chance to double-check all the prices for the furniture pieces? Does anything need to be changed?"

Bart: "What did she say?"

Birdie: "She asked..."

AND SO ON. The exchanges became a highlight of my week but somehow left an ache inside of my chest as well. I had known my two grandmothers, but never a grandpa. I'd never witnessed grandparents together before. I'd never seen the interaction of two people so weathered with age and experience and love.

Eventually, things with Duke and me smoothed over. True to his word, he didn't try to help me clean, though there were a few nights when all the garbage at RDM had been taken out before I arrived.

Our soda notes eventually morphed into texts—Anita being the sole reason. Anytime Duke wandered in my direction, I was given self-righteous looks and snide remarks. Our texting also became more informational.

> **Duke:** *Want to hear something crazy? My dad stopped by my place the other night and told me he was sorry if he'd been too pushy.*
>
> **Me:** *What did you say? P.S. Your tie is crooked.*
>
> **Duke:** *Thanks, Kiss Cam. I told him I'd much rather golf with him than talk business.*
>
> **Me:** *Nice! Very proud. Teach me your ways.*
>
> **Duke:** *It's all thanks to you. He's also terrible at golf. I win every time.*

Two days later I had my own happy news.

> **Me:** *So, guess what? My mom actually paid back some of what she owed me.*
>
> **Duke:** *Really? Only part? P.S. Red is your color. Also all the other colors.*
>
> **Me:** *Stop, you. Seriously, I'm stunned. In a good way. She's never paid me back for anything.*
>
> **Duke:** *Maybe a Lipper from Kipper's been good for her.*

Me: *Ewwwwww.*

ALL IN ALL, the final project had come together relatively easily, and having complete creative control over a project had left me on a high I'd never experienced in a work setting before. The end of the month was approaching fast, however, and I was beginning to worry that everything I had done wouldn't be enough. *I* might not be enough. It was one thing to say *may the best man win,* but I *really* wanted to win. More than that…I *needed* to win.

———

I ARRIVED EARLY at RDM's staff meeting with my nose in my phone, attempting to pay my student loan bill online. I had tried the past few days but kept getting an error message whenever I clicked send. The app had been spotty before, so I wasn't overly surprised when another error message popped up on my phone. I made a mental note to try again the next day. My payment was due in a few days, and I didn't want to be charged extra for falling behind. I sat down next to Tenisha and shoved my phone inside my pocket.

"How's your project coming?" Tenisha asked, leaning toward me in her seat.

"Good. I think. I hope." The self-doubt was definitely there.

"You got this. Just don't embarrass me."

I managed a laugh. "That's my number one priority."

"Good."

Duke and the rest of the owners came into the break room. After making the rounds, shaking hands and greeting everyone, Duke sat down in the chair next to me. He was supposed to be giving me space, but considering the way his elbow shifted into way too familiar territory with my elbow, I began to wonder if his idea of space was as spacious as mine.

"Anybody have any bucket list updates?"

"Nora was just telling me about her bucket list," Duke announced.

The entire room looked at me, and I startled, suddenly feeling like my emotions were onstage for the office.

I forced a smile, discreetly pushing Duke's elbow off the armrest. "Yeah. I rode a motorcycle." Though, to be fair, the term *motorcycle* was definitely an exaggeration.

"And was it everything your dreams were made of?" Mike asked, the orange of his button-down shirt nearly blinding my retinas.

I looked at his face. He definitely knew. Did Duke tell these guys everything?

"It was okay."

Duke coughed.

Mike grinned before turning his attention back to the rest of the board room. "Anybody else?"

Duke raised his hand. "Finally got one checked off."

To Mike's credit, he didn't look directly at me, but I could tell that it took some effort.

"Go on."

"Got my movie scene reenactment out of the way."

"Which movie was it again?" Mike asked innocently.

"That's classified," Duke said. "But I will say, Hollywood's got nothing on us."

"Us?" Anita asked, leaning forward in her chair, a wolfhound on the scent.

"Me," Duke amended, his elbow back in its place next to mine.

The rest of the office chuckled. Another employee raised their hand, talking about finally getting to take the Fun Bus to Wendover, Nevada to go gambling.

CINDY STEEL

When the attention had moved to the other side of the room,
I leaned slightly against Duke's arm before teasing softly,
"Nothing on you?"

"I didn't hear any complaints."

His smile just for me spoke of secrets and teasing and something else that made me swallow and glance away. I spent a
lovely few seconds enjoying the post-Duke-interaction glow that
seemed to happen more and more frequently. I allowed myself to
revel in it—until a certain darkness cast a pall upon me. I looked
up and met the eyes of Anita, who was staring at me with her
eyebrows raised before looking pointedly at my arm squished
next to Duke's on the armrest.

I didn't want to remove my arm. I shouldn't have to remove
anything. My arm was on my armrest. Duke's was on his. It
wasn't my fault he chose to scoot his chair a mere one millimeter
from mine. Anita shot daggers in my direction, however, and
eventually, I moved my arm and folded it across my stomach. I
felt Duke's questioning gaze but kept looking at Anita, feeling
gratified when she turned away first. I snuck a glance at Duke,
only to see him also staring toward Anita.

Very soon after, tingles shot up from my ankle to my hip as
his leg pressed against mine underneath the table. It was all I
could do to keep from soaring out of the room.

24

TWO DAYS BEFORE THE PROJECTS WERE DUE, I ARRIVED TO WORK early, sat down at my desk, and went through the motions of turning on my computer, gathering papers, and putting my purse away. I even attempted to look busy. I said hi to Shawn and gave my best smile to Anita, though she only stared vacantly through my attempt at pleasantry. She really should have taken me up on what I was offering, because I was feeling anything but pleasant at the moment. If looks could kill, I would have murdered Duke Webber a hundred times today already.

When Duke finally arrived and stepped into his office, I bolted out of my chair. I didn't even knock. I strode inside and closed the door behind me. He had just sat down and looked up at me in surprise. My hands were clenched by my side while a sick ache filled my stomach.

"Hey, Kiss Cam. What are—"

"Did you pay off my student loan?" I wasted no time on pleasantries, even though he was wearing the navy blue suit I loved, and it was honestly hard tearing my eyes away. I swallowed nervously but stood my ground.

He held my gaze for a long moment, probably trying to

gauge how to proceed. No need to think too hard, Duke Webber. I just wanted the truth.

"Did you pay off my student loan?" I asked again, slower.

"Yes." He blinked, but there was not even a crumb of remorse on his face. "It was supposed to be anonymous."

"Yes?" I repeated softly, the feeling of betrayal like a knife in my back.

"Yes," he said again.

I walked forward, pulled a wad of cash out of my jeans pocket, and slapped it onto his desk. My life savings over the past few weeks.

"I'll get you another payment next month."

I was about to walk out, guns firing, in all my dramatic glory, when his voice stopped me.

"Nora!"

I turned to see Duke's eyes blazing as he stood up, my cash in his hand.

"I'm not taking this."

I took a step closer, holding my body stiff and rigid. "If you think, for one second, it's okay to do that without even asking me, you've got another thing coming. I don't want to owe anyone anything. Okay? If you haven't understood that fact about me this whole summer, then you don't know me at all." My words were biting and jumbled and laced with hurt as I pointed and accused. He crossed the room, slowing when he grew closer, but he didn't stop. I didn't flinch, even for the fire in his eyes.

"If you think I did that to hold something over you, then you don't know *me* at all," he said, spitting the words between us. "You don't owe me anything. You could walk out that door right now and I never see you again, and I'd still do it. I'd do it again tomorrow. I'd do it a thousand times over." At his continued approach, I took a step back, bumping into the wall as he contin-ued, "I've been lucky. This new business has done well."

"But your dad—"

"It's done well for *me*. Maybe not by his standards, but I don't care anymore. The point is, this money meant nothing to me, but it was everything to you. I wanted to help, so I did."

"You can't just do that to somebody. I was taking care of it. I was getting it done."

"I know it. And you would have. But at what cost? Working yourself to the bone every night? Only to end up using the money you saved to help your mom out?" He shook his head. "I didn't do it to save you, or so you would owe me, or whatever's in your head."

I bolted forward. "Then why?"

"Because you needed a break, and you've never had one." He took a few steps closer, my chest heaving between us. "I did it because I could. Simple as that." He reached out, his fingers hooking into the belt loops at the waist of my jeans, tugging me closer as he stuffed the paltry wad of cash back into my pocket. "I don't want anything from you beyond a tiny fraction of worry to leave your face."

"I don't like the feeling of you doing that." I stared hard at him, begging him to understand.

Though his words had put out the roaring fire inside of me, the coals were still flickering. I needed him to understand that it wasn't okay. I couldn't accept his help. The audacity and the nerve heated my blood to boiling.

He closed the gap between us, bringing his hand softly to my chin, pulling my gaze up to his. "I understand what you're saying. I do. And I'm sorry if it made you uncomfortable, but I'm not sorry I did it." His eyes studied my lips for a moment, causing my insides to ache, before he lifted them to mine once more. "One day, when all the stars align for you, maybe you'll date someone. Maybe you'll get married. And I sure as hell hope that guy helps you shoulder a few of your burdens. Not because he doesn't think you're capable. Not because he wants to control you. But because he loves you." He bent down closer, the heat from his words breathing life into my ear. "And I hope you let him."

With those words, he straightened, stepping around me to yank open his door, and walked out.

———

EVERY BONE in my body felt like it had been run over by a truck as I pulled into my apartment complex at eleven-thirty that night. The extra floor had apparently had a birthday party that day, complete with a piñata. It had taken me thirty minutes to vacuum up the confetti and birthday cake I'd found smashed into the floor. I really didn't want Duke to be right about this schedule being too much for me to handle, but I was certain I could fall down and sleep like the dead for a week. But I couldn't sleep yet. I had a few things to discuss with my dear, backstabbing roommate.

Mira was brushing her teeth in the bathroom when I trudged through the door. She didn't have to work tonight. She wore joggers and an oversized sweatshirt, her hair in a bun. It reminded me of the old days, when we used to stay up late together and watch movies. How long had it been since I'd watched a movie with her? I mentally slapped myself. No time to get sentimental. I was angry right now.

She knew what I was about in one glance at my face, which honestly made me nervous about my temper after such a long, stressful day. She spit, rinsed, and turned to look at me.

"Alright, listen," she began.

"How could you let him do that?" I asked at the same time.

Instantly, her voice became defensive. "Do what? Help you out? Care about you? Do you know what you have in him?"

"How did it even happen?"

Her arms folded across her chest. "He stopped by a week ago

while he knew you were cleaning. He told me what he wanted to do, and I…gave him your bill."

"You know about my life better than anybody. How I've always felt, watching my mom's worthless boyfriends buying her crap all the time, right up until they bailed. It wasn't okay then, and it isn't now. I don't understand how you think giving him access to my bill wasn't going to break me." I walked back into my room, flinging my purse and phone onto my bed.

She followed at my heels. "Yeah, they bought necklaces and fancy clothes. They bought her affection. They used her to make themselves feel like big men. Duke took a *burden* away from you. Quietly. Because he is so in love with you he can't stand to see you hurting." She shook her head. "I don't know about you, but I kind of feel like that's a huge difference—and pretty freaking hot, if you think about it."

"I just…" I threw my arms out. "What am I supposed to do with all of this? He did this big, horrible, nice thing, and I'm just sitting with it. It's going to eat away at me as much as the dumb bill was."

She grew sympathetic, leaning against the doorway. "I get that. Your thoughts are valid, but I honestly think he doesn't want you to sit with it. He wants you to forget the whole thing. He wants to date you, and he can't do that if you're working until midnight every night." When I didn't say anything, she added, "I wouldn't have given him the bill if I didn't completely adore what he was trying to do. Sometimes you need to let people help you."

"He's not…family, though. He's…my boss."

She shot me a look. "No. Stop lying to yourself. First of all, who in your family is going to help you? And second, that guy is your best friend." When I raised my eyebrows at her, she smiled. "After me, of course. He's crazy about you, and you're crazy about him. So just shut up and let him love you."

"You shut up," I spat, like an indignant child.

We faced off against each other for a long moment until we were both fighting off smiles.

"I'm right and you know it!" She jabbed an arrogant finger toward me before she left the room. A few minutes later I heard the sound of the TV on. She generally tried to keep to her night-shift schedule even on her days off. I stayed in my room, lying on my bed in the dark.

I didn't want her words to make sense or make me feel better. My anger was justified. He had completely overstepped. But her words *did* make sense. Duke was a good guy. The best. I'd never had anyone care for me like he seemed to. It was as discon-certing as it was undeniably flattering. It scratched at the same time it caressed. I didn't know what to do with all my feelings. My head was readying for battle while my heart skipped a beat.

A perfect mix of hope and fear.

25

THE MORNING OF OUR FINAL REVEAL, AND WHAT COULD BE MY last day of work, I stepped out of the elevator, my nerves inside rubbing me raw. There was so much riding on today. It felt ridiculous to boil my entire future down to something that was now completely out of my hands. I had emailed in my project late last night, just before the midnight deadline.

Duke and I had given each other a wide berth yesterday, our argument from the day before weighing heavy on my mind at least, and I assumed on Duke's as well. He hardly walked by my desk. There were no notes either, and what was worse, I found myself craving Dr. Pepper all day long.

If I didn't get this job, I'd be back to square one. Last night, in order to rest my chaotic mind, I made plans to pay Duke back. I didn't want to completely negate his kindness, so I planned to pay him back over three years instead of one. That way, I could still save up for tuition. If, by some miracle, I did get this job, then I could pay him off much quicker because my education would be taken care of.

"Hey, Nora." Tenisha interrupted my thoughts, smiling at me

from her desk as I made my way toward my cubicle. "You look nice."

I looked down at my floral top and black pants. I had planned to go thrifting for a new outfit before today, but with all the late nights, I hadn't had any time. I wore the same outfit I wore on my first day at RDM.

"Thanks."

She nodded toward my briefcase. "You ready?"

"I think so. I've done the best I could do, so there's that."

Her eyes scanned my face as though she didn't believe me, before she waved me away. "Better get to work. I left a few assignments on your desk, mostly to keep you busy so you don't drive yourself crazy. The meeting is at three o'clock."

"Thanks. That's so nice of them to squeeze one last day of work from us all before they sack two of us."

She laughed and waved me on.

From Tenisha's desk, there was no route to my desk that didn't take me past Anita. Like any great predator, she had seen me coming from a mile away. She plastered on a smile and raised her hand in greeting.

"Good luck today, Nora."

"Thanks."

Her eyes trailed me as I made to step past her desk before she spoke again. "Oh. Guess who I saw at the gym yesterday?"

Her sickeningly sweet voice made her question feel like a trap, but I couldn't think of anybody we'd both know.

"Who?"

"Rachel." She motioned toward Duke's office. "We chatted for a while and she was asking about Duke. It's pretty clear she's still in love with him. The break up must have really tore her up."

I blinked. My mouth opened to say something before closing again. "Why are you telling me this?"

She shrugged, brushing a dark strand of hair off of her shoulder. "Oh, no reason. I would just hate to see somebody become some sort of rebound to him. Three years is a long time for feelings to just…disappear."

"Anita, shut up," a male voice at the next desk spat out. My eyes flicked over as Shawn rolled his chair into my view and rolled his eyes. I gave him a grateful nod, thankful that, no matter what happened, this was Anita's and my last day together.

I made it to my desk just as Duke stepped out of his office. He looked like he'd had about as good of a night as I had. His hair was messy up top, almost as if he'd run his hand through it all morning. His eyes were almost wild with some emotion I couldn't quite place. When he looked me full on, it was the kind of look that stopped me in my tracks. The kind that put me in a trance.

My purse made a thud as I dropped it on my desk. Duke paused outside his door and watched me. All I could do was watch him back. My heart picked up speed when he ambled toward my desk.

"How does the website look?" he asked softly.

"Want to see it?" I wasn't sure why I was whispering too. Probably because I could practically hear Anita taking notes.

"Yeah."

He stood behind me as I turned on my computer, the low hum of the machine sputtering to life the only noise between us. His hands moved in and out of his pockets, fidgeting.

"Actually, Nora. Can I see you in my office?"

My hands that were reaching to type in my passcode for my computer stilled in mid-air. There was meaning behind those words. They hinted that, one way or another, we would not be the same people coming out of his office as we were going inside.

At my hesitation, he pleaded, "Please?"

Without a word, I stood, ignored Anita's self-righteous look thrown my way, and followed him into his office. He shut the door behind him, and I moved forward and turned to face him, my legs nearly touching his desk. Duke stood in front of the door, his arms crossed.

"Are you alright?" he asked. He didn't embellish or elaborate, but I knew what he meant. I drew in a shaky breath.

"I'm trying to be, but I don't know."

"Alright. Let's have this out. Yell at me or whatever you need to do. I can't handle not talking about it."

"Are you sorry you did it?" I asked, suddenly curious if my reaction made him wish he'd handled things differently.

"Not one bit," he said apologetically.

Well, there we go.

I laughed lightly. "Why do you look like you're sorry if you're not?"

"I'm sorry it made you feel uncomfortable. I'm sorry it took you by surprise. But I'm not sorry I did it."

"Duke, it was a freaking nice gesture. So nice I can't even imagine…" I trailed off before starting again, this time with a quick breath expelled. "I'm so grateful I have a friend like you who cares for me like that. I haven't had very many people in my life like that, and I…thank you." Even amid my late night spent coming up with a payment plan, I couldn't help but be touched. Duke just looked at me, clearly understanding that was just my build-up. "But the whole thing physically makes me sick to think about. I want you to know that. I appreciate the gesture, but I'm going to pay you back."

"I'm not taking any money."

Immediately, his abrupt refusal to budge made my temper flare. I had started out so nice. "You lawnmowered me!"

He had been about to say something when he stopped, a confused look on his face. "What?"

"Just like your parents." My arms were flying now. "You tried to take this hard thing away, but you had no right. You can't do that. It's too much. I know you meant well, but what am I supposed to do? You dropped thousands of dollars on me without asking. There's this enormous pressure in my chest, and I don't know what you want from me."

I watched as shock etched itself onto his face. And then I watched that shock morph into annoyance. "Nora. Good hell, I never even thought about it like that. I didn't do it to pressure you into anything." He ran his hand through his hair. "You were working yourself into an early grave, and I had the ability to fix that. I figured you'd be annoyed if you found out, but I had no idea I'd cause a reaction like this."

"It's not your problem to fix," I insisted, taking on a fighting stance with arms folded and my heart bleeding on my sleeve.

"But I want it to be," he said softly.

At that, my breath hitched, and he took a couple steps toward me. "But even if that never happens, I wanted you to have someone in your corner. Everybody needs help sometimes. It doesn't mean there's anything wrong with you. And I have no intention of becoming my parents. But even if you're only my friend, I couldn't stand by and watch you do this to yourself. I can't watch everybody use you until there's nothing left. What's gonna happen when you try to go back to school? You're already working two full-time jobs."

"It's not full time."

"Close enough. Is your mom working that hard? Are your sisters?"

When I couldn't respond without acknowledging how right he was, he continued. "I couldn't stand it anymore. I was able to help, so I did. End of story. There's no pressure for anything. I don't even want to talk about it anymore."

My hands felt shaky, but the pressure in my chest had dissipated at his words. There was a truth and a gentleness radiating from him that spoke peace to my soul.

"Well," I blew out a breath. "If you're going to be all cute and annoying, and...really, really sweet...um..." I forced the sting in my eyes to retreat before I broke down in front of him. "I guess I'm not sure where we go from here."

"I want to date you," he said calmly. "And that has NOTHING to do with paying your bill. If you tell me no, we'll still be friends. These are completely separate entities. Alright?"

I should have known Duke wasn't going to beat around the bush. I wanted to wrap his words around me like a blanket, but my head yelled at me to wait.

"You're still my boss," I flung out the very excuse that had always kept a separation between us.

He wrinkled his nose. "Okay, the no dating interns thing was Ryan and Mike's idea. It was more like a guideline. They told the office we had rules about dating interns because they knew I was interested and wanted to help protect you during the competition."

"What?"

He laughed. "I'm sorry. I tried my best not to flirt, but it was *really* hard."

"Anita's been threatening to go to HR for the past couple of weeks."

Duke snorted."Is that the only thing that you're worried about? You do know I help make the rules, right?"

I had to be honest. I owed him that. "It's not just that. I've always planned to have a career before getting involved with someone. I keep having thoughts that I'm doing things the same way my mom did. I'm scared that if I get involved in something too soon, I might leave myself vulnerable like she always did."

He stared at me for a long moment, his arms folded as he leaned against his doorway. "I don't know what's going to happen today. It's out of my hands. Maybe you'll work here, maybe you won't. But you're not your mom. Stop hiding behind her. You're not scared of not being able to support yourself. You're already doing that. You're not scared of dating losers. You don't even date. You're scared of relationships. You're scared of trusting somebody else. You're scared of me." He took another step closer, and I could reach out and touch him if I wanted. "But I need you to see me for who *I* am. Not who your mom dated."

I couldn't speak. All this time, dancing around the nail on the board, he was finally hitting it on the head. And he was just getting started.

"But I think I figured out what the real problem is."

"What?" My ire was beginning to rise, as it would when somebody was literally spelling out all of the things you feared most about yourself.

"Even if you get this job, I have a feeling that wouldn't be enough. You'd have another excuse. Then another. Always waiting for all the ducks to be in a row."

"Duke. IF I get this job, it's still an entry-level position. I still don't have my degree yet."

"See what I mean?" He stepped closer. "You can quote every romantic comedy ever made, but you can't see the guy who loves you standing in front of your face." He let his words sink in for a moment before looking at his watch and saying, "I've got a meeting."

He turned to go until I stopped him with words that were more about saving face than dealing with accusations that burned. "What about Rachel?"

He turned back toward me. "What?"

Against all reasoning, my talk with Anita had latched itself into my mind and became something I could hold against him— fling toward him like a snake and watch him squirm. "You dated her for three years. Three. You want me to trust you, but how? For all I know, I was just some rebound. How do I know you won't toss me aside in a few years when you get bored?"

The air in the room slowed to a stop. A standstill of tension as Duke looked at me in disbelief.

"Just some rebound," he repeated, slightly in awe. He waited a beat, then to my surprise, he began to laugh—a defeated, breathy sort of laugh. He rubbed a hand over his face.

"Is that funny?" I asked, completely confused.

"Nora—" He broke off, shaking his head slightly, pinning me with his stare. "You were never the rebound. She was."

The door shut behind him, and for the second time in a week, I was left standing speechless and alone in Duke's office.

26

SHE WAS THE REBOUND.

The beautiful brunette he had dated for three years was his rebound.

After me.

After one night.

My fingers went through the motions of what they did every day. They typed. Opened documents on the computer. Returned client emails. Reached for a Dr. Pepper that wasn't there. By all accounts, my fingers were very busy.

Duke also kept busy. His office door was either closed most of the day or he was in meetings. I didn't really know. But I missed his teasing glances and countless passes of my desk. The few times I did see him, he went the long way around my desk. A few times I met his eyes unintentionally. It happened naturally. Our eyes were used to finding each other, but this time, he blinked away. Not to say he was blatantly rude or that he ignored me when addressing the whole group in the office. He met my eyes, like all the others, but instead of stopping a second too long, they kept roaming.

I decided to take a late lunch, waiting until almost everyone had gone back to work before I stepped into the break room. The thought of running into…people and having to talk and converse was too much for me to bear. When I thought the coast was clear, I flew to the fridge in the break room, fully intent on eating lunch in my car, when I turned to find Tenisha eating a colorful salad in a large Tupperware container at a small round table in the corner of the room.

"Sit down. I didn't get to see your finished product yet. Come tell me all about it."

The thought of my getaway car faded away as I took a seat next to her. With some effort on my part, I collected my thoughts enough for a casual chat. After a few questions, I ended up spilling everything Bart and Birdie to Tenisha.

My favorite part was their bio. Duke had captured the sweetest pictures of his grandparents kissing. One of them both smiling at the camera. And my personal favorite: one of Bart with his hand at Birdie's back while they both worked the saw. The dark background of the shop and the rich brown tones of the wood blended so naturally with the colors I'd chosen for their website, and its all-around vibe. It was cozy and sweet, and I fell in love with them and their business all over again when I looked at it. It had become a labor of love for me, staying up late into the night, working out every detail.

"Did you come up with a new name for the business? I remember it was a mouthful–that can be a deal breaker."

I smiled. That had been one more phone call to Birdie, telling her about an idea I'd had and grateful she had loved it.

"Two Bees Woodworking," I said. "Their names are Bart and Birdie."

"Two bees." She smiled. "I like it. Well done."

I took a bite of my ham sandwich.

She leaned closer, her voice soft. "The other designers and I were talking this morning. We both think it will come down to you and Shawn. At least, that's who we're all praying for."

A half-hearted smile lifted my lips. She gave me a once-over. "Are you doing okay?"

"Yeah, I'll be fine. Just tired."

"Huh. Well, either way, I'm happy for you. You'd be an excellent addition to this office. I wish I had a vote."

"Me too," I said, trying not to beam but failing miserably. To have validation on something I'd pinned a lot of money and dreams on meant more to me than Tenisha could have possibly known as she so casually packed her lunch containers back in her cooler.

"I've been so grateful for this opportunity."

"You can thank Duke. I just wanted to hire another designer to spread the workload, but he insisted we start up an internship program. He thought paying for the schooling of the winner would be a fun way to give back." She laughed. "'Give back to who?' I asked him." She shook her head. "But it turns out having three interns to share the workload was a great move. Y'all saved us this summer."

Her casual words wielded a sword directly into my gut.

She stood to go. "Well, have a good rest of your lun—"

"Wait. It was Duke's idea to hire the interns?"

"Yup. A couple of months ago. Had the whole thing planned in a day, I swear. Then a week later, y'all were here."

She strode out of the room, leaving me very alone with my thoughts. It was all too much. My mind tumbled with a variety of thoughts and emotions. For a girl who made it her business not to accept help or handouts, the double hitter from Duke was enough to leave me gutted.

The audacity of Duke Webber.

If my life were a romantic comedy, that would be the title.

Defensiveness and anger should have been surging through my body right now. I was waiting for it. But the feelings never came. Duke had completely unarmed me. Again. But somehow it wasn't anger that surged through my veins. It was tingles.

Awareness. It was a feeling of being grateful for a person who saw the best *in* me and wanted the best *for* me. A man who provided an opportunity to make my dreams begin. It was humbling. To have someone give something without first taking.

My family needed me. They loved me, but they needed me. Duke didn't need me. He wanted me, and that made all the difference.

Hope and fear often occupy the same space. But in reality, there can be only one. You have to choose.

It was time to choose. I'd lived my whole life with hope and fear, but now I needed to choose.

I finished my lunch in a daze and made my way back to my desk, arriving to see four cans of Dr. Pepper scattered across the top. My brow furrowed as I sat down, wondering once again at the audacity of Duke to be so brazen. For the first time since I started here, they were cans, not from a fountain.

I lifted one soda and unfolded the note. To my surprise, it wasn't Duke's slated scrawl that greeted me.

Mike: We don't want him anymore. Please take him back.

Ryan: He's a good guy. I promise. Please put us all out of our misery.

Mike & Ryan: Seriously, he's a bear when he's lovesick. At least he was three years ago. Mike & Ryan

Shawn: You are the happiest whenever he walks into the room. Go get him.

I LIFTED my head above the partition to meet Shawn's knowing grin.

"He was over here A LOT."

Half laughing and half mortified, I lowered my head back down and buried my face in my hands to block out the insane smile crawling across my face.

"Nora." I looked back over at Shawn, my hand automatically taking the can of Coke he held out toward me. "You know what to do."

"Thanks, Shawn."

I turned back toward my computer, Coke in hand, and gasped in surprise. Anita sat on my desk, patiently waiting for me to finish talking with Shawn. Her sharp nails were decorated a bold red matching her button-down top and black pants, reminding me of some sort of deranged ladybug. The colors were a power move, no doubt. I wasn't sure why she was dressed to do battle. Our portfolios were finished and were being voted on even now by the three different companies and their employees. It was completely out of anyone's hands. Maybe she wanted to look the part of a fearless leader if they called her name.

"I just wanted to wish you good luck," Anita said, though no amount of well-wishing reached her eyes. I waited for the rest of her statement, and it didn't disappoint. "I really hope that the contest is fair. It would be such a shame to have to report any disorderly conduct to HR."

My blood began to simmer. How could I have let this woman bully me for the past three months? Even the tiny snarl on her face reminded me of a snake. I had tried so hard to play nice, but the niceness would be coming to an end.

"What conduct?" I asked, folding my arms and leveling her with my own stare.

She scoffed, motioning toward the cans on my desk. "I think you know. I want to know how long it's been going on. That's obviously why you didn't want me to work with him for my projects."

"He was assigned to me. I had nothing to do with that. And he has no say in the winner of this contest."

Leaning in close, her voice turned into a snarl. "How do we know that's true? The companies who are voting are clients of Duke's. I'm sure they'd do whatever he asked."

"If you're not happy with things here, you're welcome to leave." I turned from her and faced my computer, dismissing her.

"You leave me no choice, then. I'm going to HR."

She said the words but didn't actually leave, like she was waiting for me to react first. As much as I wanted to ignore her, something about speaking my mind felt good.

"Anita," my voice was low and direct. Her eyes flashing was the only signal that she heard me. "From the moment you got here, you've tried to intimidate and threaten me. It stops now. After today, I don't ever have to see you again. You're welcome to go to HR. It won't change a thing."

"Interoffice relationships are against the rules."

"Are you just mad you couldn't turn his head?"

Her mouth dropped in outrage, and as much as I cringed even saying those words aloud, her reaction was something I'd carry with me forever.

"Are you going to leave my office space now, or should I?" I gave her a polite smile, suddenly secure in the knowledge that this woman couldn't touch me. A fire lit somewhere near my chest, the beating of my heart fanning the flame until it was roaring. Had I really never stood up for myself before? Not like this. It felt like I'd just run five miles. The hard part was over, and now I was lying on the grass, feeling bloody freaking amazing. Geez. Why didn't people tell each other how they felt all the time? The endorphins were unreal.

Anita stalked back to her desk and flung herself into her chair. For the next half hour, I got to hear every annoyed huff and squeak of her chair. Her sarcastic remarks meant for my ears stopped completely. Even the sound of her clipping her finger-nails and no doubt dropping them into a disgusting pile on the floor only resulted in making me smile.

There were more things making me smile as well. I wanted to blame my sudden frankness as an after effect of my confrontation with Anita, but I knew it wasn't. My feelings for Duke had been repressed, denied, pushed aside, and held hostage long enough. I had been scared long enough. My heart had been bruised and guarded and tucked away for so long that having someone handle it with care and sweetness had been like a red flag for me. I didn't know what to do with it. Duke had proven himself over and over, and I kept pushing him away over and over because he terrified me. I glanced at the clock.

Fear had ruled so much of my life. It was time to let hope have its day.

I waited until Duke had stepped out of his office and into the restroom to make my move.

Ten minutes later, I sat in one of the rooftop chairs, thirty minutes before the start time of our meeting. It had to be now. He had to know my feelings before the meeting. Before my fate, for better or for worse, was known. My leg shook uncontrollably as I waited. My hands didn't know what to do with themselves but settled on briskly rubbing the tops of my legs. My poor body and mind had run the gamut of emotions, and this, right here, might be what ended me.

If he actually showed up.

Suddenly, a pit dropped into my stomach as I thought of all the possibilities that Duke might not have gone back into his office. What if he went straight into a meeting with Mike and Ryan? What if he never saw the Coke on his desk? What if he was looking for me now, and he couldn't find me? I leapt up from the chair and strode toward the door. I had to tell him. I had already told Anita off today. I was a freaking lioness coming out of her cage. I'd rip Duke out of his meeting if I had to. I would—

The door to the roof burst open, and all of a sudden, Duke was there. I slowed to a sudden stop when he stepped onto the roof.

Cautious dark eyes met mine as he stopped with a few yards between us. He had rolled his sleeves to his forearms. He stuck his hands into the pockets of his blue suit and waited.

"You must have gotten my message." That was a lame way to start. I knew this, but I had just envisioned waltzing into a meeting with a bunch of suits and yanking him out. My head needed time to adjust. Time to remember all that I had practiced to say.

"I'm supposed to be in another meeting right now, but I forgot a paper in my office."

My eyes widened. I'd been right. "I'm so sorry. Do you need to go?"

"Not until you say what you want to say. You're not getting out of it that easily."

"Well, I have a whole list, so…" I sputtered out a nervous laugh, folding my arms across my stomach. The nerves hit differently in this scenario. There were only two ways this could end, and one would devastate me. I could admit that now. But there were still so many things I needed to say.

I took a deep breath of courage. "You were wrong before. I do see you, Duke Webber. Seeing you has never been the problem. You make me want to forget every plan I've ever made and run away with you. Which is why I've tried to keep my distance. You are the most terrifying thing because I've never wanted anything as much as I want you. And that kind of life doesn't happen to me."

He was listening patiently, his face passive, but I was on a roll, so I kept going. "Things work out for you. Your life is full of good things. You have a kind heart. So kind that I didn't know what to do with it when you showed it to me. A romantic kind of love was something that never felt real to me. It was a movie. A fantasy. That's what you are. You're the fantasy. Not real life. I had to stop thinking I could—Hey! Don't look at me like—I didn't mean fantasy like that. Don't smile. DUKE."

I waited until he had gained control over his facial expression once more. But my impressive speech had been stalled, and the way he was slowly moving toward me wasn't helping my memory.

"Stop. Please. I have to get this out." I closed my eyes to finish. "I thought I was mad at you because you paid my bill, but the more I thought about it, it wasn't that. I hated that my life was so messed up that you thought you had to rescue me. Trusting other people hasn't been easy for me. But I hated that, in the end, all I could feel was incredibly grateful that you would do something like that for me. But for the record, I will kill you if you do something like that again without asking me. But..." I hesitated, blinking back the emotions sprouting in my eyes. "Thank you for caring so much."

He ambled another step closer, hands in his pockets, a sexy, smoldering hot man in a suit, before I stopped him. "No! I'm still not done. This next part is what I'm the most scared of. You think you want me, but I'm not what you think I am. I was fun a handful of times. And all of that with you. I feel bad that you might have carried some torch for me all that time and then now you're seeing the real me. I'm a snooze fest. I'm controlling. I have a mom who acts more like a child. I'm not good at making time for fun." I folded my arms and sent him a pleading look. "I feel like you keep forgetting all of that."

"Can I talk now? Are you finished?"

I shrugged, my little heart on pins and needles.

A little smile crossed his face then as he shook his head. "I know exactly who you are, Nora Griffin. You have the biggest heart of anyone I've known. You gave up your childhood so you could give one to your sisters. You have a work ethic like nobody I've ever seen. You selflessly give and give until you break. For better or worse." When I glared at him, he only smiled. "But you also make me laugh. You're sometimes a wild woman who breaks the rules. You tease and flirt with me even when you try not to. I fell in love with all of those parts of you."

I wiped at my eyes and looked down at my feet, unable to take the sweetness oozing out of his face. I felt so inadequate, hearing him tell me these things. So wholly inadequately, and completely swept away. And he wasn't even finished.

"I've seen you laugh until you've cried. I've watched you clean the company toilets. I've watched you ride a motorcycle and love it. I saw you help my grandma cheat playing cards." I sputtered out a laugh, a crying mess of laughter and tears. He continued, "I've seen your heart, Kiss Cam. And I must be selfish because I want every bit of it. I have since the night we met."

Duke spoke again. This time, his words were hoarse and a bit downtrodden. "If you don't want me, fine. Tell me, and I'll go. I'll leave you alone. But don't stand here and tell me you don't deserve me. Because from where I stand, I don't deserve you. Not even close. But I want you."

"I started loving you the night we met." The words came out soft. I hadn't planned to say that. I had always denied its truth, but there it was, leaping between us, like it had been there the whole time. "I'm sorry I've been so scared. I still am, if you didn't notice."

I heard a nearly imperceptible snort before his dark eyes raked over me, a wary flicker of hope in their depths.

"It's always been safer to shut off a part of my heart that might get hurt. I've done that my whole life...until, one night, I went to a random basketball game with an annoying stranger and met you."

His eyes flared with humor before he stilled, folding his arms. "Wait. Am I the annoying stranger?"

"Shh. I'm telling the story. I showed you pieces of me that I never showed anyone. And I told myself it was because I'd never see you again. But then I did. And you were here, and I was at the lowest I'd ever been in my life. But you kept showing up, and that terrified me." I cleared my throat, my decision made. "It's hard to feel like I deserve someone so good, so I'm going to tell you some of my flaws to make sure you know what you're getting into before this goes any further."

He stopped, scrunching his nose into an adorable face. "Is it the Dr. Pepper thing? I already know that. We can work through it."

I cleared my throat. "Number one, I know how to cook, but it's stuff like Hamburger Helper and Rice-a-Roni. Things from a box. I can also boil noodles, but that's about it."

"No worries there. I like to cook."

My eyes narrowed. "Of course you do."

He laughed and took a step forward. "Are you done?"

"No." I kicked my foot out to stop him from moving toward me. "I think making my bed is stupid, so I never do it."

"I haven't made my bed in ten years."

That one surprised me, but I felt a tiny bit better. "That's what I like to hear."

He stood still, as if waiting for a signal from me to come closer. But I wasn't finished. This was a big one. "I have a mom who I love but who sometimes makes bad decisions. Hopefully, this time, she's found her happiness, but she might be sleeping on my couch in a month or two. Or asking to borrow money. I never really know. And I usually help her. I really want to work at setting healthy boundaries, but it might take me a while to figure that out."

Duke nodded. "That's good. I figure we can help each other out there because I also need to set some parental boundaries."

"I can do that," I added. "And I want you to try to see my mom's good qualities too. Because she has them. Lots of them."

His eyes grew soft. "You came from her. I already love her best quality."

My eyes welled even as I threw him an exasperated look. "Stop with the adorable lines. I need to get through my list before I kiss you, or else none of this makes sense."

He laughed and motioned for me to proceed.

For this last one, I took a ragged breath. My hands were trembling until I folded them across my stomach.

"For the longest time, I have only been able to trust myself. I had a lot of people in and out of my life, and it's been difficult for me to trust people. I'm trying to be better, but it might be hard for me sometimes. You might have to be patient with me."

He nodded. "Done. Now are you finished?"

"Nope!" I held out my hands and took a step back, once again warding off the advance he no doubt had on his mind. "Now I need to hear a list of your flaws. From what I can see, you're pretty much perfect, so you'd better let me have it."

He bit his top lip as his gaze was steady on mine, the look of a man with his mind whirling, probably trying to think of some stupid flaw to tell me. I'd know if he was lying, and I told him so.

The smile that crept across his face started a chain reaction in me. A smile of my own began to form, matching his until it threatened to grow even wider. I tried to contain it. I still hadn't heard his flaws, after all. He began walking ever so slowly toward me again, the tiniest dimple forming in his cheek. I swallowed and held out my hand—a finger, to be exact—warning him away.

"Hey! No! Stop walking. You can't charm me now with dimples and smiles. Flaws, mister. And they'd better be good."

He stopped, his hands in his pockets. "I leave my socks all over the house."

I lifted my chin. "That's definitely annoying."

"I leave my shoes in the middle of the floor. I trip over them all the time, but I still do it."

I raised my eyebrows. "You don't leave them by the door?"

"Nope. And my towel goes straight to the bathroom floor, crumpled and wet, until the next day."

I gasped, my hand covering my mouth as he moved closer. I was nearly crawling out of my skin. But then I remembered something, eyes narrowing dangerously. "Wait a sec. Ryan and Mike always accused you of being a neat freak. Are you just telling me what I want to hear now?"

He stopped, nodding his head in shame. "I do like having the dishes done. And the countertops wiped down. And I'm a master loader of the dishwasher."

I shook my head. "Tsk, tsk, tsk. You were so close."

"I'm usually late wherever I go. At least five minutes. Sometimes ten."

"Now we're talking."

He closed the distance between us, gathering me slowly into his arms. "When I do laundry, I put everything in one load. On cold. Whites, colors…" He leaned in closer to my ear, whispering, "Reds."

My body shivered at the puff of warm air from his mouth that sent goosebumps down my neck. I sighed, leaning into him and resting my hands on his chest. "That's almost fatal."

"One more thing. And this might be the worst of all." He bent forward, placing his forehead on mine. "With the exception of the lift in the water, I absolutely hate the movie *Dirty Dancing*."

I laughed then, a sound of pure happiness surging out of me, when I felt his arms tighten around my waist, pulling me flush against his body. His face was millimeters from mine, his eyes dipping toward my mouth.

My arms moved to his shoulders as I nestled into his neck, a lightness surging out of my soul that I hadn't dreamed of feeling. "With the exception of the last epic dance scene, minus the moment Patrick Swayze jumps off the stage and the camera has that super cheesy angle of his face, I also hate the movie *Dirty Dancing*."

He laughed, but only for a second, before his lips found mine. And I suddenly knew what heaven tasted like. It tasted like hope. It was light and giddy and left me teetering over the edge with dizziness. One of his hands skated up my arm to hold my cheek before getting lost at the nape of my neck. As for me, I pressed myself even tighter against him. I couldn't get close enough. My fingers trailed along his shoulders and neck as his kiss worked a spell over me. My soul released a great sigh as our mouths began creating a dance. Our dance.

And it was perfect.

27

I WOKE UP THE NEXT MORNING WITH A SMILE ON MY FACE. BY
all accounts, the smile shouldn't have been there. I had lost the
job to Anita. Her marketing package for the dermatology office
had been the perfect amount of chic and function. With one
company in particular, she had won by a landslide. The disappointment that bloomed inside of me had felt muted. Dulled. It
didn't make any sense. This was everything I had been working
toward for months—the past four years, really. Anita got it over
me. And Shawn. I had seen his design, and the results had
visibly stunned me. By all accounts, I should have been devas-
tated. But...then Duke took me out to dinner and dessert. We
were that couple sitting on one side of the table together because
I discovered I would literally die if his hand wasn't on my leg at
all times—or caressing my cheek or tucking my hair behind
my ear.

I had received a scorching blow regarding my career. Everything I thought I wanted had been taken away. Except, now I had
a secret weapon on my side by way of a man who loved me for
all my petty flaws and failures. Nothing else mattered beyond
that. All the other senses had been dulled. Perhaps I was more

like my mom than I thought. The only difference was that I had refused to settle on just anyone. Duke was the jackpot. Not the consolation prize.

I was jobless.

Degree-less.

And happier than I'd ever been in my entire life.

MY PHONE BUZZED WITH A TEXT.

Duke: That was the longest six hours of sleep ever. When can I see you?

Me: Don't you work today?

Duke: I took the day off. I heard there's a pretty girl who loves me living in an apartment. I'd never get anything done at work.

Me: I'm about to pour myself a bowl of Lucky Charms. If you don't already have breakfast plans…

Duke: I'll be there. Should I bring some eggs and bacon?

Me: I think I have eggs here. Unrelated, but how long do eggs stay good for?

Duke: I'm bringing new eggs. Need anything else?

Me: Just you. And bacon.

I MOVED INTO THE KITCHEN, the smile still on my face, and I made no attempt to wipe it away. How many years had I lived in fear of the one thing I had hoped for more than anything else? Now I wondered what might have happened if I had allowed myself to exchange numbers with Duke after the kiss-cam date. I'd kept myself so tightly guarded, and now it seemed like there was a whole world out there for me to explore. My heart felt like it had been trapped in a box for so long that all it wanted to do was dance.

Or…you know…something that *resembled* dancing.

Hence the reason Mira's mouth dropped open when she came home from working her night shift to find me shaking it to a pop song from one of my old playlists. I had made it a habit to listen to podcasts while working for Cathy, but today called for a happy love song.

"Who are you, and what have you done with my roommate?" she yelled, yanking my headphones off. "Did you get the job?"

"Nope!" I said, regretfully turning the music down. "Even better."

"What?"

"Duke loves me."

"Well, duh," she said, throwing her purse on the couch. "Did you two make up?" She looked at me, and a big grin crossed her face. "Never mind. I already know the answer. Tell me everything."

I quickly filled her in on the last twenty-four hours.

"Wow. I mean…he's no Brock or anything, but…you are the luckiest," Mira said as we lounged next to each other on the couch.

"I know."

"And he's lucky too." She nudged my elbow. "Although, just out of curiosity, does he know you make me use a chore chart in the apartment? I feel like that could really change things."

I laughed. "I'm hoping to surprise him with those extra adorable parts of my personality."

A knock at the door had me almost running to open it. So imagine my surprise when it was not only Duke standing outside, but Mike and Ryan as well.

I stepped back in surprise. "Hey."

Duke was the only one not in a suit. He was Casual Duke today, and something about his jeans and baseball hat was really working for him. Or maybe it was the smile on his face as he stepped inside, snaked an arm around my waist, and kissed my temple.

"Okay, that's enough," Ryan said, turning away.

I laughed and motioned the two of them inside. After introductions to Mira were made, she left us alone so she could go shower, and we all squished in together on the couch and loveseat, Duke's hand on my knee. Then, they got down to business.

"We're here to formally offer you a position with RDM," Mike said, a knowing smile on his face.

I stared at him blankly for a minute. "What? How?"

"Anita cheated. We just fired her, and we want to give a position to you and Shawn."

My mouth dropped open, and I looked to Duke for confirmation. He nodded.

"We thought it was strange that there was one company who voted almost 95 percent in Anita's favor. The other two offices were mostly split between you and Shawn. So Mike made a phone call, and it was discovered Anita had a cousin at that company, and she had threatened the cousin to bribe the employees to vote for her."

My hand flew to my mouth. "Are you serious?"

"Yup."

All the accusations made about me using Duke to get ahead in the company, and she was the one cheating?

"Can't say I'm that surprised," I said.

"Us either."

"But how can you hire both me and Shawn? I thought you could only hire one."

Mike nodded toward Duke. "We, and your man over there, have been working nights and pulling in extra clients, trying to bring in more income for the company. We recently had some big clients sign on with us, and we're bringing in more revenue. We can afford it. And we want you."

"That's why we came to tell you instead of Duke," Ryan added. "It's pretty obvious that he wants you no matter what, but we wanted it clear that we also want you. Professionally speaking."

A smile broke out across my face. I was getting hired for my dream job, and I also didn't have to say goodbye to Shawn, who —besides Duke—had become one of my favorite things about RDM. I turned to meet Duke's eyes and found them warm and crinkly and already on mine.

"What do you say? Do you want it?" Mike asked.

Duke kissed me, much to the groans of our audience.

"There is definitely going to be a handbook of rules at the office now," Ryan muttered. "No more of this guideline crap."

I pulled out of Duke's embrace. "I accept!"

We stood so I could walk Mike and Ryan to the door. "Don't worry about coming in today," Mike said. "Get whatever you need to do out of your system before you're an employee again. And you too, Nora."

I laughed and gave Mike and Ryan each a hug of gratitude, feeling, once again, how amazing the effect of one random night could be on a life.

After closing the door, I turned back to face Duke.

"So all this time, you were working to add new clients so two interns could potentially be hired?"

He shoved his hands in his pockets. "Just doing my best to keep up with the work ethic of this amazing intern we had at the office."

I looked at my watch. "I don't mean to tell you your business, but it's been exactly four minutes since you last kissed me."

Watching me carefully, he closed the distance between us, this time a smile playing across his lips.

"You gonna make me come the whole way?" he asked.

"I've always wanted to see if a guy would go the full hundred."

His hands found my face, and his forehead touched mine. "In *Hitch,* they said it's supposed to be 90/10."

I drew in a breath, stars in my eyes. "You've seen *Hit*—"

Then he was kissing me.

EPILOGUE

THE CROWD CHEERED AND STOMPED THEIR FEET IN THE STANDS when the Jazz scored another point right at the buzzer. With our seats at the top of the nosebleed section of the arena, the sound was deafening in my ears. It had been almost four years since I'd been back to a Jazz game. This time, I could lean into the good-smelling guy without it being weird. There was no body hair in my face. This time, we skipped the armrest altogether, and instead, Duke had his arm around my shoulders. Dancers from the Jazz dance team began filling the court.

"Can I buy you a foam finger?" Duke asked as he stood up to grab us some snacks for the second half.

I grinned. "I think I'm good."

Duke leaned all the way down to give me a quick kiss on my lips before sliding out onto the stairs. As he walked away, my eyes couldn't help but take note of the way his jeans hung low on his hips, the basketball hat, and his soft-blue t-shirt. It was some-times hard to believe he was mine. Being back at the Delta Center with Duke felt surreal in the best way possible. Our seats were at the bottom half of the second level, which I found I liked. And most importantly, we had quick access to the stairs for easy snacks. A pretzel with cheese sauce for me—and a Dr. Pepper. Though Duke and I were together every day at work and hung out at his house whenever we could, I still found it difficult to get enough of him. He always left me wanting more.

The Jazz dancers began dancing to an enthusiastic beat a few moments later, and I was immediately captivated. I wouldn't tell Duke, but the dancing was by far my favorite part of the game.

My mom and Kip are still married and living in his RV down in the south of Florida somewhere—near a beach, if the bikini-clad pictures she sends me by the water mean anything. She seems happy, but maybe that's just what happens in such close proximity to a beach. I hope she really has found what she was looking for, but I wouldn't be surprised to find her on my couch one day. Years of this cycle weren't easily forgotten. Duke and I have had several long talks about ways to set boundaries with our parents while still maintaining loving relationships. Having someone in my corner, to help me make decisions and set guidelines, has made all the difference for me.

A man wearing a ratty t-shirt and a blue beanie covering up his stringy blond hair slid past me and sunk into the empty seat at my left. He looked to be in his mid-forties. I re-adjusted, scooting closer to where Duke would be sitting and put some space between me and the man. I couldn't help but be disappointed that out of the hundreds of empty seats I'd seen littered throughout this section of the arena, his seat had to be the one right next to mine.

All too soon, the dancers finished their routine and left the court. A smile lit my face as "Kiss Me" by Sixpence None the Richer came blasting over the speakers. The kiss cam started off strong with a couple who'd been dancing in their seats. They pointed and laughed when they saw themselves, and she jumped into his arms. Two more couples got on screen before I saw my face on the Jumbotron.

Instantly, my smile left, and I blinked again, not quite sure how this was happening. I stared in horror at my open-mouthed, terrified face gracing the screen. And my blond seat neighbor.

Are you freaking kidding me?

"Hey!" the blond man leaned toward me. "Look at that!" He looked over at me, laughing. "It's us!"

My eyes were as wide as plates. Panic flooded my insides. Frantically, I waved the camera away, except I had no idea where the camera was, so it looked like I was motioning toward someone in the opposite direction on the screen. After a moment, big and bold words appeared on the screen. *Kiss him, kiss him, kiss him!*

What in the—?

NO.

"They're kind of intense about this," my seat neighbor said, looking down at me with a small, uncomfortable laugh. You and me both, buddy. "Should we just kiss real quick?"

"No," I blurted. "I have a boyfriend. He just left."

"He left the arena or…" came his mumbled reply.

"He's grabbing snacks."

Our eyes were still peeled on the Jumbotron. We were starting to get booed. Was the camera broken? I planned to write a strongly worded letter to the kiss-cam people as soon as I got home.

"Let's just kiss on the cheek real quick. We're going to get food thrown at us if we don't give them something." He was eyeing the Jumbotron in confusion. The crowd behind and in front of us began shouting, motioning through very specific gestures of what was expected.

But they picked the wrong girl this time.

"No. It will leave us alone eventually." Although, in my experience, that was very much not true. But the song would eventually be over.

AND HOLY CRAP MY FACE WAS STILL ON THE JUMBOTRON.

Where was Duke?

The crowd had started out thinking our reluctance was funny, but the uproar at the moment was riddled with near-hostile intent. I sent another pleading look out into the universe, begging for the camera to pick one of the other ten thousand couples in this stupid arena.

"Let's do it." The man turned to me, leaning into my space. "Just a quick one."

Suddenly, the guy was pushed away from me, and warm hands were pulling me to stand. The crowd cheered wildly as a grinning Duke pulled me close, his hands encircling my waist. My arms wrapped around his neck as I breathed in his cologne, the distress over the past thirty seconds gone in an instant. I hadn't had time to think when my face was suddenly on a TV with twenty thousand people watching, but something about this had my Duke suspect meter pinging.

"What is it with you and kiss cams?" he mumbled, both of his hands on my cheeks, breathing me in. "I can't leave you alone for two minutes to get you food."

"If you did this, I'm going to—"

His lips were on mine, asking and taking all at once. My heart sighed as my body melted against him. His strong arms locked around me, my fingers toying with his shirt. The hostile environment around us had quickly turned into roaring enthusiasm. The crowd finally had their show, and by the sound of the excitement, it had been worth the wait.

He pulled away for a brief second, his warm eyes meeting mine. "I had to make sure you wouldn't kiss just any good-looking guy sitting next to you."

"You set it all up?"

"It's all in who you know." Duke reached out a hand across the empty seat to my neighbor. "Hey, thanks, Jim."

Jim grinned, his white teeth gleaming as he nodded toward me. "Sorry about that, Nora. I was beginning to think Duke just wanted to punch me in the face on camera."

"Sorry, man, I wasn't supposed to be gone this long. The line for the pretzel was crazy."

He laughed and stood, shuffling past us. "Well, I'm going to go back to my seat."

After he left, I turned to Duke, cradling his face in my hands. "How do you know Jim?"

"He's my electrician. He's got season tickets to all the games."

"And you knew the camera guy?"

"I knew how to get ahold of the camera guy."

"Why are you whispering?"

His voice was low as he leaned close to my ear. "Because I have something else to ask you."

He sat down in his seat, pulling me onto his lap. His chair was next to the aisle, and my feet dangled that direction while I curled into his chest.

The stadium had moved on, another kiss-cam moment stealing the show, leaving Duke and me lounging together in his seat. I was being cradled on Duke's lap, our foreheads pressed together, and the entire arena reduced to a muffle of noises. While inside this cocoon, we had our own private show. My entire world held me on his lap with such a look of tenderness that my eyes filled with moisture. My breath caught as he removed one hand from around my waist, reached down in his pocket, and pulled out a small box. Immediately, my hand covered my face as my eyes welled up with tears.

"I fell in love with you the night we met. I tried to forget you, but it was impossible. And then, when I saw you again, I knew my life's mission would be your happiness. But in all actuality, you've made me the happiest I've ever been. I'm just trying to keep up." A warm hand began brushing at the tears spilling down my face. "Will you marry me?"

If tenderness had a color, it was the deep, rich brown of Duke's eyes. If sweetness had a flavor, it was his kiss, soft and hot against my mouth. It was a timid thing, opening my heart up enough to fuse it to another. To give someone the very thing I'd guarded so closely. But there was freedom in it as well. Without movement forward, we become stagnant. I didn't know where our love might take us. But I had chosen hope over fear, and so far, hope felt like a warm wind in my face, looked like smiles that wouldn't stop coming, and a feeling of pure happiness that was all-consuming.

And then he pulled away. I growled in outrage at his mouth, which was no longer kissing mine.

"Are you going to answer me, woman?" he demanded, laughter in his eyes.

"Yes." I nodded, smiling up at him as I added, "I love you too."

I only caught a glimpse of his grin before he kissed me again. This time, I pulled away.

"Duke."

"Yeah?" His voice came back soft and gravelly as he leaned forward and stole one more kiss.

"I'm all for a good romantic comedy. You know that, right?"

"Yeah."

"That being said, I'm really glad you didn't propose to me over the Jumbotron."

He grinned. "I wanted to marry you. Wasn't sure you'd say yes if I did that."

"I would have definitely hesitated," I teased, my hand fingering the collar of his shirt.

"I'm not sharing you anymore."

He kissed me for a good long while. With a respectful nod to all the grand gestures and Jumbotron moments in all my favorite romantic comedies, *our* moment was a thousand times better.

The End

AUTHOR'S NOTES

This book started when a scene about two strangers on a Kiss Cam came into my head over a year and a half ago. I sat down and within two days, I had written the first two chapters, almost like the pen was writing it for me. And then...crickets. I loved the premise. I loved the dynamic between Duke and Nora. It was fun for me to attempt to create tension and banter out of thin air. Before this book, my main characters had always known each other before their books started. After writing the first couple of chapters, I put it away to write another book, Faking Christmas. But every so often, I'd sneak back into this story and tweak and add a few things and jot down ideas. I had the first few chapters locked down, but absolutely nothing after that. That's one of the difficult things about being a writer that nobody talks about. The decisions to be made when I could potentially take this story anywhere. Eventually, I settled on knowing two things:

The meet cute was going to take place in Utah at the Delta Center, where I once went on a date with a nicer version of my own Jason, uncomfortable back massage and all. And I was going to get these characters to Idaho somehow, even if it was just across the border. I am who I am.

Like most of my books, the process was full of ups and downs. The idea of a light Cinderella theme began circulating in my brain. The idea of a bucket list and one fun night together took hold and wouldn't let go. I grew to love the image of a janitor down on her luck and a guy who'd never quite gotten over her. I loved the idea of a good man with a really good heart.

I'm raising two little men right now and more than anything I want them to grow up to have a heart like Duke's. The world is full of so much that is ugly and harsh...I want them to cultivate goodness. I want them to work hard to pave their own way to success and happiness. I want them to have the instinct to help others and to see the best in those around them. I want them to understand their enormous value when the world might be telling them otherwise.

A few other things of note...

The kiss scene on Nora's phone that Duke overheard when he startled her was from my novella, A Christmas Spark. My friend and critique partner, Karen, convinced me to add a kiss scene from one of my own books so obviously I picked the most heated moment I could find to make it as cringeworthy as possible.

My little family lived in Fargo, North Dakota for four months while my husband worked as a travel nurse. Most of the state seemed as flat as a pancake, but the people were great, and Fargo really is a cool little city.

The pink and blue carpet mentioned in Bart and Birdie's home was similar to the carpet I grew up with in my home. My mom also inherited an over-sized porcelain cat with creepy blue eyes and it continues to terrify my husband and kids at every visit.

The "town" truck and "work" truck Birdie told Nora about is a very real thing with farmers.

Thank you for reading!!

ACKNOWLEDGMENTS

James - This book couldn't have been written without your help. Thanks for your good heart and for all those times you got home from work and sent me to my office while you fed the kids dinner and put them to bed. You're the best.

Dawson & Stetson - Thanks for having all those movie nights with Dad so I could write. And for only giving me a small guilt trip about writing so much. Love you guys.

Lucy - You've rocked our world in the best way. Thanks for teaching me that you are not the distraction. Writing is. Thanks for the post-pregnancy brain fog that refused to lift those first few months so I could spend all my time snuggling you.

Mom & Dad - Thanks for letting me stay over to write and do edits and spoiling me rotten with all the food and plot chats. Mom, thanks for coming up with the business name of Two Bees Woodworking. Dad, thanks for mulling over my plot and calling me with any ideas you had. Mostly, thank you both for caring about any and all of it.

Lisa - This book literally wouldn't have gotten written without your help. I'm sorry I'm so annoying, but thanks for the daily phone calls and inspiration from our chats.

Karen - As usual, thanks for all your insights on this plot and these characters. And for building up my confidence when I really needed it.

Sue - Thanks for answering all of my questions and for helping me understand what goes on in a marketing office. And for being a pretty amazing cousin.

Kate & Annie - Thanks so much for all the babysitting so I could get some uninterrupted writing done. You guys are the best.

Karen, Hollijo, & Whitney - Best critique group ever. Thanks for the encouragement, support, and beta reads!

Jana Miller - Thanks for squeezing me in last minute and helping me find what was missing.

Jenn Lockwood - Thanks for a beautiful copyedit.

Amy Romney- Thanks for your time and care with my book. You have such a gift for language and have helped make this book shine.

Melody Jeffries - I adore this cover! Thank you so much for bringing the vision to life.

Hannah @thebookmaiden - Thanks for being excited, being a friend to me, taking the time to make graphics, and for loving my books.

Lauren @thebookscript - Thanks for being the biggest cheerleader for me and my books. You are brilliant and so creative and I love following your account. I'm so happy to know you.

I have so many author friends who have helped support and cheer me on. There are too many to name, but you know who you are. I'm so glad to call you all friends.

To all the bookstagrammers and readers who have read, loved, promoted, purchased books, told their friends, made reels, took beautiful pictures, requested my books at their library, and messaged me lovely things…you are my village and your support has been everything to me and this crazy job I now get to call a career. Thank you.

ABOUT CINDY

 Cindy Steel was raised on a dairy farm in Idaho. She grew up singing country songs at the top of her lungs and learning to solve all of life's problems while milking cows and driving tractors—rewriting happy endings every time. She married a cute Idaho boy and is the proud mother of two wild and sweet twin boys and a baby girl. She loves making breakfast, baking, photography, reading a good book, and staying up way past her bedtime to craft stories that will hopefully make you smile.

She loves to connect with readers! She is the most active on Instagram @authorcindysteel and her newsletter but she occasionally makes her way to Facebook at Author Cindy Steel and her website at www.cindysteel.com.

Made in the USA
Monee, IL
25 October 2024

68676287R00177